The Day After Always Comes

Rod Hacking

To my dear friends:

Joy and Henry Moule

Her finely-touched spirit had still its finest issues, though they were not widely visible...but the effect of her being on those around her was incalculably diffusive: for the growing good of the world is partly dependent on unknown historic acts: and that things are not so ill with you and me as they might have been, is half owing to the number who lived faithfully a hidden life, and rest in unvisited tombs.

(George Eliot: *Middlemarch*)

1

I am convinced that my husband knew he was going to die on that day, though gave me no warning. He had said that he wanted to go down to Dittisham, the place we often walked to the river, the river he loved, the Dart. Our two-year-old, Sam, came with us and André carefully lifted him from his car seat into the buggy, and we made our usual walk. On our way in the car he had asked we listen to Elgar's *Sea Pictures* but stopped it after the fourth song, *Where Corals Lie*, which he claimed was perhaps the most beautiful piece of music he knew, especially when sung by Janet Baker who like him, hailed from Yorkshire. Not for the first time, as I drove, I could see his eyes fill with tears, but it was to be for the last time.

We mostly walked the small pathway in silence, at ease as a threesome together. We had a favourite bench, and we sat down.

'It's just perfect here,' he said, as I took out a drink and handed it to Sam.

When I looked back at André, I knew at once that he had just died. His was face showed all the signs of being content – there had clearly been no pain, but I had no doubts. I took hold of his hand and told him I loved him. Then I took out my phone and made a call. I sat on the bench with André to my right, and Sam in his buggy by my side, chattering to me. It was so unbelievably peaceful and although there were tears rolling down my cheeks, I knew that the little man on my left now demanded all my attention.

A police car came first. It was a woman officer, and I could see she was taken aback when I said to her: 'My husband has just died.'

'Are you sure? The paramedics will be here shortly. They will try to resuscitate him.'

'Oh no, they won't. Come and see for yourself.'

As she cautiously walked towards the bench, the ambulance arrived, and Sam's attention was immediately directed to it. I moved the buggy round so he could see it more clearly.

The two paramedics, one of each, came with a bag to the bench where André was seated.

'I had no warning. He has not complained of any sort of pain but wanted to come to his favourite seat by the river. I was giving our son a drink and when I turned round, I could see what had happened. It was a wonderful way to go, so please don't even think of doing anything to him other than carrying him into the ambulance.'

They looked at one another hesitantly.

'How long ago did this happen?'

'Twenty minutes, more or less.'

'He looks so peaceful, it seems almost a shame to move him,' said the police officer.

'Oh, I think it would best,' I said, with a smile. 'Others come here and might be a bit surprised to find a corpse.'

The paramedics returned to the ambulance and brought a chair onto which they lifted André. Sam was fascinated. As they did so, there was information I needed to give the police officer.

'My husband was Sir André Beeson, and we live in Foxhole Lane on the Dartington Estate. Although retired from active service, he was still a senior member of the security service. They need to be informed and will almost certainly want to ascertain the cause of death themselves. Your Chief Constable will know what to do and I would like you to notify her as a matter of urgency, please. And please instruct the paramedics to take him to the Royal Devon and Exeter, not Plymouth, as that's where he will need to be seen by someone from London. I'll take my son home and you or anyone else can come and take a statement there.'

'I don't know your name.'

'I'm Dee Beeson, technically Lady Dorothea Beeson, and this is our son, Sam. André was a little older than me, forty years as it happens. I'm 34.'

Dee noticed a tear on the cheek of the police officer.

'You're being very brave,' she said, taking hold of my arm.'

I shrugged.

'What is your name?'

'Nicola Fairchild'

'Thank you, Nicola.'

'I'm sorry, Lady Beeson, but I cannot let you drive yourself home. It would not be fair to other road users after you've had such a shock. I'll call the Chief Constable's office, and speak to the paramedics, but then I will drive you and Sam home in your car and get someone to pick me up and collect my car.'

Dee smiled and did not argue.

Sam was amused that the car was being driven by someone different but asked where daddy was.

'Daddy's safe,' said Dee. 'Let's get home and get you something to eat.'

Once inside the cottage, Nicola set about making a cup of tea, and almost immediately my phone rang, as I had known it would, though perhaps not so quickly.

'Oh, Dee, I'm so sorry, but I can be with you later this evening.'

'Oh, Sharon, that would be wonderful. Sam will be over the moon to you see you.'

'Is he ok?'

'He's enjoying the presence of a nice police officer who drove us back and who's making me a cup of tea. I imagine the Chief Constable called it in.'

'Yes. Kim called me at once. I'm hitching a lift with the pathologist, and there's a car on its way to get me to Northolt. I'll pick up a car in Exeter. Love you.'

'News travels quickly,' I said to Nicola. 'Your call was relayed to London. That was my closest friend. She's coming by helicopter to Exeter airport with the pathologist. They must be careful that nothing sinister caused André to die.'

'I should warn you that the Chief is on her way here to see

you.'

'A warning isn't necessary. She and André were close friends, but please, can you remain with me a while at least?'

'I've been told to stay as long as you need me.'

'That long?' I said with a smile that surprised us both.

2

That was exactly one year ago today – July 1st, and I sat on again on the same bench as Sam ran around playing. He already looks so like his dad that just to glimpse his face when he gave me a sideways look was to remember André, who had been so happy and amazed that at his age he had become a father.

'I can hardly believe a year has passed,' said Nicola, as she kept one eye on Sam and the other on the beautiful Dart. 'I love this place despite what happened here.'

'There's no need to say "despite", Nicola.'

She came to the bench, sat down and took my hand.

'Well, it is special. And it's also where you and I met, a year ago today.'

'And a lot of water has flowed under the bridges of the Dart since then.'

Sam came towards us.

'Is it time to go home, mummy?'

I had first met Sharon Atwood (as she was to become after her marriage) on a singing course. She was the headteacher of a posh girls' school in Cheshire, but left to pursue a career in journalism with *The Times*, where she was first, the Education Correspondent and then the Features Editor.

In the past, Sharon had married her tutor at Exeter University, but left him after he converted to Islam. He became known to the nation as the Portsmouth Bomber, planting a bomb in the dockyards which killed two teenage girls and sentenced to life imprisonment. By means of deep cunning he had escaped from

Rampton High Security Prison with the single intent of killing Sharon, whom he regarded as an apostate. Armed police came to protect her on the singing course and at breakfast one the second morning there, dressed as a waiter, he made an attack on her with a knife, but was shot dead by the police officer just two metres short of Sharon.

Needing to get away, I invited her to Yorkshire where I worked as the manager of Betty's, a well-known tea shop in Ilkley. Concerns with Islamic terrorism followed us and we both met MI5 in form of Kim who she went on to marry, and André. More by accident than design I played a minor part in the eventual arrest of a prominent person plotting terrorist acts. André offered me a job in London with the service, and then asked for my hand in marriage. He retired, and we moved to a house on the edge of Dartmoor.

I can't deny my attraction to Sharon back then, but she moved to London with Kim, an army officer and now the Deputy Director of the security service. They have a daughter, Olivia, who shares her mother's beauty. I never hid from either Sharon or André my feelings for her, but it was a long time ago and comprised nothing more than an attraction, which was never reciprocated, but we became close friends.

She was with me too on the day my first pregnancy ended in bizarre circumstances. There had been a credible warning that an IRA splinter group were to make an attempt on André's life, though that warning was simply a cover to divert attention from the attempted killing on another person. My pregnancy already had difficulties but the decoy event set in motion a uterine haemorrhage in our cottage. It turned out out that the unwitting decoy was an experienced gynaecologist from Ireland who immediately saw what was happening, without whose immediate intervention I would undoubtedly have died along with the unborn twins I was carrying. Brendan has since become a good friend and works as Obs & Gynae consultant at the Royal Devon and Exeter Hospital.

All in all, Sharon has played a major parts in my life and circumstances, and arrived that evening and stayed until after the funeral. From the start, however, there was an unusual tension between us, kindled by the constant presence of Nicola, who had taken annual leave to come and stay and look after Sam. I had not expected that Sharon could be jealous. After all, she had Kim, and had shown only love and support for André and me together, but it was quite different with Nicola.

Sharon was older now and some of the glamour of earlier years had faded, and Nicola was 29, unattached, and whilst not beautiful by the standards of the former Features Editor, had become a rival for my friendship. Nicola and I were just five years apart and laughed at the same sort of jokes. She had also won the affection of Sam, and in the first days after André's death, often took him out in his buggy. Sharon had always hitherto been his favourite.

Nicola had picked up a sense of smiling hostility and in the immediate pre-funeral period returned to her flat each evening, but the hostility remained and seemed so inappropriate. The only person in my bed with me was Sam, though Sharon brought me in an early cup of tea and drank hers alongside me, lying on the bed.

'It's good that Nicola can come and take Sam out, but she strikes me as a needy person, and you need to make sure she doesn't cling.'

'I don't know about that, but she's been a real help with Sam and doing the shopping.'

'Can't you get it delivered?'

'Of course, but André and I always enjoyed going to the giant Tesco in Newton Abbot. He would carry Sam and they would giggle their way round. If I get a delivery, it will prevent an opportunity for us to get out.'

'So, Nicola is only temporary.'

'Oh yes, she's taken some of her annual leave to be of use here with Sam.'

'That's kind of her,' she replied, with a hint of sarcasm.

I was dismayed that Sharon was behaving like this and hoped that when Kim arrived, things might improve.

Just six days after André had died, Nicola and I walked Sam in his buggy along the road, leaving Sharon at work on her laptop. Suddenly Nicola stopped.

'Dee?'

'Yes,' I had said, with a slight sense of foreboding.

'She doesn't like me, does she?'

'She's jealous.'

'I'm happy for her to do the shopping and washing up, if she would like to take it on,' she said in a gently mocking tone.

I laughed.

'She can't come between us, Nicola, and I don't just mean that I shall stop her doing so – she can't. I know that even after just a few days, the highlight of my day is when I hear your car stop outside. I'm sorry if I shouldn't have said that and Sharon would just say I'm bereaved and vulnerable. But I'm not behaving stupidly, I'm just telling you how it is, and Sharon can do nothing about that. You could, of course, having heard what I've just said, might want to disappear and never return, but I've said what I have because I mean it.'

'Dee, I'm 29 and I've had no experience of love other than in books, but for the first time in my life I wake up and my first realisation is a face and a person. That's never happened to me before.'

'I suppose I should be feeling guilty about it. After all, we haven't even had the funeral yet, and I'm supposed to be the unhappy widow crying all the time, and I do sometimes when Sam's not around, but you're not a replacement for André, Nicola. You're totally you, and I'm dreading your return to work after the funeral, just as I dread each evening now when you go back to your flat in Totnes. I know enough already that I will put up with all this nonsense of Sharon but only if afterwards you will be there.'

'Did you ever think I might not be? I said to you last week by the river that I had been told to stay as long as you need me. I intend obeying orders, but if it makes your life easier, I'll just come as your child minder. I shall hate it, but just to see you will have to suffice.'

That was the occasion, in the lane, with the buggy containing

Sam, of our first and long kiss.

On the day after Sharon had arrived, Nicola told me that two people from the security service would be coming to removed André's computer which belonged to the service and such papers as they needed. Sharon seemed to know about this and when they arrived the two men had worked quickly and quietly in the study, but, as I discovered, had removed just about everything other than the books.

Neither André nor I took part in church life, though I had taken Sam into St Mary's occasionally. The information available said it was not a separate parish, but part of the Totnes team ministry, whatever that was. I was under constraints regarding the funeral. Once it had been confirmed that André had died of nothing other than heart failure, I was given instructions from the security service, which were explained to me when Kim and Olivia arrived to join Sharon and me.

It was "recommended" (a highly unlikely rubric!) that those who had seen active service, as had André in Northern Ireland during the Troubles, should be laid to rest with the minimum of information broadcast – no mainstream obituaries and no memorial events. I suppose I understood why, but it seemed such a pity. André loved obituaries, and had 60 volumes of the Oxford Dictionary of National Biography in his study, but he had chosen a life of secrecy and had to leave the world in the same way.

The funeral, meant to be a simple affair (paid for by the service) was attended by the Chief Constable of the County, the present and former directors of MI5, and two former Home Secretaries. Funeral directors from Exeter were asked to deal with the arrangements, and a priest sent from London to take the service, which did not include any sort of tribute or address that might have referred to the fact that for 20 years André had worked as the leading interrogator of terrorist subjects with a unique style which obtained a great deal of information useful to the service, and more importantly, to the safety of the realm.

The clergy of the Totnes team ministry were instructed to stay away from me and from the Church as the day of the funeral approached because of security implications, and I learned later that police with dogs were in and out the building on the morning of the funeral.

The priest sent by the service was a woman of mixed race who was delightful and extremely pretty. She was known to Sharon and Kim, though I didn't ask how, and she didn't say. She was called Judith, but her name was not disclosed, even on the order of service. I liked her and discovered we shared obstetric calamities. I told her of mine, and she told me she had developed pre- and then full eclampsia at 28 weeks, the pregnancy no longer viable was terminated ended. She and her female partner had broken up almost immediately afterwards.

The way she took the funeral using the old Prayer Book Service, and then conducted the burial was remarkable, especially as she had told me when we met that although the words had great sonority, appropriate for someone who would have appreciated them, she was wholly unconvinced by the content! I should have welcome further contact but it was recommended that I should not attempt it!

My mother had wanted to come from Lancashire for the funeral, but I told her that only those with security clearance could attend. This ameliorated her a little, but only a little, and she came three weeks later and stayed five years! Ok, it was only five days, but I know what it felt like.

On the eve of the funeral, as I was putting Sam to bed, I overheard Kim speaking to Sharon.

'I've run a security check on the child minder,' said Kim. 'There's nothing much to report – very average in every way. She was told to stay with Dee for as long as she was needed on the order of the Chief Constable.'

And so here we are, a year on, with Nicola still obeying orders and the three of us, in the words of the old song: "Happy Together".

There was nothing "very average" about Nicola. Her mum, Fiona Fairchild, is Deputy Principal of the Ashburton Cookery School and Chef's Academy, just a handful of miles away, and an amazing cook, as I have sampled on most Sundays in the past twelve months – a talent also shared by her daughter! Her dad, Ben, is a qualified dog groomer, and works in Ivybridge for a company based in Plymouth.

Nicola grew up in Ashburton, where her mum and dad still live in the same house (and where parking is almost impossible). Her elder brother, Mark, and his wife Helen, with their children Maisie and Angus, live and work in Newton Abbot. He's the manager of a large restaurant attached to a well-known hotel group. Nicola and Mark both went to school in Ashburton and Newton Abbot, and Nicola decided to enter the police force which had necessitated attending Police College in Coventry, before returning to work, first in Plymouth and more recently as a community constable based in Totnes, and that is all Kim knew – very average!

However, Nicola Fairchild is also known and published (so much for the scrutiny of the security service!) as Chloe Thomas, one of a new generation of women poets whose works are widely appreciated and, needless to say, bringing her next to nothing in the way of royalties. Her closest friend, another poet, Viv Manville, with whom she speaks regularly on zoom, was also a police officer and is married to a GP in an obscure village in Cumbria. Every year, Nicola, Viv and two or three other women poets meet up in the Derbyshire Dales in the house of another friend, Emily Elliot who, oddly, is married to a retired Church of England bishop who caused considerable controversy when he resigned aged just 42!

When Nicola told me all this, I remember sitting there with my mouth wide open. She laughed and kissed me, before producing her three published collections of poetry for me to see.

I knew nothing about poetry and at first all I could do was look at her photo on the back covers.

'You are allowed to look inside, you know.'

I felt I was handling something so precious I was frightened that I might cause them harm, and certainly anxious that if I did open them Nicola would discover exactly what sort of illiterate cretin she was now living with. I wanted to share in her obvious joy but didn't know how.

'You must be so proud of these,' I said, 'but Nicola, I know nothing about poetry.'

'That will be your school's fault. It makes me weep to know how just about everyone is forever turned off poetry by those who are supposed to be teaching it, when it is so simple. All they have to do is to get people to read it aloud in the open air.'

I looked at her, somewhat incredulous.

'Are you serious?'

'Oh yes, my darling Dorothea.'

She leant forward and kissed me again.

It was the start of a new and passionate love affair. We don't have many neighbours but the few have become accustomed to the sight of the obviously eccentric Lady Beeson, walking up and down reading a book aloud and obviously enjoying it! I didn't care. It was as if I had suddenly discovered the door to a room I had never even known existed and found it to be the repository of a treasure chest of wonder. Poor Sam is growing up with a mother who's slightly crackers!

Nicola only met André once when he was already dead, seated on a bench by the river Dart, so she had no idea of how and what he was. She understood intuitively when I needed to grieve for my loss and encouraged me to talk both to Sam and herself about life with André.

She came to live with me on the day Sharon, Kim and Olivia returned to London and, risking everything, told me she had that morning resigned from the police force, adding that if that meant she was wanted by me as only the child minder, the role for her cast by Sharon, she would accept it provided she could see me every day. I burst into tears and took her into my arms, where she has been, metaphorically (and usually physically) most of the time, since. That night, less than three weeks after André had died, she came to my bed, and it had never occurred to me she would be anywhere other.

André at first had assumed that at his great age his performance in bed would be muted but it didn't turn out that way. On the contrary, it seemed he was determined to make up for lost time and in his sex drive was considerable – it's little wonder his heart gave out in the end.

Being alongside Nicola in our bed was obviously going to be a very different matter even though from the beginning I longed for her, body and soul. Her one previous sexual experience with a fellow male police trainee at college had been far from glorious, and neither of us had ever had any a sexual relationship with another woman. But, little by little nature took over, and we discovered the joys of making love. It was a totally different experience from my nights with André who sometimes gave the impression that he had to catch the late bus home. Instead, it was slow and punctuated with laughter and occasional conversation as together we learned from what we knew from our own bodies what could bring not just delight but also ecstasy to the other.

Each morning Sam joins us and is wholly accustomed to us together. Nicola is more often than not awake before me and brings tea back to our bed, together with Sam's "milky-cup". After breakfast I have Sam to myself whilst Nicola writes for up to two hours. For lunch, when it is not too crowded, we walk to the Green Table Café by the Hall at Dartington. We take it in turns to cook our evening meal and both of us being talented cooks, we live well even though, as I suppose is the case in most families, we have a pattern of dishes we most enjoy over each fortnight On Sundays we go to Ashburton for lunch where Fiona cooks us something special, almost enough to make us feel it will last us the week.

Fiona and Ben took to Sam immediately but seemed uncertain how to handle someone who was a Lady though quickly learned that at heart I was just a lass from a Lancashire village and just like them. I quickly abandoned any use of the title, though my mother was horrified when I told her. I love Fiona and Ben. They are good and true people and have fully accepted that their daughter and I are a couple who live and love together, not least because they can see how happy Nicola is. I like Mark and Helen too, though she is very quiet, and spends most of the time we are with them attending to Angus who is not yet one-year-old.

But what can I possibly say about my mother? Not allowed to attend the funeral she eventually came, by train via London. She lives in Hoddlesden, near both Darwen and Blackburn, a village on a hillside at the bottom of which was once a pipe works, a cotton mill and a hideous Congregational Chapel. My mother always had airs and graces above her station, and proved a constant source of amusement to those living about us. She had five children, and besides myself, Dorothea, my siblings are Hermione, Hippolyta, Oberon, and Fyodor! Quite where Fyodor comes in A Midsummer's Night's Dream I don't know, though neither of course does Dorothea, the central character in Angus Eliot's *Middlemarch*. It was redeemed for me by Nicola, who made me watch the BBC production on DVD, since which time I have been trying to live up to Juliet Aubrey's portrayal and have subsequently read the novel and adored it. Dorothea Brooke is a lot to live up to, so I am still Dee, except to my mother,

She was dismayed to discover that Nicola and I were living together with all that implied. I hadn't warned her, and on the first day she assumed Nicola was some kind of live-in help, but I won't ever forget her face when I told her that Nicola and I slept in the same bed! I think even Les Dawson might have been impressed by the shapes her face assumed. That night I'm certain she lay awake, scheming, devising ways she might use to break us up.

My mum is a total snob as everyone in the village of

Hoddlesden has always known, and often enjoyed, though usually she is too self-regarding to notice when she is being mocked. With her daughter a "Lady" she was almost in heaven, and I was wondering how she would take my news that I no longer made use of the title as to all intents and purposes its significance had died with André.

She was quiet at breakfast and when she saw Nicola going into the study and closing the door demanded to know why.

'Nicola is a writer, a published and well-known poet though she doesn't write under her own name.'

I sought the three collections that had been published by a major poetry publishing house and handed them over. Now my mum is also a literary snob – hence the names she gave her children, though, ironically, is not and never has been much of a reader! There are no books in her house.

'Who is Chloe Thomas when she's at home?' she asked with a puzzled look.

'You've just had breakfast with her.'

She was struggling to take it all in.

'Nicola wrote the poems in those books and in the places where such things are taken seriously, she is highly regarded. So every morning after breakfast she goes and writes, leaving Sam and I for some quality time together.'

Mum twitched her eyes and then her entire head, desperately trying to find something more to say.

'Famous, you say?'

'No. I said highly regarded where people still read.'

'I've always loved poetry,' she burst forth. 'Tennyson is my favourite and I'm sure nothing written since could ever be better than that.'

In my mind, albeit for only a moment, I considered matricide.

'It's just possible, mum, that not everyone would agree with you,' I said.

'Nonsense. But now I think of it, I've read in the Lancashire Telegraph that there's a literary group meets in Darwen. Do you think Nicola would come and talk to them?'

'Are you a member of the group, mum?' I asked, somewhat

incredulously.

'I've been thinking about it, but to have a genuine published writer to bring along to my first meeting would be a great way to start, and I'm sure they would want to buy her books.'

Suddenly Nicola was mum's friend and a ticket to a new form of respectability in Darwen.

'She'll have to put it to her agent, as he arranges everything for her in the way of appearances.'

'An agent? Gosh, she really must be important.'

'She is,' I said.

I heard an extended cough from the study and went in to see if Nicola was ok.

'She was doubled up with laughter, coughing to disguise it.

'An agent?' she spluttered, tears running down her cheeks. 'My love, you've got a richer imagination than me,' once again coughing to cover up her intense giggling.

My mum has a loud voice, almost certainly because she's far too vain to get her hearing tested, so I had known that even with the door closed Nicola would have heard her every word.

I lifted up her face and planted a big kiss on her lips.

'Now listen, you. Get on with your work and maybe, just maybe, you'll write something even the author of *In Memoriam* might smile upon, let alone the Darwen Reading Group, and no more of this coughing.'

'To be fair to your mum, that really was a great work, but I promise I'll try, provided you don't report me to my agent.'

'Oh, alright. I promise,' and kissed her again before returning to mum who was talking cheerfully to Sam. She looked up.

'Is she alright?'

'She's fine now. It was just one of those coughs that last whilst you're trying to clear your throat.'

'I sometimes get them, often worse than that. Haven't you got any *Gee's Linctus* in the house. That would help. If we go out today and pass a chemist, I'll see if I can get her a bottle.'

My head did not actually spin round 360° but for a brief moment I thought it had and I'm sure Sam would have noticed, but at that moment he gave me a look that said something akin to

"Rescue me". I did so, leaving my mum to remove the breakfast things to the kitchen maintaining throughout a smug-looking smile on her face. Clearly her daughter did not want to be a Lady anymore but was living with a well-known author! It wasn't quite the same, but considerably better than nothing.

'You need a dishwasher, Dorothea,' she called out from the sink. 'It was mean of André not to get you one.'

It had never occurred to her I was the one who opposed André's regular entreaties to install a dishwasher and the very last description appropriate to my former husband was mean, though to be honest, in his will there was no mention of a supply of funds for household equipment, though his will did contain some surprises.

4

André had insisted from the time of our marriage that there was no need to talk about money, other than when after Sam's birth he made a day trip to London by train to make some changes to his will and, when we moved here to the cottage, which, he insisted, was to be wholly in my name.

When Mr Gleadall, our solicitor in London, telephoned me a week or two after the funeral to say that he wanted to bring his wife down to Devon for a short holiday, and that, if I wished, he could come to discuss André's will with me. That seemed eminently sensible, and I agreed, not least because in the hurly burly of events, I had not actually given any thought to the matter of the will.

Nicola took Sam out during Mr Gleadall's visit. It was the first time we had met and, unlike some of those holding an important office, he didn't treat me as an idiot.

'Sir André, Lady Beeson, prepared properly for this eventuality, but can I assume you are already aware of its contents?'

'Not at all. I had no reason ever to mistrust André. I know he came to see you after Sam was born and I assumed he was doing something for his benefit, but as his death seemed further off than it proved, I gave no thought to it.'

'Your late husband, Lady Beeson, was what I would call a moderately wealthy man and, in addition to the house you own, the majority of his estate comes to you, which means you are now a moderately wealthy woman.'

'What does "moderately wealthy" mean?'

'It means you will not what want for a great deal. The legal
processes following a death, probate and the like, can be
prolonged, and these will be complicated by inheritance tax,
though in his will, my firm is preferred to do these things for
you, but this is now your choice. I estimate that by the time of
their completion, you will be in receipt outright of over two
million pounds, with a further £500,000 set apart for your son to
be invested until his 18th birthday. By modern standards, this
will not number you among the rich, but you might understand
what I mean by moderate wealth.'

I was shaking and desperately trying not to show it. Mr
Gleadall assumed my silence to be consent to continue.

'As one might have expected, Sir André made a number of
generous bequests to military and other charities, but there is one
outstanding bequest, about which you may already know, of
£100,000 to Michael Donahue of Tullymore Park, Ballymena, in
Northern Ireland.'

'I've never heard the name. Who is he?'

'I do not know and all I did was to fulfil Sir André's instruction
when he drew up his will?'

I was puzzled.

'Was this an addition when André added the instructions about
Sam? I mean, was it in the original will?'

'The only change made by Sir André to his will was by codicil
to provide for your son's 18th birthday inheritance, which with
investment should be considerably more by then.'

'So, this bequest has been there for a long time?'

'This was Sir André's second will, made when you and he were
married. The first was destroyed but to the best of my
recollection it was also in the earlier will.'

I drew in my breath and then let it go with a smile.

'André would know that I will use such capital coming to me
for Sam's benefit even before he reaches the age of majority.
Thank you, Mr Gleadall for coming and bringing me the details
of the will. I will happily leave all legal and taxation matters in
your hands, though I imagine there will be documents to be
signed and so on for which I imagine I might have to come to

London. I am intrigued as to the identity of Michael Donahue, but trusting my late husband as I did, I have no reason to question his intentions, and whoever he may be, I hope he can benefit from this legacy. Does he know yet?'

'Oh no. That will have to wait until the demands of probate have been met, but I agree that Sir André will only have acted for the best of reasons.'

'He worked in Northern Ireland for the security services, and it could be anything. Most of what he did has remained a secret even from me, and I will let this remain so.'

I watched Mr Gleadall as he drove away, and at once summoned Nicola on the phone. She was now living with a moderately wealthy woman, news I knew would make her laugh.

We fed Sam and put him down for a rest, giving us the chance to talk.

'So, tell me,' began Nicola.

'Apparently, your partner is now a moderately wealthy woman, but only moderately, not rich.

As I had anticipated, Nicola burst out laughing.

'What does moderately mean?'

'The very question I asked Mr Gleadall, and he told me it amounts to the house in which we live, plus a moderate two million pounds plus half a million for Sam invested until he is 18.'

Her face at first showed no obvious expression, but then became visibly pained.

'I can't stay. I shall have to leave at once and live with my mum and dad until I can find somewhere.'

'Did you have a drink whilst you were out with Sam?'

'What are you talking about?'

'I assume you took him to our favourite café, and I'm wondering what you had to drink.'

'Coffee, of course, a flat white.'

'You'll have to change beverages if it affects you like this, ya daft haperth.'

'But if I stay, it'll look like I've been gold digging.'

'Well, I don't know about you, because I have found gold, but true gold called Nicola, and I had rather hoped you felt the same about me.'

'Of course, I do – gold, diamonds and riches beyond price, but this is quite different.'

'So, you were aware of the contents of André's will before we began to live and love together, even before Mr Gleadall's visit this morning?'

'Don't be silly. How could I?'

'In which case you can hardly be accused of being a gold digger, can you? This news will not change our world at all – not one bit, though we should have a talk about our day-to-day finances sometime soon. But as for leaving, do you really want us to be apart, because that would plunge us both into terrible grief? The thing is, Nicola, and I have only ever said this to one other person in my life, but I say it now and mean every word: I love you. We fit together perfectly, as if we were designed this way.'

By now we were both crying, and Nicola came to me on the sofa.

'I love you, Dee, and I will never part from you, ever.'

'Even from a moderately wealthy woman.'

'I have no need of wealth. I have everything I need already, if I have you, and would continue to do so even if we had nothing.'

We kissed and held each other close. Having professed my love, I felt this was a commitment, and that we were now was engaged to be married and said so.

She sat sharply back.

'You've been a widow for only a few weeks. Sharon would tell you not even to think, let alone say, such a thing.'

'I'm only interested in what Nicola has to say,' I said, reaching out and taking her hand. 'Perhaps we should wait until the autumn but, Nicola Fairchild, will you marry me?'

'Mummy, Nicola,' came a demanding voice from Sam's room.

We looked at one another and laughed.

'I'll go,' said Nicola, standing.

'Will you think about it, please,' I added quickly.

She stopped and turned.

'Considering I'm a daft haperth – whatever one of them is – I've already thought about it. I'll see to Sam, and the answer is yes, my moderately wealthy wife-to-be!'

We agreed to say nothing to anyone for a little while, and especially to neither my mother nor Sharon. However, at our first Sunday lunch after my mum had returned home, we agreed that we would each wear our newly acquired matching engagement rings and see if anyone noticed them and that I had placed my wedding ring onto my right hand. Nicola's mum missed nothing.

'What's going on?' she said only minutes after we had arrived and were together setting the table.

'I really prefer the original 4 Non Blondes version, don't you?' Nicola said to me with a huge grin.

'Oh, I don't know,' I replied with a look at Fiona, 'I quite like Pink.'

'Stop it, you two, and just tell me your news, or am I getting ahead of myself?'

'No, you're not, mum,' said my fiancée. 'We've decided the love we have for each other is such that we want to get married, not just yet, but soon.'

'But you've just lost your husband,' Fiona said to me. 'Making a decision like this at such a time is not sensible, and you've hardly known one another for more than a very short while. Don't you think you should wait a couple of years at least?'

I sat down.

'Fiona,' I said gently, 'My husband and I both knew that being 40 years apart, our marriage would end sometime and that most likely I would survive him. Though perhaps sooner than I had expected, André had spoken about the inevitability of his death and told me that I must not hesitate to find someone to love and live with, and to help bring up Sam.

'Nicola knows how much I adored André, but I'm not sure I didn't adore him more than love him. He died so incredibly wonderfully – I could not have wished for a more perfect ending to his life, with Sam and the River Dart and me. And then, as if by magic your daughter came into my life just minutes afterwards and shared in that incredible moment of his passing from life to death. I'm not religious nor, I think, superstitious, but it was as if it was all meant to be. From the first moment I felt as if Nicola and I were two halves meant to fit together, and I have been able to find that I love her. André and I together produced Sam, but I love Nicola and as they say, "end of".'

It was hopeless. Three women, now joined by Ben, were crying together. However would lunch get cooked now? This was serious!

5

It was just three days later that I received an unexpected call from Helen, Mark's wife. Until then, we had hardly spoken and Nicola had said Helen had been troubled with postnatal depression following Angus's birth.

'Helen, how lovely to hear from you. Is it your sister-in-law that you want because she's out at the moment with Sam?'

'No. It's you I wanted to talk to. In fact, I am ringing to ask whether we might meet somewhere to talk, you and me. I recall you saying you had a miscarriage. You may know that since Angus was born, I have been struggling. My GP has prescribed tablets, but I don't want them, though Mark is getting frustrated with me and begs me to take them, but I just wondered whether you and I might talk, woman to woman. I don't know, but I think it might help me.'

'Do you know *The Grange* on the grounds of Buckfast Abbey? The three of us have been there sometimes for lunch and it's good and there are places where we can walk too. Could we meet there?'

'Yes, I would really like that. Do you think Nicola would mind?'

'Don't be daft, lass. Of course not.'

For the first time ever, I heard Helen laugh.

'Clearly you've been taken out of the north, but the north can't be taken out of you.'

'Such flattery means I will pay for the soup and roll.'

Again, I heard a small laugh.

'When?' I asked.

'Please, soon?'

'What about tomorrow? Meet me in the Abbey car park at 11:00?'

'That will be fine. My mother has Angus tomorrow, so it means I can come easily.'

'And Nicola always has Sam at that time, too. Helen, thank you for calling. I look forward to seeing you.'

I reported the conversation to Nicola when she and Sam arrived back.

'It would be wonderful if she could open up to you. It's been tough for her, and Mark too, since Angus was born. When they were first together, she was a lively person and, well, you've seen what she's like when we're together for Sunday lunch.'

'What did she do before the babies?'

'She was a waitress. That's how they met – working for Mark.'

'I don't know what I can do, but if you're happy for me to meet with her, I'm more than willing to listen and share my own experiences, though it's totally different from hers.'

The Abbey Estate at Buckfast is an enchanting place to visit and they cater well for the many who come each day. Besides the inevitable shops selling alcoholic beverages made by the monks and a bookshop, there is a good exhibition on the Benedictine way of life I had once visited with André. Neither of us liked the inside of the Abbey itself, but from the outside it is splendid. There are also ornamental gardens of various kinds and the whole place is uncluttered, offering the chance to walk and just be.

The Grange is the café/restaurant which I was most interested in, having managed the outstanding *Betty's* in Ilkley (and "outstanding" is not just my description but the view of just about everyone who came in – just look it up on TripAdvisor and see) and where I lived and worked when I first met André and Sharon.

I was a little early but enjoyed the summer warmth as I waited for Helen to arrive. I recognised her car and waved, seeing her smile in recognition.

'Hi,' she said as she walked towards me, and we gave each other a hug.

'I thought this might be a good place to meet,' I said. 'It's not too busy just now so we can get ourselves a drink and something to eat and sit outside if you like.'

Once we were seated, Helen chose not to waste time on niceties.

'I imagine Nicola will have told you that since Angus was born, I've been having a rough time, and I imagine that if you were to ask him, Mark would say he was having an even worse time. His job is very demanding timewise, so I've learned to rely on my mum and dad to look after the children.

'Although the doctor describes it as PND I can't help thinking that is more use to him than it is to me, you know, a convenient label, but it ignores the fact that the depression, if that is what it is, began before Angus was born, at least two months before, when I would have been about 32 weeks. I can remember a sense of horror when I came away from an ante-natal appointment knowing that I didn't want this baby, and though I love him and do my very best to care for him, my feelings haven't changed. In fact, I'm sure I don't want my life. Dee, I'm not saying that I'm suicidal. I want a different life. I've even fantasised about being swept off my feet as you have Nicola and having the chance to start again.'

'How much of this have you said to Mark?'

'Nothing at all. I just don't think he would have the first idea what I was going on about. He thinks everything in the garden is rosey – nice house, good income, two kids; he doesn't want for more. I just wondered if by talking this over with you it might make some sort of sense.'

'It does, Helen, it does. What I would say, however, is that I'm not a professional counsellor, and at the most I can tell you a little of what has happened to me that ties in with what you're saying, if you would like to hear it.

'I really would.'

'There's two things. The first is that like you I wanted my life to change when I was manager of the tea shop in Yorkshire. That could quite easily have become an end in itself and a dead end at that, so if that is what you're saying, then I can more than empathise with you.

'The second, the only other thing I can offer, is my experience after my miscarriage and near-death experience. I was saved by only the most bizarre and unlikely of circumstances. An Irishman we initially thought was a terrorist come to kill André, turned out to be an obstetrics and gynae surgeon. By the time it happened I had passed out from loss of blood, and he realised that this was an emergency and dealt with me only as he could by pushing his fist into my vagina to staunch the bleeding as we were driven at great speed into the Royal Devon and Exeter in the back of off a Land Rover. On arrival, he did an emergency operation, even though no one there knew he was qualified to do so. He saved my life. When the department consultant turned up towards the end of the operation, she said what he had done was quite brilliant and offered him a job there and then. But, and there is a point to this, Helen, it was afterwards, as I recovered, that the difficulties began.

'I could not get my mind away from the thought of this other man with whom I had now had the most intimate contact. It wasn't just the fact of the wound and the intense bruising and pain, plus the loss of my babies – it would have been twins – I was no longer sure I wanted any more intimate contact with André. This lasted quite some time and though he was understanding, he couldn't see the complete picture. I know I could have had intercourse with him before we eventually did again, but the fact is I didn't want to. But when we did, I soon became pregnant again and I had to go through the whole rejoicing saga. Now, I love my son with every ounce of my being, but I didn't want a baby and when I was pregnant, I didn't want this baby. Now I have him, he fills me with joy every day and since André died, he's a constant reminder to me of his father, who rescued me from my first life in the tea shop.'

'On my goodness!' exclaimed Helen when I stopped. 'Why am I complaining?'

'You're not complaining, Helen, you're telling how it is, and we can't compare someone else's experience with our own. I didn't tell you this to make you feel bad. You feel bad and I just wanted you to know that some of what you're going through, I can understand. The only thing that matters now is you, and how you might discover that life you are longing for, and which, in its absence, you are depressed because you cannot see even a tiny light that suggests a way through to it.

'There's a story of a man who falls into a deep hole. He cries for help and a priest throws him a prayer book, followed by a lawyer who promises to take up his case. Then his friend sees him and jumps in to join him. "Now we're both stuck" the man protests. "Ah", says his friend, "but I fell in here once before and I know the way out".'

Helen laughed and took a drink of her apple juice.

'All I can say is that I'm wholly on your side. I will not leave you on your own. I'm sure I speak for Nicola too, when I say you can to come be with us, call me or meet with me. at any time.'

'Nicola is Mark's sister, remember, and I'm not sure I could tell her any of what I've told you.'

'I know and I fully understand, but she's also much more than Mark's sister and I truly think that if she heard what you have told me this morning, she would be wholly alongside you, too. It's not about taking sides. I don't know if you've ever read any of her poetry, but it is all a powerful expression of the longing for a life that any of us might want. She would want only the very best for both you and Mark, but like me, must accept that something fundamental might have to change. Depression is not life.'

I could tell that Helen was feeling more positive. We left the café and walked slowly around the gardens as she told me more about her life before working as a waitress, and I could have cried as I listened to her because I realised that she had not been helped to get more, the more she knew inside that she longed for, and had accepted jobs that were clearly less than she could have risen to.

We returned to the car park and gave each other a warm hug.

'Nicola is so lucky to have found you.'

'I'm the lucky one, but the circumstances of our meeting, with my husband dead on the seat, weren't exactly the most propitious. But even in the darkness, there may be the hope of light and life. Oh, God, I sound like a vicar.'

'And you one of those wicked women called lesbians!'

After she had driven off, I sat in my car pondering her last words. I had never thought of myself as a lesbian. and I refused to accept any label. I knew I was simply a woman in the happy position of being in love with a poet whom I was intending to marry in a matter of weeks. Definitely, end of!

6

Eventually, packing for a small child being far more demanding than even for two women, we set off on our way to Derbyshire, my personal qualified police driver behind the wheel. As we passed the sign for Newton Abbot on the A38, Nicola asked me if Helen had known that all that she had disclosed to me two days earlier would be repeated to her.

'Since my earliest encounters with Sharon and André in Yorkshire, I have been surrounded by secrets of various kinds, most of which I have not been aware. I dare say that it was the same in the police force. I will no longer live like that. I may know some things that the Official Secrets Act forbids me to reveal, and I bet you do too, but to my mind they don't matter one whit to you and me, and I want there to be no secrets between you and me because I believe they are destructive. They're a sort of cancer in relationships. I didn't say I wouldn't tell you all she told me, but that's quite different from telling others in the family. But Mark's your brother and if you'd rather...'

'Oh no,' she interrupted. 'You're right about no secrets. I love Mark, of course, and he will always be my brother, but I can imagine he's not necessarily the most patient man to live with.'

'And what about me?' I asked, playfully. 'Do you think I'm patient?'

'You're a superb cook, better than me. Cooks have to be patient. My mum says that's the hardest message for her students to take in. You would pass easily.'

We were on our way to the Buxton Literature Festival, an

event masterminded by Nicola's friend Emily. She was once a somewhat wild "performance" poet much loved by left-wing youth and her publishers because, unlike most collections of poetry, they sold well. And then, much to the chagrin of audiences and publishers alike, she stopped. She abandoned all her previous work and, as it were, reinvented herself as quite a different sort of poet, writing a different sort of poetry.

'Her publishers sent her on a tour of America to try and get it out of her system, accompanied as her manager, by a man who needed a break from England,' said Nicola with a delightful laugh. 'He's called Alex Elliot and was once a philosophy professor at Cambridge, and then, astonishingly, was appointed as the Bishop of Truro. He couldn't stand it and resigned after two years, and so a trip to America seemed a good idea. To cut a long story short, they fell in love and then were killed in an airbrush in Vancouver.'

'What?' I burst out. 'What on earth do you mean?'

'It was in the papers and on the television. A plane they were on crashed with complete loss of life, but they had missed their flight though their names were released to the press as having been on board, and they only found out they were dead 24 hours later. They came home, married and have twins, though he's had a bad nervous breakdown since.'

'I'm not surprised after all that.'

'They're a smashing couple and I'm fond of them both, and I can't wait to show you off.'

'My greatest fear is opening my mouth, to be honest. I know so very little about literature and the only poetry I now know is by you, though that's saying a lot.'

'In which case, just walk around repeating that to everyone you meet and I might sell more books,' she said with a laugh.

Once on the M5 Nicola kept a constant speed but drove with her eyes continually checking behind, at the side and in front, as she had been trained to do and I felt perfectly safe. We did, however, have to make several stops en route for both for ourselves and Sam. It was about 250 miles and especially when we converged with the M6, the traffic was heavy.

'Did I mention that we're not actually staying in Buxton?' Nicola said, as we passed by Stafford.

'No,' I replied, wondering what was to follow.

'We're staying with Emily and Alex. They have a big house on the eastern edge of the Dales, so we'll leave the motorway at the next junction and go via Uttoxeter.'

'Do they know about me?'

'I've told them I'm bringing Lady Dorothea Beeson and her son, Samuel.'

'Nicola! How could you? What on earth will they think?'

'Do you care what people think, my love?'

I paused and asked myself the same question.

'No, you're right. I don't care one bit.'

'They will love you and you them. They have twins, Chloe and George, so Sam will have some friends.'

'Alex and I could play my Lord and my Lady games too.'

'I wouldn't put it past you.'

The person who met us at the door was Amy, Emily's mum.

'They'll be back any minute but it's lovely to see you again, Nicola. You look great. And a special welcome to you, Lady Dorothea, and Samuel. It's lovely having you here.'

I gave a quick glare at Nicola, who laughed.

'Amy,' I said hurriedly, 'I'm called Dee, and this is Sam.'

'Blame your fiancée.'

'She told you that too? Excuse me while I thump her on the arm.'

'Be my guest, but I'd noticed the rings. Congratulations, both of you.'

'Amy was apparently once a nun, but I think she might have been a witch,' said Nicola.

'Let's just agree that I'm a noticing sort of person. Now then, most important of all, Sam, would you like a drink and some cake, and I'll show you the playroom where Chloe and Angus will come and see you when they get home?'

'Ooh, yes please!' said Sam, causing my eyebrows to rise with sheer amazement at the "please"!

Before taking Sam to the kitchen Amy directed us upstairs to a room with a wonderful view looking south. To me, the Dales meant North Yorkshire, but these were undoubtedly dales too, though obviously not as good.

Nicola and I held one another and kissed, releasing only when we heard the front door opening below and the sound of adult and children's voices eagerly wanting to greet their visitors. At once we went down to be with them. My eyes almost fell out of my head. Alex was tall and handsome, wearing a Hawaiian style shirt and shorts, but how could I find the words to describe Emily? Nicola hadn't told me she was stunningly beautiful, or at least I thought her so. Also tall with short dark hair, her skin a colour which suggested her father must have been non-white. She smiled and came towards me whilst Alex gave Nicola a hug.

'And you must be the amazing Lady Beeson my friend Nicola told me about,' she said, almost engulfing me in her arms.

'She'll soon stop being *my* friend if she continues telling tales.'

'I don't think that's at all likely. She's quite wicked or have you not yet discovered that of the lady hugging my husband, whom I imagine, from what I can see of your left hand, you intend to marry?'

'Blimey, you're as bad as your mother!'

'I will take that as a genuine compliment, but it's great to have you here. I assume it's ok to call you Dee.'

'Of course and thank you for your welcome.'

It was now the turn of Alex to squeeze me tight.

The children had already disappeared, determined to meet Sam, and probably also to persuade their granny to hand over cake and a drink for them too.

Eventually, we all sat together in the large sitting room and chatted about the festival they had set up.

'I'm really chuffed about some of those coming to speak and read, especially Rebecca Watts from Cambridge and Viv.'

'I hope this is alright for me to say so, Dee,' began Alex, 'but I met your late husband once and really liked him.'

'Of course. Tell me.'

'It was one of those utterly ridiculous things the Church of England sets up to pretend it still has an important role. to play in national life. The Director of MI5 and André were invited to dinner at the Athenaeum with me and the Bishop of St Edmundsbury and Ipswich, because he'd once been a naval reservist. God knows what they must have thought about this, but the Director and André were so interesting about everything other than their work, though I did manage to learn that André had served in Belfast during the Troubles and that the Director was a highly decorated soldier, so I left with great respect for them both.'

'That must have been before my time,' I said, 'and to be honest, I know little more than you about what André did in Northern Ireland. He never spoke about it, though I'm sure that's for the best.'

'Yes, soldiers rarely talk about their war experiences.'

'But thank you, Alex, for telling me that.'

'Have you plans for getting married?' asked Emily.

'Ideas rather than plans,' said Nicola, but we want it to be sooner rather than later, perhaps in October.'

'I'm sorry the Church of England won't let you do it,' said Alex.

'I'm certain we wouldn't want a religious ceremony even if they could offer one,' I said, looking towards my fiancée. 'Marrying Nicola is much too momentous for that.'

I swear Nicola blushed though she later, unconvincingly, denied it.

The plan for the three days of the festival was that Amy and Alex would take turns looking after the children, whilst Emily, Nicola and I attended each afternoon and evening. It took me a little while to remember that I was soon getting married to Chloe Thomas and that the woman I now knew as Viv Manville, was known by most others there as Olivia Doyle. Even Emily was better known as Emily Cunningham than the Mrs Elliot we were staying with.

I marvelled at the reception Nicola received when she did her reading. I was so proud of her but was almost knocked out by a new poem she read about me, of which she had told me nothing in advance. As I sat there, I really did blush, and felt everyone must be looking at me, but of course they weren't, focusing all their attention on her words which held them spellbound. As she concluded her reading I could only cry, though Viv, sitting next to me, assured me it was the appropriate response.

Viv and Nicola had both been police officers and often, as we ate supper together, they would share knowledge and experiences far removed from the world of poetry into which both led us when they performed. Viv lived in an isolated part of the world. Few know about the Cumbrian Dales, a secret the residents do their very best to keep, and where her husband worked, mostly among farmers. With two small children she was not now writing as much as she had formerly but had acquired the art of making the most use of stolen moments when the children slept in the daytime. I found myself wondering whether Nicola and I would ever want a baby. At the moment, the thought of all the intrusive processes involved filled me with disquiet, but were it to arise, then Brendan O'Callaghan, who had saved my life, was the person I knew I could talk to. Still, I thought, we were both young enough to think about babies later.

I missed the last day of the festival to allow Alex to attend the final reading which to be given by the lovely Emily Cunningham. He was so proud of her, just as I was of Nicola. Our two poets had gone out for an early walk and as Amy cleared away the breakfast things, Alex and I had the chance to talk whilst the children played with cars around our feet.

'Your husband died what I would call a perfect death,' he said.

'I know and that has made it almost impossible for me to grieve over-much, especially as within ten minutes Nicola came into my life, but I'm not so daft as to know that I miss him, and Nicola is wise enough to allow me the necessary time and space to live with those feelings.'

'Have you enjoyed the festival?'

'Yes. Nicola read a poem about me about which I hadn't known, which astonished and delighted me, and I've so enjoyed being here with Amy and you and getting to know Emily and Viv. I have to say, though, that some poems I've heard have been way above me. They sound as if they are saying something that matters, but I can't always puzzle it out.'

'I think, then, there's hope for you,' said Alex with a smile. D H Lawrence said that if you nail down a poem, you either kill the poem or it will get up and walk away carrying the nail. I've learned so much from Emily, not least that a poem is an invitation to explore much more than a definite location on a map that you can put your finger on. You are in the enviable position of being an explorer with so much still to discover and enjoy.'

'I sometimes feel stupid when people throw around names I've never heard of.'

The poet T S Eliot, just one letter 'L' by the way so no relation, included a line in one of his earliest poems: "In the room the women come and go talking of Michelangelo", and I've also heard what you are referring to. It's a way of exhibiting their cleverness and is utterly boring. I bet you've not heard Viv, Emily or your Nicola doing that.'

'No, I haven't. I'm afraid my education was seriously lacking.'

The children were engrossed in a game as I left the room, and then my phone rang. I saw at once it was Helen.

7

'Helen?' I said. 'Are you safe?'

'Oh Dee, I'm at my mum's with Maisie and Angus. Mark hit me this morning, and I took the kids out straight away and came here.'

'I'm so sorry. Are you able to tell me what happened?'

'Yes. Mum's taken Maisie to her nursery and I'm just here with Angus. I've been doing so much thinking since our time together the other day at Buckfast and trying desperately to consider how things might change. Last night, Mark said he had lost patience with me and demanded we had sex again. I told him I couldn't and when he tried to force me, I upped and went into the spare room. He didn't follow me, I'm pleased to say, but when I got up to get the children their breakfast, he got furious and hit me across the face.'

'In which case you've done the right thing, but I imagine he will know you've gone to your mum and dad's.'

'Yes. I told him I was coming here and I imagine he will have gone to work.'

'Did he hit you in front of the children?'

'Maisie was still in her bedroom, but Angus was in his high chair with me.'

'Do you have a visible injury?'

'No.'

'And have you told your mum what happened?'

'I can't, Dee, not least because I think she'd be on his side and tell me to get home and pull myself together.'

'Mark has to understand the seriousness of what he has done if things are ever to recover, and if that is, either of you wants them to recover. It might not do him any harm if, when he gets home this evening, he finds the house empty.'

'But where could I go?'

'We're not back until tomorrow, but you could go to our place. Nicola's mum has our spare keys and I'll call her and let her know you might be coming. We live in the first cottage you come to on the right on Foxhole Lane. If you can get yourself some milk, everything else is there for you to use."

'Fiona will wonder what's happening. She is Mark's mum, after all."

'Go back home and get the things you need for the children and yourself. I'll call Fiona in the meantime.'

'Thank you, Dee.'

Oh dear, I thought. What have I set in motion? This could turn into some kind of nightmare, tearing Nicola's family apart. I waited eagerly for her to get back from her walk and saw them approaching, both laughing and talking. The laughter was about to stop. I opened the door to meet them.

'Nicola,' I said with urgency, 'I've just had a call from Helen. Something's happened and I have an awful feeling I might have caused it.'

'I'll go in,' said Emily, concerned, but leaving us to it.

I told Nicola about Helen's call and my offer.

'That's so typically generous of you, Dee, but it's not the right way forward. If she leaves the matrimonial home and takes the children, she may lose every legal leg she has to strand on. She must go back. Domestics are always complex and, having refused the help of the GP, she needs all the protection she can get. I need to call her.'

I was impressed that the former police officer had taken charge and felt rather foolish that I had reacted as I had, which I know she saw on my face, as she reached into her bag for her phone.

'What you suggested was good, just not the right thing.'

Her call was answered.

'Helen? Hi, it's Nicola. Dee's just told me about my idiot brother, but I'm not calling to defend him, but as the former police constable who's had to deal with this sort of appalling behaviour before.

'If you are to safeguard your future and that of Maisie and Angus, you mustn't leave your home, or you could lose every right you have. I know he's been horrible, and that he doesn't understand how things are for you, but you need to be there when he gets home. His day will have been ruined by guilt and remorse – we both know him well enough for that, and at this stage, whatever might belong to the future you discussed with Dee, you must start from a position of security. He won't assault you again, I'm sure. Nor do I think it would help for me to alert someone from the Newton Abbot police to call in and have a word, but if he turns violent again, and we both know him well enough to know he won't, because he'll be devastated by his behaviour this morning, then call me and I'll call it in.'

She listened to Helen for a while and then responded.

'She's here, standing alongside me, and I'll tell her that,' responded Nicola. 'Text me later and let me know you're back home and even later, to say how things have been when Mark gets home? One other thing, though. Your first concern must be to safeguard Maisie and Angus. That's imperative. Ok, my lover? Bye.'

She put the phone back in her bag.

'I've had to attend several domestics in the past year. They always preferred to send a woman. Whatever Helen needs to do for herself, foremost must be the well-being of the children, not that my brother would ever hurt them, but she needs to know how the law works if she is to benefit from it.'

'I'm so sorry. What a total idiot I've been, utterly seduced by thinking how clever I had been when talking to Alex. I was completely out of my depth, and I really could have messed things up for her.'

'Don't worry, my love,' said Nicola, taking hold of my hand as we remained standing by the front door facing the fields onto which the sun was not shining for me. 'It'll be ok if she does what I've told her. In the meantime, I need to give thought to how I can get some sort of support for Mark. What he did will be a terrible shock to him, and I don't just mean his pride will be hurt. It will go deeper. And she sends her love and can't wait to see you again.'

As Alex, Emily and Nicola got ready for the drive into Buxton, I sat with Amy drinking coffee outside as the three children played happily together in the garden.

'I gather something's happened back in Devon,' said Amy.

'It's what the police call a domestic, involving Nicola's brother and his wife. She was brilliant on the phone to her sister-in-law, whereas I had said things that were obviously far from helpful.'

'Oh good,' said Amy.

'Good? What on earth do you mean?'

'I couldn't help overhearing snippets of your chat with Alex as I cleared away the breakfast things, and I kept thinking how wise you were. So, you got something wrong because you lacked Nicola's police officer experience. I'm hugely relieved to know you're human after all!'

I couldn't resist a laugh, but it didn't make me feel much better.

The afternoon was sultry and, whilst the children had their post-lunch rest, Amy and I compared recipes in the kitchen.

'You worked in *Betty's,* didn't you?'

'You've obviously been,' I replied.

'Oh indeed, though the York shop, not that in Harrogate.'

'I was manager of the Ilkley branch – in the Yorkshire Dales. After school, I did a cookery course in Blackburn and then applied to *Betty's* for work as a cook. It was to get away from my mother as much as anything. I worked first in Harrogate and then became assistant manager in Northallerton before taking the reins in Ilkley. It was a good job, and we had very satisfied customers in both the café and the bakery shop. Then my life changed, wholly unexpectedly, as it has done so again.'

'I was widowed shortly after giving birth to Emily,' said Amy. 'As will be obvious to anyone who looks at our daughter, my late husband was Indian, and he was such a good man. He was overjoyed to see his daughter, but within three months had died of a brain tumour.'

'That's awful, Amy. How did you meet, because weren't you a

nun before you got wed?'

'Yes, in an enclosed order near Wakefield, and I can't deny that
I was happy there. It seemed to me such a good life. Then one
fine day I was sent out to collect something from a local shop,
when I tripped and fell. Ronan picked me up and led me inside
his house to have a drink and recover, though I had obviously
broken my finger in my fall, so he then took me to hospital. It
was called Casualty in those days, and within a few minutes as
we sat there, we knew there was something special going on
between us and by the time we left the hospital I knew I could
abandon the good life for the even better. Mother Superior was
singularly unimpressed when I telephoned from Ronan's house,
but I never returned to the convent. He swapped my habit for the
clothes I had originally arrived in. Ronan stood at the convent
door and did the deal as I had nothing yet to wear other than the
somewhat peculiar underwear nuns in that order were required to
wrap around themselves sexlessly.

'Did you get married?'

'Yes, believe it or not, in a Hindu Temple in Leeds. Oh, it was
glorious and although occasionally I talk Christian spirituality
with Alex, I think of myself as Hindu and I'm ever so proud of
that.'

'And how long was it before Emily appeared?'

'Two years, so Ronan and I had very little time together. That's
a bit like you and your husband.'

'Amy, forgive me, but I'm dying to know...'

'If I slept with Ronan on that first night? 'Oh Dee, how could
you think such a thing? I was a dedicated nun and he a devout
Hindu, so of course we did, and fabulous it was too!'

They both laughed.

'Is Emily Hindu?'

'Emily has only ever been Emily, but she has huge respect for
my Hindu beliefs, as does Alex.'

In the late evening as we prepared for bed, Nicola having
returned exhilarated from a highly successful last event in
Buxton, she told me Helen had texted to say she was feeling safe,
and that Mark was deeply ashamed of what he had done. I was

relieved and made a mental note never to interfere in the affairs of others again!

8

I was a little anxious about Sunday lunch in Ashburton two days later, wondering whether Mark knew anything of my interference or that Nicola and I knew about what had happened, but there was no sign of this in the way he was with us, though I noticed Helen was no more voluble than before, though just before they left, she mouthed the single word "coffee". I nodded.

'I'm not sure seeing Helen again is a good idea, Dee,' Nicola said as we drove home. 'I don't want her to break my family up.'

'What if I suggested she come when we're both able to meet with her in *The Green Table*, perhaps, or even the *Cider Press Centre*, and besides which we don't know yet how things lie.'

'There was no obvious atmosphere today. I don't want us to stir up something that may be settling down.'

'By us, you mean me. I learned a hard lesson from you the other day, but I can hardly just drop her as a friend.'

'It's not only about Helen. She has two children, and it's also about my brother, don't forget.'

'Oh help! I've done it again, going where angels fear to tread.'

'That's the first time I've ever heard you quoting from a pope?'

'A pope? Good heavens.'

'Yes, "*A* Pope", Alexander Pope, in a poem he wrote in 1709.'

'Oh Nicola, why are you marrying me? You're much cleverer and now I'm threatening your family's life because I just don't have what I see in you every day.'

'I'll tell you something, Lady Beeson,' she began, as we left the A38 at Buckfastleigh to follow the Dart downstream. 'Everyone, and I mean every single person who met you last week, congratulated me on my extraordinary good fortune. Driving into Buxton on Friday, Alex said that he thought you were a woman of great courage and wisdom, and Emily said that she'd become a little scared of talking poetry with you, so taken aback was she by some of your observations about one or two of her poems. And at supper in the evening, Viv said to me you would have made a first-rate detective because you not only look at people, you seem able to see into them as well. She really liked you and begged us to come north and stay in Dentdale with them.'

'You should have pointed out my far from wise efforts to destroy your family.'

'Oh Dee, don't be such a daft haperth – what a wonderful phrase, by the way, and you must tell me what it means sometime – because all you've done is to be there when Helen asked you. It's not your fault that I've been more involved in domestics, and I don't want to stop your support for Helen, but we must think out the best way to do that.'

'A haperth is short for a "halfpenny worth", though most people drop the "h". There used to be a chip shop in Hoddlesden, and I've been told that in days when people were much poorer than now, they would sometimes ask for a haperth o'chips, mostly comprising scraps. It was quite a social service.'

'When did you last visit the place?'

'I don't think they ever served plaice.'

'Ha ha, hilarious.'

'You've met my mother, so you'll understand when I say it was quite some time ago, but if ever we were to go and visit Viv in Cumbria, on the way I could show you a very different sort of village to the one you grew up in.'

'Did you ever take André?'

'Oh God, no. He'd been in Belfast during the Troubles, but even that wouldn't have equipped him for a night in Hoggy, as we call it, visiting the Con Club or the Ranken. He'd have opted for a haperth o'chips and a rapid escape.'

As she parked the car, it was difficult to stop Nicola laughing and Sam joined in the fun too.

Helen must have called as soon as Mark had left home on the following morning.

'Dee, I haven't mentioned to Mark that you and I had coffee last week, but I'd still like us to meet. And thanks so much for the generous offer you made, though I fear it got you into trouble with the police!'

'It's ok. Nicola knows more than me about some things and I must bow to her superior knowledge, but my concern was that you might get hurt.'

'I know and I love you for it, Dee, but he's been so full of regret it's unlikely he would do it again. But nothing has really changed since we spoke and I want to meet with you again, for two reasons. The first is to help me sort out my thoughts. You made a start, but I need more. The second is because I really like you and just enjoyed being with you as a friend. Surely Nicola can't object to that?'

'She doesn't, but has warned me off marriage guidance, because there are people properly trained to do that, but we agreed last night that for you and me to meet for coffee, agreeing not to discuss you and Mark would be a good idea. The *Cider Press Café* here in Darlington is a good place if you can get here.'

'I like cider, so it sounds ideal. I assume it's easy to find. Can you manage 11:00 this morning? You mentioned that's the time when Sam gets taken out by Nicola, and my mum can have Angus whilst Maisie's in nursery.'

What Helen had said actually sounded more like "Oi loik coider", her Devonian accent even stronger than Nicola's lovely lilt and in total contrast to my hard East Lancashire consonants and rolling r's, though my wife-to-be says she loves my r's, or at least I think that's what she said and hope it wasn't!

The Sunday-silent Helen was not in evidence when we met. She had been busy on the internet looking up courses on the Open University and elsewhere. She was already thinking long term in the recognition that with small children "and no more!", she needed to do her learning at home, but clearly our earlier encounter had set off ideas. I didn't say that I was thinking along the same lines for myself though I said I had spent some days in the previous week with a group of talented women that had made me reflect on my own limited education and how it might be improved.

'But you've been married to a Sir and you're a Lady.'

'Helen, I ran a café, albeit a very good one, and had trained as a cook. Just because a man who really *was* clever, took a fancy to me, doesn't mean I had the sort of education the women I was with last week had. One of them was married to a former professor who'd even been a bishop.'

'I thought Nicola said on Sunday that those you were with had small children. He must surely be an old man.'

'Ah well, he was a sort of failed bishop and jumped off the ecclesiastical chess board early in the game, and accompanied a stunning young poet on a trip to America and couldn't resist sharing more than her poems! The only one who had married an old man was me. André was forty years older than me.'

Her head went slightly backwards, and she did a double blink.

'Forty?'

'Nearly forty-one, actually.'

'Did that mean you got a regular good night's sleep?' she said with a grin.

'Shame on you, Helen, for being so ageist. Until my miscarriage and haemorrhage, it was difficult to stop him making up for lost time. I began to look forward to my periods.'

Helen laughed.

'I know all about that and sometimes it's surprising how long they can be made to last.'

It was my turn to laugh.

'This is not an advert for a same-sex relationship, and we've only been together for a short while, but I'm enjoying sexual intimacy for the first time, real intimacy and not just the occasional orgasm.'

'I can't think what that means with another woman.'

'In which case, use your imagination, but as I'm talking about your sister-in-law, I think we should attend to potential courses for you. Tell me, what has excited you as you've looked at the website?'

'Do you think I'd be up to tackling a two-year certificate in Creative Writing, doing it part time? I mean, I would prefer to do a degree, but that would take six years and if I'm no good and had to stop, I'd have wasted the money.'

'I don't understand how creative writing can be taught, but obviously it can, but why not try it? Think of something and let your imagination roll.'

'Alright, but only if you will read it and let me know what you think.'

'I'm not any sort of guide as to literary quality.'

'No, but I'd like you to read it.'

'Well, ok. Use WhatsApp and send it to me.'

'You can tell me if it shows enough skill to make a creative writing course worthwhile.'

I smiled at her, loving her enthusiasm, such a contrast to the Helen I saw each Sunday.

'How was coffee?' asked Nicola when we were sitting down to our sandwich lunch.

'I've encouraged her to follow up an interest in creative writing by contacting the OU.'

'That's a good idea. Well done.'

'No, it was her idea, not mine.'

'And how are things at home?'

'I think she realised that the call from the former police officer who was in my bed again last night and this morning, has helped her see that I mustn't become involved, so I asked nothing and that's exactly what she told me.'

'Good. It was always a very messy part of the job and on the day I was called to you by the river, I assumed I would be attending some sort of domestic.'

'And you tell me not to get involved!'

'Best day of my life.'

'This is a terrible thing I'm going to say, Nicola, and perhaps I should be ashamed to say it, but it was mine too and I don't mean because of what happened just before you arrived.'

I walked around the kitchen table and kissed Nicola.

'Mummy,' said Sam, 'why do you and Nicola keep kissing?'

'For the same reason we keep kissing you. It's called love.'

'I kiss teddy as well as you both.'

'Of course,' said Nicola, 'because you love him and we kiss everyone we love, and I love you and your mummy.'

He seemed pleased and was ready for his post-lunch sleep with Teddy.

Returning to the kitchen, I said, 'My conversation with Helen made me ask what I might do, apart, that is, from kissing you and Sam.'

'It's a good question though perhaps you should form an orderly queue in your mind: first, our wedding; second, what we do about our finances; and third, whether we might want further children. I know you've got a lot of money coming and have access to immediate funds, and I've got savings, but at the moment you pay for it all – the food, the utilities, the cars and everything else. It isn't fair to you.'

I sat down at the table.

'Yes, we should think about some of these important things, and I'll return to them in a moment, but I also need to use my brain not just for day-to-day decisions, even though caring for Sam and you top my agenda every day and night. You have your writing; our time away has made me wonder whether I'm also capable of something more than being a wife and mother. I'm not in the same league as Viv, Emily or you in terms of intellectual ability, but surely I could do more and learn more.'

'Viv was a police officer like me. Neither of us were in higher education. We've just read a lot more than you've had the chance to do, but trust me, my darling, I know no one with a sharper brain than yours and I think you'd be more than capable of anything you put your mind to.'

'I want any decision made to be ours together, because I want everything to be ours, including the response to all those other issues placed in a queue. As for money, let's wait to see how things are affected by our being married and leave things as they are now. I'll do what I recommended to Helen and see if anything

I might see on the internet sparks a light in me, but you're quite right, the wedding has to be sorted first.

9

We both wanted something simple and non-religious which the local Church could not offer, even had we wished it. Having heard Amy's account of her own wedding I rather fancied a Hindu ceremony, but as neither of us qualified, I might have to accept something a little less colourful and noisy! Perhaps inevitably, we decided on the Upper Gatehouse ceremony room less than a mile away at Dartington Hall and we met with two members of the team help us make all the preparations. It was set for the first Thursday in October.

We decided on a limit of 30 friends and family, though it would not be easy deciding who to include and who to leave out. Informing my mother, who I did not wish to be present, led to unforeseen consequences. She, (and I should add "wouldn't you just know it"), published an announcement in *The Times* of the "forthcoming wedding of her daughter Lady Dorothea Beeeson to Chloe Thomas, the well-known poet".

I learned of this only when Sharon telephoned, and immediately regretted not having murdered my mother during her stay!

'I saw the notice in the paper today. You've kept that secret quiet. What a catch, and please accept the congrats of Kim, Olivia, and me. Can we come?'

'Thanks, Sharon.'

'How did you meet her? By all accounts, she's a highly regarded young poet and I've already ordered one of her collections from Amazon.'

'Do you mean how did I, a humble cook and café manager,

manage twice over to get hitched to someone special?'

'Everyone who has ever known you, Dee, knows how remarkable you are, and presumably Chloe does too. I was so concerned about that policewoman you had taken on and I suspected she was a bit of a gold digger.'

'Do you mean Nicola Fairchild?'

'Was that her name? I felt she was taking advantage of your newly bereaved state by giving you and Sam so much attention. How is he and what does he think of the prospect of two mums?'

'He's well thanks and beginning nursery next week. He's thrilled about us getting married and asks why we keep kissing each other.'

Was I going to tell her, or should I just hang up?

'We're still planning but we want to keep it small, but you're such a special friend, Sharon.'

I hadn't extended an invitation and wondered if she'd noticed.

'But I'm so glad you know about it. The announcement came from my mother, but I was intending to let you know. So please give my love to Kim and Olivia.'

I put my phone down and made a loud raspberry noise.

Sam looked up, somewhat puzzled, from where he was playing on the floor, and Nicola came out of the study. I told her what my mother had done and that the call was from Sharon, and I reported what she had said.

'I'd been thinking only the other day that considering she is your closest friend, or at least was, she hadn't been in touch since the funeral. Do you think that has to do with that awful Nicola woman?'

'She used to be a headteacher of a posh girl school before she went to work for *The Times*, and she's married to the deputy director of MI5 and at one time was said to be very close to the wife of the former director. Perhaps constant exalted company and the fact that my important husband has died has altered her affections, but if so, it makes me sad. We shared a great deal.'

'Are we going to invite her?'

'We've only got space enough for 30. They would be 10% of those present, and part of the past I've left behind, but it's helped me decide something important. I want to leave the name of Beeson behind, not least so my wretched mother can't manipulate it again. If you're happy, I want to be Mrs Dee Fairchild.'

'What about your son?' she said, not wanting to mention his name whilst he was in the room with us.

'I don't know. What do you think?'

She looked at me blankly. We both knew this had to be my decision only.

Helen sent me her first piece of writing just a few days later; I was stunned by what I read. Whatever literary merit it might have, was completely obscured by the content. It was an account of an older woman forcing herself sexually on a 14-year-old schoolgirl. As I read it, I desperately hoped she had found the whole thing on one of the seamier pages on the internet, but surely even there it would be illegal. If it really was only the product of her imagination, there might be a cause for anxiety.

I read it through again and the detail was scary. It started with laughter and ended up with what I can only describe as violent rape – seduction leading to violence. I was at a loss as to know what to do. As far as I could recall from our coffee together, I hadn't promised not to show it to someone else, but was it implicit in suggesting WhatsApp? I can't imagine she could have shown Mark what she had written, but did that preclude me showing it to Nicola?

Nicola was still in the study and her mum had come over to take Sam out, part of our hope of adapting him to spending time with her so we could have a honeymoon alone. When she came back from her writing, she could see at once a measure of consternation on my face.

'What's the matter?'

'I know what the matter is, but I'm not sure how to handle it. You'll recall I suggested Helen have a go at creative writing and send it to me. I told her to use WhatsApp, assuming she would want her earliest efforts to be private. What I couldn't possibly have foreseen was what she would send me, and I don't know what to do with it. And having told her to use WhatsApp, does that mean I can't show it to someone else who might help me respond?'

'Do you need some advice from someone who knows about teaching creative writing? I'm sure we could find someone.'

'Definitely not – Oh God no! I think that might break the law.'

'And you don't think you can let me see it? You could print it where I could accidentally come across it?'

'I'm not sure I want anyone to read what's she's written or even if receiving it isn't in itself an offence.'

'I think you're going to have let me see it, Dee. Not for Helen's sake, but yours. Something is making you seriously twitched, and even if you had said the content would be confidential, that's no reason for not seeking help. If some of it had been in Spanish, say, you would have to let an interpreter help you. Is this different?'

'As far as I can recall, I only said to use WhatsApp, but added nothing more.'

'Then you cannot possibly be held to be breaking a confidence.'

'Ok, though it's not pleasant reading.'

I stood up from the computer and she sat down and gave her attention to the screen. I went to make us both coffees. When I returned, she was sitting back from the screen, obviously weighing up in her mind how to respond. She closed the file and came through to the sitting room with me.

'It's possible, I suppose, that she has made use of the internet on which to feed her imagination. Lesbian porn can probably be found simply by using a search engine, but I have to say that her written style shows promise.

'I imagine a sex therapist frequently hears things like this. Unless this is an account of something Helen has done, which I think unlikely, it is a powerful fantasy, not necessarily of something she wants to do but which is there inside her all the same, as many things are inside us, and don't get put into practice.'

'Like murdering my mother?'

'Oh no, that would be perfectly acceptable! But she, herself, might even be shocked or at least surprised by what she has written, but there is nothing illegal about our fantasies, unless we feel driven to enact them to the detriment of others.'

'But how should I respond?'

'Just by doing what you've said you'll do, which is to offer your thoughts on how well she has achieved in words what she set out to communicate. You mustn't disallow the content and act as some sort of censor. I agree that her writing shows promise and if she can be encouraged to write about a variety of other things, it may well be that a course in creative writing might be just what she could well use.'

'And say nothing about the content?'

'Well, you could always say it had an effect upon you, as it certainly did on me, assuming you could get past the thought that you shouldn't possibly feel even slightly aroused by it. Surely that's part of what sex on the internet is there to provide – stimulation and excitement for those who cannot otherwise find it. I always watch ballet feeling aroused – all those beautiful bodies.'

'Male or female?'

'I've always thought men in tights ridiculous.'

I smiled.

'Oh Nicola, I have so much to learn about everything.'

'Not quite everything. I haven't yet suggested we look at the internet in bed!'

'No dancer could be as beautiful as you, but at this time in the morning, I can't do a great deal about it.'

'No, especially when I can see my mum and Sam approaching. I love you, though, and perhaps we can consider this further later tonight!'

'I'll be there!'

We decided that the four of us should go out for lunch and I immediately chose the Cider Press Café again, though I only understood why when we got there and allowed myself to look, without my inner censor, at the waitress who had served Helen and I on my last visit. For the first time, I even allowed myself the brief thought that perhaps I really was a lesbian – after all, it was my attraction to Sharon that had first raised the possibility – and I gave myself a smile. The waitress smiled back and the hairs on the back of my neck stood on end.

I replied quickly to Helen, focussing almost exclusively on style.

"Thanks for this, Helen. My most immediate observation is to do with the pace of your narrative: this happened and then that and now this and so on. I didn't get a great sense of either woman other than their relative age. Were they tall, short, thin, fat, blonde, brunette, etc? What were they wearing at the start? Had either of them been drinking? What time of day was it? The back story is important to give the action context. BUT, if you can attend to these things, I think there are clear signs that you can tell a story and a good story will always hold a reader's attention. I look forward to your next contribution and perhaps one that doesn't quite as much take away my breath! x"

Nicola read it through and having her approval, I pressed the Send button.

'Perhaps I should have said she needs someone different next to make comments for her, and by that, I mean you. I can't think she would have sent that to her sister-in-law.'

'And I wonder what her sister-in-law's brother would have made of it,' said Nicola, 'because I'm blowed if I know what it might mean, but I can't think it doesn't mean something, even though it's only inside Helen's head.'

'How well do you know her?'

'Hardly at all. She's never been all that communicative, and I've never been invited to their home. She's an only child and grew up in Exeter, as far as I can recall. Her parents moved to Newton Abbott, and she started work in Mark's restaurant. Ironically, you've spent more time alone with her than I have.'

'Are both her parents still alive?'

'Oh yes. Her dad works on the ground staff at the racecourse and her mum's a part-time hairdresser and looks after Maisie and Angus sometimes.'

'Does your mum ever have them?'

'No. She sees them on Sundays, but Helen mostly uses her

mum as she lives a short distance away.'

'That makes sense. I only ask because I'm more puzzled than ever by what she wrote and wondering where it comes from. Is it just from the internet or does it come from inside her? I don't mean she is coming out or anything, I just worry about the vivid description of a seduction and rape of a 14-year-old, just as I would if you or someone else were to write a poem describing it.'

'Your friend, Alexander Pope, wrote a poem called "The Rape of the Lock" but it refers to the seizing of a lock of hair, not the sort Helen has written about. The only poet I know of who might have written something like it would be John Wilmot, the Earl of Rochester, and there are several sexual references in the work of Restoration playwrights. John Donne's love poetry should be compulsory reading for every young person, often sexy in wonderfully unexpected ways but never lewd. You should read them as I'm sure you would enjoy them, but so should Helen.'

'Did you spend all your youth reading?'

'Most of it. I was waiting for you.'

'That's unfair, Nicola. How can I ever match the words of a poet and tell you I love you without sounding banal?'

'You just have.'

She leaned forward and kissed me.

10

A formal-looking letter for Lady Dorothea Beeson arrived on the next morning. It was an invitation to accept the Presidency of the Royal Devonshire Show for the next twelve months. As I looked through the lists of my would-be predecessors, I could see how desperate they must have been to secure anyone with some sort of title.

The letter did not spell out what would be required other than to attend social events, to have my name on the headed notepaper for a year, and to open the glorious event itself and award prizes. It was so ridiculous that I almost thought it was a spoof but a telephone call late in the afternoon was made to confirm the safe arrival of the letter and to urge my almost immediate acceptance. I was so discombobulated that I accepted there and then, only later, when talking it over with Nicola, realising what a mistake I had made.

'What was it you said about no more rushing in where angels fear to tread?'

'Hilarious, but I can hardly back out now. It will almost certainly be in the local papers tomorrow.'

'True, but just think how much delight this will give your mother.'

'Oh God, I never thought of that. But I know nothing about the sort of things that happen in country shows – cows and sheep and horses.'

'I rather suspect they're not asking you because you do. It's your title.'

'But I'm shedding my title when we get married. I can't think

Mrs Dee Fairchild will exactly excite the punters.'

'She does that for me.'

'I'm glad to hear it. Anyway, we have visitors from the Hall this evening, to go through the details for the wedding, so we need to be sure we're agreed on everything before they arrive, especially the music.

The man and woman who came were already known to us and were clearly used to active disagreements among couples about such things, but finally we agreed, mainly because I recognised Nicola knew considerably more than I did.

During our conversation, I received a call from a reporter from the *Exeter Daily* seeking an interview.

'Congratulations on your appointment, Lady Dorothea. Shall we meet in the morning so I can be sure of my facts before we go to print?'

'Meet? Meet where?'

'Your place?'

'No. Come to the *Green Table Café* at Dartington at 11-00 and be sure to be wearing a reporter's trilby and carrying a notepad, so I will know who you are.'

I was sure I could hear his smile!

'It's a deal. There'll be two of us; the photographer will come as well.'

I returned to the wedding planning to find that Nicola had wrapped things up. The next stage would be the three-week legal publication of the forthcoming nuptials on a noticeboard in Newton Abbot Town Hall. And then the big day itself.

'Are you having a honeymoon?' asked the woman, named Anna.

'Yes, four nights in Florence. Our three-year-old son will have a holiday with his Granny. We're flying from Exeter to Pisa and then getting the train into the city for three days of beauty and unrestrained sex,' I said, to the obvious embarrassment of Barney ("short for Barnabas" he had told us apologetically, though I would have thought the longer name preferable to bearing the same name as the character from the Flintstones).

'I'm envious,' said Anna, covering up for her colleague, and not saying which part she most envied.

Once they had gone, Nicola and I opened a bottle and decided my hopes for our honeymoon would become a wonderful reality.

My meeting with "Scoop Andy" Smith and his photographer, began with food and drink on their expense account.

'It's not been easy to find out a great deal about you,' he began, 'so the editor suggested we meet and run the story tomorrow.'

'Perhaps you have found nothing because there's nothing to find.'

'You're from the north, I would guess from your accent.'

'Lancashire is where I was born, but I worked mostly in Yorkshire, managing the Ilkley branch of *Betty's,* which you can learn about on the internet. My greatest claim to fame is that I was a metre away from a Moslem fanatic shot dead by the police as he attempted to kill his former wife. Later, I was asked to marry by a civil servant in London and we moved to Devon. He was much older than me and knighted for services to the Crown, and that is why I am called Lady Beeson, though sadly my husband has now died. I have a son, a constant reminder of his father. That's me, more or less.'

'Do you have parents and siblings?'

'My mother is still alive, and I have two brothers and two sisters?'

'And what do you think about being invited to be President of the Count Show?'

'It's a great honour, especially when I consider the names of some of my predecessors, but I will do my best to serve as well as I can.'

'You're the youngest person to be asked.'

'It makes me think that 34 must be older than I had thought.'

'Have you plans to marry again?'

'My late husband cannot be replaced, but I am hoping soon to marry someone who is special in a totally different sort of way. A wonderful friend, with whom I can still hope for happiness as I grow older.'

'More children?'

'We haven't given thought to that yet. Give us time.'

'Does that mean you won't be Lady Beeson anymore?'

'You're very old-fashioned, Andy. These days it's quite common for people not to change their names when they get wed, as we say in the north.'

'Is there any chance we might meet your husband-to-be?'

'I'm sure we will appear often enough at events in the year's course and Emily can get the photos she needs then, but let's say I am receiving wholehearted support as I take on the new role.'

'Do you work?' added the photographer.

'I suspect you haven't yet given birth. When you do, you won't ask such a question.'

She blushed.

'I am a full-time mum, though my son is about to start nursery, so I might give thought to other possibilities.'

I could sense a certain frustration at my replies, but they were getting no more from me. I wondered how they would dress me up in the paper. Emily took some photos against the background of the Hall where, I said, I would get married again. I was soon to regret saying this!

The article on the following morning was anodyne and made me sound very boring – a widow from the north who had managed a cake shop and café. I was satisfied with my photo and story on page five. I came over as wonderfully dull, for which I was extremely grateful.

As she looked it over, Nicola said, 'You realise that this might lead to other local groups ensnaring you as their patron. You could make a career by attending meetings and fundraising events! Still, what's done is done, Madam President.'

'You may mock, but I'll have you know you're marrying a Lady.'

'Guilty, your ladyship. Hey, and that could be next, a magistrate.'

'Silence in court!'

I went to collect Sam from nursery in Totnes and it was clear he had enjoyed his morning and had already made new friends, about whom he chatted all the way home. We had lunch before he went for a rest and I sat down on the sofa with a cup of tea.

That was when I began to sob. They were not tears, but cascades of water pouring down my cheeks. Nicola was with me at once, putting her arm around me and holding me close to her breast. The sobbing went on and on, and she had the good sense and sensitivity to say nothing.

I suppose ten minutes went by before I could speak, though even then the words were broken up by repeated sobs.

'What have I done? Why isn't André here to stop me from being ridiculous?'

I felt my words were a kind of betrayal of Nicola's love but of course she was much wiser and knew better. She was to say that evening that she felt huge relief that I had been able at long last to let go of the pain of my loss she knew I must have inside me.

Now, however, she took my phone.

'I have to call someone,' she said, though I couldn't work out why she had not used her own, which lay on the table in front of us.

'Hello, is that Sharon? I, that is we, Dee and I, but especially Dee, need your help. But first, let me tell you who I am. I'm the Chloe who is marrying Dee next month, but that's the name I use for my writing. I am still Nicola Fairchild, you know, the gold digger, but that's not why I've called you.'

'It's ok, Nicola, I know who Chloe is and I apologise, but what's the matter with Dee?'

She explained the circumstances of the invitation and the Press who had come this morning and were intending to do a story about me. She turned on the phone speaker.

'Why on earth didn't you stop her?'

'Let's save that for the post-match analysis, Sharon. For now, we are facing a story all over the Exeter Daily and syndicated papers across the county.'

'That will involve the name of André and there is a security bar on that.'

'Do I need to do something?'

'No. I'll call someone who will make sure the story is spiked immediately. Is Dee there?'

'She's not in the best of states, but she can hear your every word. I'll put her on and turn off the speaker.'

She handed me the phone.

'I'm so sorry, Sharon. I just never thought when I stupidly said yes in the first place to being Show President that it was bound to lead the press to want a story.'

'Do they know of your wedding plans?'

'They know I'm getting married, but they assume it's to a man.'

'They'll find out. Did you tell you tell them where it's due to take place?'

'Yes.'

'In which case by now they will have found out and the headline will be, "Show President is Spy Widow Lesbian Bride", or some such. Don't worry, Dee, it won't happen. And when is it?'

'It's on the first Thursday in October. I can't wait to see you.'

'Now go back to the gold digger and tell her that her poems are very good indeed.'

'I will. Thank you, Sharon.'

I passed on the message.

'I'm sorry about everything, Nicola.'

'I'm not. It was worrying me you hadn't expressed the grief you must feel. I'm sure there'll be other days when you feel the same and you must allow them to happen and not worry about me. They don't mean you love me any the less, nor I you. But at least the decision about inviting Sharon to the wedding has been made. She said she already knew my identity.'

'She has lots of connections in the literary world.'

'It might also help that her wife is the deputy director of MI5!'

'Once you get to know her, you'll love her as much as I do.'

We were experimenting with Sam staying overnight for the first time in Ashburton and looking forward to a quiet evening together. As I was preparing our supper, I heard a car pull up outside, and Nicola opened the front door.

'Inspector!' I heard her say.

'Hi Nicola. Is Dee in?'

I recognised the voice at once.

'Ro!' I said, as I walked from the kitchen to greet her. 'Oh, my favourite police officer in all the world now that Nicola isn't one any longer. Come in. I imagine at this time of day you might manage a drink.'

'Dee! How wonderful to see you and congratulations on your forthcoming big day, but first let me tell you that the splendid story in the paper tomorrow isn't happening. I spent an hour with the editor this afternoon telling him that instead there will appear a brief paragraph announcing that because of an error they had misreported that you had accepted the role of President. It will come with an apology. The Show Committee will say something similar.'

Ro, is Rowena Lehmann, who for five years had worked closely with André in the security service, and on an occasion threw herself on to an Irishman to save her own life when I fired a gun in her general direction. I will never forget her words: "If you fire that fucking gun again, Dee, I promise I will shoot you!" A short while later, she helped saved my life by driving a Land Rover at great speed to hospital with a gynaecologist keeping me alive in the back.

I poured her a g & t, and she sat on the sofa.

'I didn't know the Regional Crime Squad had such powers,' said Nicola.'

'We don't. Your saviour this time, Dee, was a service lawyer who threatened the editor and his lawyers with the Tower of London if they went ahead with the story. The Chief Constable thought a DCI might help hammer the point home, which it did.'

'A DCI?' I said. 'You've gone up in the world.'

'Two months ago. It was Nicola or me, so when she pulled out, it had to be me.'

Nicola and I laughed.'

We chatted for an hour or so, but throughout, I was feeling ashamed of what I had brought about by my stupidity. I could tell Nicola had picked this up even before Ro left, but afterwards she at once came and sat next to me on the sofa, taking hold of my hand.

'It's been quite a day.'

Once again, I began to cry, and she took me in her arms and didn't say a word.

When I finally surfaced, I looked at her lovely facing smiling at me.

'I'm feeling so ashamed. I've failed everyone, but mostly I've failed you in just about every way.'

Listen, my darling, I'm going to speak a poem to you. Not one of my own, but perhaps the best written in the English language. It's by George Herbert, a priest in the early 17th century and is called Love.

'Love bade me welcome. Yet my soul drew back
Guilty of dust and sin.
But quick-eyed Love, observing me grow slack
From my first entrance in,
Drew nearer to me, sweetly questioning,
If I lacked any thing.

A guest, I answered, worthy to be here:
Love said, You shall be he.
I the unkind, ungrateful? Ah my dear,
I cannot look on thee.
Love took my hand, and smiling did reply,
Who made the eyes but I?

Truth Lord, but I have marred them: let my shame
Go where it doth deserve.
And know you not, says Love, who bore the blame?
My dear, then I will serve.
You must sit down, says Love, and taste my meat:
So I did sit and eat.

'That poem is almost enough to make me religious but even without that, it's about love triumphing over any sense of shame and unworthiness we might feel about ourselves, and whilst I'm not God, I am your Love.'

I looked at her and cried once again, but not tears of shame and self-pity this time, but those of love for this wonderful woman. I didn't really understand the poem, though its words were strangely soothing and helped me see my shame was perhaps just hurt pride. So I did sit and eat.'

11

I awoke at just after 4:00 in a panic about where Sam was and rushed to his room before Nicola came to me and reassured me that Sam was perfectly safe and fast asleep at her mum's. I felt so silly and went back to bed. Nicola made me a cup of Rooibos tea, which whenever I had trouble sleeping always has acted like a sleeping draught and, cuddling up to Nicola, did so again now.

Fiona was going to discharge her duties as a grandma by taking Sam to nursery before going off to train chefs for the rest of the day, allowing us something a rare lie-in.

'André must have been over the moon when Sam arrived,' Nicola said, as we luxuriated under the duvet.

'He was. I think he would have preferred a girl, hoping he could name her after his own mum to whom he was devoted.'

'You've never told me about her. I assume she has died.'

'Oh, years ago, when André was at Oxford. I'll tell you something that will surprise you. André grew up in inner-city Leeds and he and his mum lived in a small, newly built council house on an estate. She had a most interesting occupation – the oldest profession.'

'You don't mean...'

'Yes, I do. She was a prostitute, but only entertained clients brought to her by a few local taxi firms who could control the sort and numbers of men who came. From an early age, André was not only aware of this, but made sure the punters knew he was in the house and wouldn't tolerate anything his mum objected to. Actually, he was so very proud of the way she managed her life and they were extremely close. When she'd built up enough to send him to Oxford, she packed it in, only to die of cancer whilst he was at college.

'I love to think of him chatting with his posh friends comparing notes about home life. In those days, most of them came from public schools, though I bet a fair number of their parents played away from home too. Perhaps one of their dads had visited André's mum.'

'Does your mum know about this?'

'Oh, how I wish she had done when she found out my husband was to be known as *Sir* André. He had achieved a First in History at Balliol, but André was not given to talking about his own past. Somehow or other, he was recruited into the security service, and I know he served in Belfast during the Troubles, but that's the full extent of my knowledge. He became the senior interrogator for the service, which is what he was doing when I met him, but again he told me nothing of his work there, other than that he worked with Ro, and she'll tell you nothing either.

'For most of our married life, he was in his study, though never told me what he was working on and I have found nothing among his papers to show what it might have been. He immersed himself day after day in the 60 volumes of the *Oxford Dictionary of National Biography*. He liked us to walk together each day and I regret to say he took only a minor part in care for Sam. I was cook, cleaner, mother and bed mate, and though he tried to love to me in his own way, he didn't really know how. Who knows? Perhaps if I'd had a steady stream of gentlemen visitors, he would have had more idea.'

'Yet you miss him?'

'André rescued me from mediocrity and for the first time in my life, I felt I mattered. I don't miss what wasn't there, and I mean by that the total love I now know all about, but he provided the key to my release and whenever I was with him, I recalled that. He was an important part of my landscape.'

I reached out to Nicola.

'But you know well enough, and of course I don't need to tell you, but I will just for the joy of it, that you are much, much more, and every day I wake up rejoicing that you and I are together, and that I love and adore you. The George Herbert poem made me realise you are Love, you are my everything.'

'Does that mean, with Sam away, for once we have the time for morning love?'

I didn't hear the noise of a car but when I answered the knock on the door, I was startled to see standing in the light rain the figure of Helen. I quickly brought her in and sought a towel to dry her off.

'I parked behind the café and walked. I've not been here before. It's lovely, Dee. Are Sam and Nicola about?'

'Sam will be on his way to nursery, care of his Granny Fiona, with whom he stayed last night. Nicola's working. But tell me, has something happened, and where are Maisie and Angus?'

'My mum's got Angus and Maisie's begun school – mornings only this week and next, and Mark's gone off to work, but nothing's happened if you mean like the other day.'

'I'm glad of that,' I said, wondering what she was doing here. There was a look on her face that made me feel a little uneasy.

'I just needed to see you.'

'About your writing, do you mean?'

'No. Just to see you and be close to you and tell you that you're about to make a huge mistake.'

I assumed she meant about my would-be Presidency of the Show, though I couldn't think she could have known about that.

'Oh, don't worry, that's taken care of.'

'What do you mean?'

'What do *you* mean?

'Isn't it obvious? Dee, you are about to make a dreadful mistake, none bigger, and I must stop you.'

'Oh?' I said, sufficiently loud, hoping Nicola might hear. 'You must tell me then.'

'You can't get married to Nicola. She is evil and only after your money.'

'But I don't have that much money.'

'Don't lie, Dee. You've inherited millions from your husband, and Nicola wants it for herself. She's just like her brother, a greedy schemer. I could tell you all about the amounts he has stolen from his work and hidden away for when he gets rid of me and will go off with his assistant manager, "Randy Mandy" I call her. He thinks I don't know, but I have spies there who tell me the truth about him, the slimy bastard.

'But it's you I'm here to protect. I have to stop this stupid lesbian wedding. You saw what I wrote. I want to do that to you. I want you for me. Nicola only wants more and more money. Everything else she'll pretend. Just as her parents pretend everything. Oh, they're nice to us on Sundays, but for the rest of the time they're making money and I bet they've got it hidden away like squirrels with their nuts.'

I kept thinking that I must keep the conversation going and hoping that Nicola was not using headphones to listen to Radio 3 as sometimes she did.

'How do you think they're doing it?' I asked, trying to feign interest with a puzzled look.

'The idiots who bring their dogs to him are being fleeced by him, paying a fortune for a wash and blow dry. It's obvious, and she has a scam running with all her trainee cooks and chefs, just like the son has in his restaurant. He learned it from his mother.'

'So what should I do? What you're telling me is scary. I don't want to get hooked in to such a family if what you're saying is true.'

'It's not *if*, Dee, it's actually happening, and I've got to stop the wedding.'

'I agree, but how do we do that? Everything's arranged.'

'The first thing is to throw out that bitch, my sister-in-law, and if she won't go, then I'll have to deal with her. I want you to do that, Dee, because if you won't, I'll have to stop you marrying her. Unless you agree here and now to keep her locked out, for your own sake, I would have to stop you permanently but first I would have to do those things you know about that I have wanted to do to you since ever I saw you.'

'I take it you mean you want to seduce and then violently rape me.'

'It wouldn't be rape because you're already an utterly corrupt lesbian. You would love every moment, and then we can be together.'

'I won't deny that what you wrote got me feeling a little hot as I read it, and I've read it again and again, thinking about it and thinking about being held and touched by you.'

'Yes, yes, yes.'

Her handbag had opened slightly, and, to my horror, I could see something shiny and feared it was a knife.

I heard a car stop outside.

'Who will that be?'

'I'm expecting a delivery from Tesco. I'll just open the door for them, and they'll put it in the kitchen.'

'No, just leave them. They'll go away. I'm not sharing you with anyone. You understand that don't you?'

'Of course, I do, and I'm just as desperate for you as you for me.'

As she moved to do so, I "accidentally" knocked her bag onto the floor, but she was not intent on holding back and had her face on mine and her arms around me. And that was when two male police officers appeared in our sitting room and took hold of Helen, separating us. Behind them, Nicola rushed towards me and as the two officers moved Helen away from me, she came and held me.

'I think there's a knife in the bag,' I said, 'so don't touch it.'

One of the two officers had a firm hold on Helen, who kept shouting foul abuse at Nicola and me.

'You'd better call backup,' said Nicola to her former colleague. 'Mrs Fairchild needs to be provided with help and that would probably be best provided in Plymouth, but all she said has been recorded by me, and this assault may well amount to attempted murder.'

'I'll call CID.'

'No,' I said, though by now I was shaking and struggling to speak. 'Please call DCI Lehmann at the Regional Crime Squad. Insist on getting her and only her and tell her what's happened. She'll come.'

The constable looked at Nicola, who nodded.

Helen had by this time been taken out to the car and I was becoming distraught. Nicola did not let me go and led me through to our bedroom and sat me down on the bed, where just a short while before we had made love.

'I'm thinking I must be a gold digger after all. Helen obviously agrees with Sharon,' she said to bring a little light humour.

I managed a smile.

'I couldn't give a damn about the money. I hate it before it's even here. And Nicola, my love, why has this happened again? Why has someone come into my home intent on killing? It happened just before my miscarriage and near death, and I thought all that association with a horrible world was over with. And now it's invaded our home and our family. Thank God Sam wasn't here, and we're going to have to inform Mark and Helen's mum where Angus is, and Maisie will need collecting.'

'Leave all that to me, as we can leave to Ro all that happens to Helen now. I was listening and recorded everything on my phone, and I'd called for help as soon as I heard her speaking. It was in her voice. I knew something was not right. Had they not come, I was on the verge of coming to protect you from her. I signalled to them through the window and threw them my door key. I would never have let her hurt you.'

She remained with me, holding me, until we heard sirens, and then we both went through to the sitting room. Helen's bag remained where I had knocked it to the floor. Outside there was an ambulance and two cars, all with flashing blue lights, out of one of which came Ro.'

'Dee, this is not fair,' she said as she came and put her arms around me. 'Nobody should have to experience what you did once, let alone have it happen again.'

With gloves on, Ro opened the handbag, discovering that there was a kitchen knife inside. She left it there for the scene of crime officers when they arrived.

'Nicola, why didn't you act as soon as your sister-in-law got close to Dee?'

'She'd come to see Dee, and it never occurred that she might have criminal intent. Why should it? But I soon knew something was wrong, so I listened and immediately summoned help, recording everything she said on my phone. Had the boys not arrived as they did, I would have been in there as soon as she attempted to take hold of Dee. But I also knew we would need evidence.'

'What's going to happen to Helen?' I asked Ro.

'She's being taken by ambulance to the Glenbourne Unit in Plymouth where she'll be assessed. After that, I don't know, as it depends on what they find.'

'You need to give full access to Ro all your correspondence with Helen, including her writing,' said Nicola. 'It can't be confidential anymore. I'll put the kettle on and make us some tea, and then I'd better call Mark.'

'That's in hand, and a family liaison officer will soon be with him.'

'He's my brother, Ro, and I need to speak to him.'

Tea never tasted better and gently, Ro asked me to tell her everything, which I was more than relieved to do. Nicola returned and joined us.

'I've spoken to Mark, who told me there's been something wrong for a long time and feels bad that he didn't get Helen back to see the doctor once she'd refused the tablets. He then told me that last week they had yet another row about her needing to see the doctor and she picked up a knife in the kitchen and slashed his cheek, for which he still has the wound. He said she also told him that if ever he tried to approach her sexually, she would kill him, that there was someone else, though thought it was just words.'

'Well, that's going to make it easier knowing how best to deal with her,' said Ro.

She turned to me.

'As for you, Lady Beeson, as you still are for a little while, what are we going to do with you?'

'Forget all about any sort of title, which drew to me what happened yesterday and perhaps also today. In three weeks, I shall be plain Mrs Dee Fairchild, and I can't wait.'

'What about Sam?'

'There's a process to be gone through which will be complete long before he starts school. In the meantime, for convenience, he will be Sam Fairchild, as he already is known at his nursery group.'

'I can't know, but I imagine Helen will be held under Section 136 of the Mental Health Act 1983, which will give us 24 hours to consider how best we should deal with her. I should think she will then be moved to a place of safety for observation, before we have to decide whether to press charges, but whatever the next stage, your safety will be paramount.

As the crime scene officers had been late in attending, Nicola and I together went to collect Sam and took him out for lunch, by which time our home was much as he had left it on the previous day. But I was not!

12

Everything is followed by something else. When someone dies, that day is always followed by the "day after", and all that we do has consequences of a sort. Yet so very often such sequels surprise us.

I was surprised by the "time after" the morning happening. We arrived back at an empty house and Sam ran at once to find the toy animal friends he had missed and my own first gaze was towards the sofa. It was perfectly normal, and I decided I must sit there with Nicola beside me. She took my hand.

'You're going to be ok, you know.'

'I know that, my love, but it's strange to think about what happened here just a few hours ago and that I might even have been dead by now.'

'I'm sorry. I should have come out as soon as she arrived, but I wanted to get the evidence not to send her to prison but so that she can receive the help and treatment she urgently needs. Killing you would never have happened, and once I saw her touching you, I couldn't stand it anymore. I could see the guys and held them back until the last moment.'

'You did right, my love. As always. What I wonder would your friend George Herbert have to say to me now, I wonder? I have been such a fool.'

'No. These things, yesterday and today, came about not because you're a fool, but because you are the most open and generous person I have ever known, and I think the many others who love you know that is so. That some will look to take advantage of that means vigilance, but no closing down of who you are. These two events have made me proud of you. No one has ever asked a brilliant poet (ahem!) to open anything, and I've been known to Helen for some time, but never once has she made advances towards me. Please, whatever else, don't start writing poems – I would fear knowing just how good they would be.'

'Oh no, they wouldn't. Yours are superb and even Sharon knows that.'

We laughed and through one of those coincidences in life (which Nicola told me Jung, the eminent psychologist, called synchronicity), my phone summoned me, and the name of Sharon appeared.

'Hi Sharon.'

'Are you ok?'

'How on earth did you find out? I'm fine, here at home sitting with Nicola, who rescued me.'

'Ro informed the Chief Constable who informed Kim who informed me.'

'I forgot you knew Ro, who was with us the last time I nearly died. Well, it was unpleasant. Helen is Nicola's sister-in-law who seems to have found in me a focus for her far from calm mind. There's much more to what's being going inside her than any of us had realised, but I guess that will all come out in the wash, as they say.'

'No, they don't all say that, just them what live in t'north,' she said with a laugh, 'but it brought me out in goosebumps when Kim rang. You were also there with me when I nearly died from a knife attack. I can hardly believe that we've both had that experience.'

'She hadn't got hold of the knife when she grabbed me. You were about a second away from being fatally stabbed until that protection officer shot him dead.'

'I'm still in touch with Sandra, and she always laughs when I tell her she made me gay, though a former husband about to kill me no doubt also played its part in bringing it about!'

I laughed.

'At our wedding, Sharon, Nicola's dad's going to accompany

her – not "giving her away" – and I would like you to do the same for me, if you will.'

'I will need to give that some thought, Dee...Ok, I've thought about it, and of course I will. In fact you have turned my fears when I heard what happened, into joy. Thank you.'

'If Kim and Olivia get time off, we would love you to come and stay here with us before the day and have a holiday here whilst we are in Italy. It's only a four-day honeymoon as we don't want to leave Sam with his Granny too long – for both their sakes.'

'That would be wonderful, not least because I'm dying to get to know the wonderful poet who produced such amazing collections and saved your life. Don't get jealous if I kiss her on both accounts!'

'I'm sure both her accounts will love being kissed by you, Sharon. I always have!'

After the call, Nicola was completely taken aback by all I told her.

'What? Kissing the gold digger?'

'You don't know Sharon. She's in love with you now and I wouldn't be at all surprised if this doesn't lead to a feature in *The Times*. She's not Features Editor now but works freelance and I suspect that if she wants something, she gets it.'

A call came from the Chief Constable. She had regularly called in to see André, not least because he was still "in the loop" regarding security precautions and received weekly security briefings.

'I know you won't like it, Dee, but even with André dead, you remain an obvious target, not just in matters to do with Shows and the mental health difficulties of members of your family-to-be. There will still be those in Ireland who know who and where you are, so the recommendation from Milbank is that we equip your home with modes of security and provide you with any security briefings we notice that might involve you. It is, of course, only a recommendation.'

'Oh, Arleen, you know as well as I that a recommendation from the deputy director of the service, is a bit more than that, but I'm not likely to object given what happened to me this morning. I just hope it won't be a barrier between us and normal Dartington life.'

'Dee, there is nothing normal about life in Dartington, trust me!'

I laughed.

'Is there any chance you might investigate it on the first Thursday in October at about 11:00? After all, Nicola was once one of yours.

She took out her diary.

'I have a finance meeting, so yes, I'll be with you. A double thank you!'

I told Nicola about the "recommendation".'

'I'm perfectly happy about that. I'd always wondered why it wasn't already in place, given that André had worked in Belfast.'

Nicola had been on the phone to Mark, who reported that a gentle woman detective had called to see him, and he wondered whether he might come and call on us before he collected Maisie and Angus.

I could hardly believe it was still only five'oclock 5 when Mark arrived, given that so much had happened in the day. Sam was pleased to see Mark, but immediately pointed to the plaster he had on his face.

'Poor uncle Mark,' he said, almost immediately reducing Mark to tears. I offered to take Sam into another room, but Mark begged me to stay, and Sam quickly became caught up in a game much more important than our conversations.

Mark sat on the sofa next to Nicola in exactly the place Helen had sat earlier in the day.

'She's called Sergeant Abigail Molloy, and I wanted to throw myself into her arms. She was so kind and understanding and says she would leave making a formal statement until tomorrow, and I would like you, sis, to be with me, if you will.'

'Of course. I know Abi. She's an experienced family liaison officer. What were you able to tell her?'

'I said that Helen had begun to act strangely a couple of

months before she gave birth to Angus. I had persuaded her to talk to the doctor after she didn't improve, and he said it was undoubtedly hormonal changes which had led to peri-natal depression but that it would lift in time. She wasn't breastfeeding, so he prescribed anti-depressants, but she never took them and he suggested Cognitive something or other.'

'CBT,' I said. 'It's a short-term therapy the NHS makes use of sometimes. Cognitive Behavioural Therapy is used in a brief series of sessions. It helps some people, but not everyone. Did Helen take it up?'

'No chance. I could see her getting worse and whenever I said anything she became aggressive towards me and I worried about how she would be with the kids, but my job is extremely demanding at the present – huge rise in our energy bills and so on – so I wasn't able to do much. I suggested the kids should stay with mum but she wouldn't agree and as you've probably seen on Sundays, when she's there, she just shuts up.

'She then accused me of having an affair with my assistant manager, which honestly, sis, is not true. I mean, I'm running faster and faster at work just to stay standing – however could I have an affair at the same time?

'When you two got together, she decided you, Dee, were going to be her special friend, someone she could turn to and benefit from. I'm so sorry, Dee, but you became her project.

'On a day off, when she was at her mother's, I went on to her laptop and, to my horror, discovered pages and pages of videos of women doing things to other women that could only be described as sick. I found none of men doing any of these things, just women.'

'Have you told Abi?'

'Yes, and she's taken the laptop away. Anyway, I told Helen that I had found some of this stuff on her laptop and that was when she grabbed a kitchen knife and slashed my face. What's going to happen now?' Mark asked his sister.

'After assessment, she'll remain where it's safe for her to be, but proper account will be taken of her being a mother whose children will need her as much as their dad. But it's going to take a while. It will be easy to blame your GP, but I imagine he was just too busy to attend properly to her, though he will have to answer questions about it.

'There are conditions other than those associated with peri-natal depression and the doctors will seek to explore the best way to restore Helen to you.'

'But won't she be charged with attempted murder?'

'She didn't attempt to murder me as such, Mark,' I said, 'though made threats and it may have been in her mind having brought the means.'

'She might be charged with cutting your face, but personally, brother of mine, I think the plaster actually improves you!'

By the time Sam was in bed, we were both exhausted. I said to Nicola that it was a good job we had started the day so amazingly because when we got into bed shortly I'd be out like a light.

'It hasn't been all bad. We've sorted out who will give you away at the wedding and that the Chief Constable of Devon and Cornwall will be in attendance. We're about to be descended on by the security people with their devices and I've learned a great deal about just how many love and respect the person I'm going to marry. But perhaps, most important of all, we've learned something of the truth about what a family has been going through and the effects it can have on others, in this instance, you. We can only hope that Helen can be helped to return home safely before too long.'

'Only *something* of the truth?'

'Oh yes. I'm not doubting the story my brother has told, but it's only his account. He will inevitably have left out what he didn't want us to hear, and I don't think for one moment that Abi, the officer who saw him today, will have overlooked that. He's asked me to be there, and of course I will, but Abi will know that he might have requested my presence to protect himself. She's no fool, believe you me.'

'And   neither   are   you!'

13

Instead of writing poetry, Nicola left early to meet with Mark and Abi. An early phone call from the officer has said the statement would be taken at the Newton Abbot police station, not at Mark's home, to save neighbourly nosiness about the attention being focussed there.

'That's thoughtful,' I said, when Nicola told me.

'Perhaps,' she replied, 'but also clever. Mark needs to know that what has happened is serious. To you, Helen accused him of hitting her first and acting in self-defence, so the interview is not just an informal chat, as even given what we think is the case with Helen's mental state, it might end up in court. She can't be charged with attempted murder, but assault with intent could certainly be considered.'

I took Sam to nursery but didn't particularly want to be alone at home. I therefore took a punt, as they say, and called on Brendan O'Callaghan. It was, I knew, his day off and I called, hoping he might be there. It was Mary who answered his phone.

'Has he even got you answering his phone, Mary? It was bound to happen once he became a consultant.'

'He should be so lucky,' said the wonderful Irish voice, 'but himself is in the shower. He's been out for a run.'

'I'm so sorry to hear that, Mary. I hope he feels better soon! But I'm calling to see if you're both in for a wee while. There are things I'd like to share with you.'

'We have no plans. We make sure we get the same day off, but sometimes that just allows for us to do nothing together and to do it well. Come over.'

'I've just dropped Sam at nursery so if it's ok, I'll come straight away.'

They lived in a lovely big house in Bovey Tracey, between Exeter where he worked, and Ivybridge where she did, and I hadn't been to see them since André had died, though Brendan had called me a few times. He was working hard to set up a specialist unit at the Royal Devon and Exeter for multiple pregnancies in which one baby was starving the other of blood, so that it would be possible to enable invasive intervention to put this right in the womb, to help the smaller child survive.

'Welcome Dee,' said Brendan, 'this is the first time you've been here since André died, but already I gather congratulations are in order. I saw the announcement though I was a bit surprised. It said you're getting married to a poet called Chloe Thomas.'

'You've met my mother, Brendan, and it was she who placed the announcement. Chloe Thomas *is* Nicola Fairchild, who's been with me since minutes after André's perfect death by the river he loved, with Sam and me beside him. Chloe is just the name she uses for her books. She was the police officer who came to where we were, almost as if it was meant to be, but only almost, as I haven't yet got religion.'

'I was a surprised to learn that you were getting married to anyone so soon after André had died. Three months seems somewhat hasty, Dee.'

'I have never doubted that I would get an honest word from you, Brendan, and you're probably holding back on the fact that I'm getting married to a woman.'

'Bren and I live in the modern world, said Mary, 'and even back in Ireland such a union would be possible now.'

'Well, we're getting married in Dartington Hall on the 5th October, and it would mean so much to me if you could both come, but there's so much to tell you, I'm not sure where to start, though if I start at the end and say I narrowly escaped death yesterday, I hope I can retain your interest.'

I told them everything about how I had discovered in Nicola someone wholly different from André, and a love, not his fault, that had been lacking in my marriage. They listened intently. I then spoke about my recent idiocies regarding the County Show and my involvement with Helen that finally got out of control on the previous morning.

'Thank you for telling us this,' said Brendan. 'What a relief that the poor lassie didn't kill you, and all you've said seems to me to flow out of your wonderfully generous nature, but, and I'm risking our friendship now, perhaps no one else will ask you, might what you have described as your idiocies include getting married in just a couple of weeks' time?'

'I won't deny I miss André, especially when (excuse my French) I've fucked up as I have in the last few days. André would have stopped me – that's certainly true. But he had started stopping me doing anything. After you saved my life, I had to be protected like some sort of exotic plant, and he became increasingly paranoid.

'It became worse once Sam was born. He even told me that he had not ruled out the possibility that you were still providing information to Republican Groups. That's how bad it had become. We moved house because he feared the layout might have been passed back by you to Dublin. I told you – real paranoia.'

'Were you able to tell anyone?' asked Brendan.

'I thought it would get better once we'd moved.'

'And?' asked Mary.

'He died.'

'Oh my God, you didn't kill him, Dee?' said Brendan.

'Don't be such a daft haperth, Brendan. I would never have hurt André. He was the one who saw something worthwhile in me that no one else ever had, who rescued me from a life wasting away in a tea shop. You and Mary are both sciences trained and have regular access to drugs, so how on earth do you think I could have arranged André's death? I wouldn't have known how to do it even if I'd wanted to.'

'What's on the death certificate?'

'Coronary thrombosis.'

'A local pathologist?'

'No. Someone was sent from London, but it took place in

Exeter. Sharon came to stay that day and Kim phoned through to say that it was what the death certificate said it was. He just died.

'Do you know, Brendan, I learned a great deal from growing up in a village, and mostly it was the realisation that behind front doors lie realities, sometimes distressing and unimaginable misery, concealed in public behind smiles, and women who remain. for where else would they go? I have learned to disregard the front doors presented to the world, not least because I found myself behind one.'

'Dee, I'm sorry to have spoken as I have. I guess I just never thought your own front door was like that.'

'Do you know, Dee,' added Mary, 'when I first heard what had happened to you back then, I thought Bren had done something heroic in saving your life, but I now think the hero was you, and this morning you've proved to me just how true that is.'

'Ah well, you might think better of that when it sinks in just how stupid I've been accepting two ludicrous invitations, both of which could have been catastrophic had it not been for others pulling me back when I'd gone where angels rightly fear to tread.'

Brendan looked thoughtful before he spoke.

'André should never have told me because of the Official Secrets Act and I promised never to repeat it to anyone, even to Mary, but I'll risk it now. He told me how shortly after you had met, you had shown extraordinary courage, putting yourself at great personal risk, in enabling the arrest of a leading and extremely dangerous Islamic fanatic. Angels may fear to tread, but I don't think you know what the word fear means, and the latest sign of that is, I would imagine, that your Nicola knew she could leave you whilst she sought help.'

'I agree,' said Mary. 'And are we to meet Nicola?'

'October 5th.'

'I've never been to a lesbian wedding before.'

'I prefer to think of it as just a wedding, Mary.'

'We'd love to be there to celebrate with you both, and Sam,' said Brendan, 'and I look forward to meeting a real live poet.'

'Even though she's not Irish?'

'All poets are honorary Irish.'

'And all Irish doctors have kissed the Blarney Stone!'
They laughed.

I began my journey home down the A38, crying almost all the way. That time with Mary and Brendan had been painful, not least because I realised in recounting my story, that I had closed the door on myself, colluding with André's coercion (unintentional no doubt, but wasn't that always an easy excuse for it?) because of the terror of being without him. I remembered the last lines of Hilaire Belloc's poem *Jim* about a boy who ran away and was eaten by a lion: "And always keep ahold of nurse / For fear of finding something worse". And this person, declared by Brendan to be without fear, I knew to be the same person too scared to face the empty house earlier. Tears continued as I left the main road and headed towards Dartington, alongside the river Dart. It was such a lovely river and although for September it wasn't all that warm, I thought the three of us should later go downstream to our favourite place.

14

Nicola was back before me.

'I wondered where you were as there was no note or a text.'

'On the way back from taking Sam to nursery I diverted to Bovey Tracey to call on the O'Callaghans to tell them about our wedding.'

'And what happened to make you cry? Your eye makeup is all down your cheeks.'

I told Nicola about the conversation and how, simply by talking, I had revealed to myself things to which I had never given conscious expression.

'The greatest poet of the 20th century, W H Auden, included a line that says it all: "There is always another story, there is more than meets the eye". I suspect he must have feared losing you to a younger rival and although you colluded, fearing losing all that being married to him gave you, it was a form of control.'

'He missed the younger rival by about ten minutes! But Brendan is a wise old bird, and if ever we were to consider children, he'd be the one to talk to. But tell me about your morning.'

'I collected Mark for his meeting with Abi. It took place in one of the special suites used for victims of sexual assault, so it was comfy chairs and subdued lighting.

'Abi is a real pro – gentle as can be, reinforced by steel, if you know what I mean. He repeated his account from yesterday, but I could tell he had been rehearsing it, though that's fair enough. She took him back as far as when Helen became pregnant with Angus. "Did she want another baby?", "Was she sexually resistant?". He hadn't been expecting this sort of questioning and he struggled, even whilst she was reassuring him she regretted having to ask.'

'It can't have been easy for him with you there.'

'No. But he had wanted me to be there so could hardly now ask me to leave.'

'Should he have had a solicitor?'

'Technically, he was being interviewed as a witness, so it would not have been necessary. He was there just to make a statement.'

'But did Abi know that?'

'He signed his statement, but I don't think my dear brother was telling everything, and I'm sure Abi knew this too. As I drove him home, he was flippant and giggly, as someone might be if they think that've got away with something. It's our friend Auden again for there is always more than meets the eye.

'He accepts he'd begun to find her withdrawnness, and not just in the bedroom, difficult. This had gone on for well over a year, but he said she suddenly perked up when you came on the scene and talked endlessly about you. He thought she resented you and me together, though thoughts and feelings don't go on to a statement but will have been logged in Abi's brain. I wouldn't be at all surprised if Sergeant Abigail Molloy comes to pay a friendly call to meet you. But now we must head off to Totnes to collect Sam.'

As she drove, I asked, 'Why might she want to talk to me? Hadn't Ro got what she wanted? I handed over everything.'

'Abi is looking into background, context, and you're a key player, because no matter what else characterised Helen's strange behaviour over a long period, and as far as I know, there's no report from the shrinks yet, so Abi is still investigating a possible crime in which you have played an unfortunate part as victim, and I imagine she will want to know if and how you might have triggered something.'

'But doesn't that make me complicit?'

'Of course not. I think Abi simply wants to see for herself the lady who has stolen my heart and Helen's brain.'

'A likely story! Isn't there always more than meets the eye?'

Sunday lunch was inevitably a somewhat subdued affair. Helen was being cared for in the Langdon Hospital in Dawlish, and Mark had been asked to attend a case conference with her and the doctors on the Monday morning. As yet, we had heard nothing further from the police, but Nicola pointed out that it was probably because as yet they had heard nothing from the medics.

'Would I be allowed to say I don't want to press charges?' I said to Nicola as we loaded the dishwasher after lunch. 'I don't want to do anything to harm Mark, the children, or your mum and dad.'

'To be honest, I very much doubt the matter of charges will even arise. No damage was done after all.'

'Good. Do you think I should tell Mark?'

'Yes, I think he'll appreciate it.'

In the absence of Helen, Mark and the children stayed much longer than normal and the grandparents took all three out, providing us with the chance to talk.

'Mark,' I began, 'I want you to know that there is simply no way I would press charges against Helen. No matter what you learn in the morning, I would do nothing to cause further pain to you and our whole family.'

'Thanks, Dee, though after everything that's happened for well over a year, of which her slashing my face is the final straw, I don't know if I want her back. If she is discharged tomorrow, I think she should go to her mother's.'

'I can understand that,' said Nicola, 'but a lot of thought will be given to the needs of the children. They will take precedence in the minds of the social services.'

'What might that mean? Surely they won't let her have access to them?'

'It will be a joint decision, including you.'

'Will Helen be present?'

'I don't know. I've never taken part in a psychiatric case conference, but I imagine it will depend on what they have been thinking since beginning their assessment, though we've had a weekend, so that may slow things down somewhat. It's a case of wait and see.'

'Would you come with me, sis?'

'I would happily do so, but I know in advance that they wouldn't let me. I'm about to get married to Helen's potential victim, and she also threatened me. It's on the tape.'

'She slashed my face with a knife!'

'Yes, but she is married to you and the mother of your children, Mark. You need to hear what they are saying.'

I had more or less forgotten the matter of André's will until I had a phone call on the following afternoon from Mr Gleadall, my solicitor.

'Hello, Lady Deeson, please accept my congratulations on your forthcoming wedding.'

I'm sure he must have heard my sigh of exasperation at my mother.

'I am a little surprised that this should be taking place so soon after the demise of your late husband, but I wish you and Miss Thomas great joy. I can't say I know her work, but I have been informed it is of the highest quality.'

'Thank you, though Chloe Thomas is simply her pen name. She is called Nicola Fairchild.'

'Oh!'

'And in that context, I hope to continue to make use of your good offices to enable Sam to change his name to Fairchild.'

'Is that altogether wise, Lady Beeson?'

'Sam will never have cause to forget his father. I can guarantee that, but I have been informed that for reasons of security it would be preferable for the name of Beeson to be occluded – their word not mine. I shall become Mrs Fairchild.'

I understand and perhaps we can talk this through, because my call is to invite you to pay a visit to Salisbury. I have a complex legal matter to deal with at the Cathedral which will take me at least a week's residence in the city. Papers relating to the will of Sir André are now ready for you to sign.'

'I've never been to Salisbury but there is a direct railway line there from Exeter. When are you going to be there?'

'I am travelling there tomorrow and will be staying with friends. I know this is somewhat short notice, but I have only this morning received probate for your late husband's will and thought it might save one or other of us a longer journey.'

'A visit to Salisbury is more than possible, Mr Gleadall. Getting everything sorted before I marry is more demanding than I might have hoped for, so I must thank you for the speed with which you have dealt with it.'

'Perhaps those advising your security issues have also been a source of encouragement to my expeditiousness, if you take my meaning.'

I laughed.

'Oh, I do, Mr Gleadall, I do.'

We made some arrangements and agreed to meet in two days' time in the offices of a local firm of solicitors where he was doing his business, just outside the main Cathedral Close arch. It would be a wonderful outing for the three of us and Sam's first train ride.

Nicola's eagerly expected call from Mark came whilst I was talking to Mr Gleadall. I waited, hearing only snatches from the bedroom. It was also Sam's waking up time after his afternoon sleep, so I brought him into the sitting room and told him about his forthcoming train ride, which excited him no end. I was wondering what I might get him for a wedding present, and if he took to trains, perhaps a train set would be ideal for his stay with his granny.

'The doctors said they need more time with Helen,' reported Nicola when she joined us.

'We're going on a train,' announced Sam.

'Ooh, that's exciting,' she said, giving me a puzzled look.

'I'll explain later. Your news is more important.'

'Well, in fact, there isn't much to tell. She'll be remaining in the unit. She is refusing to speak to anyone, other than repeating a demand to see you, not Mark, nor the children or her parents, only you.'

'How on earth do I respond to that, presuming it would be allowed, given her intention last time?'

'I'm sure your safety would be guaranteed and there will be someone in the room with you throughout.'

'You've said yes?'

'Of course not. I wasn't there, was I? I'm just reporting what Mark said. If you don't want to do it, no one is going to blame you and he said Abi told him she would drop by on you later.'

'Brendan told me this morning I was fearless, so I guess I'll have to do it for Helen's sake, but I'll wait to hear what the lady with the hand of steel in a velvet glove has to say before I agree. In the meantime, let me tell you about our trip on Wednesday to Salisbury.'

I was recounting my call from Mr Gleadall when my phone rang. It was Sergeant Molloy.

'Hello Lady Beeson. I'm Abi Molloy. First, please accept my very best wishes for the big day and beyond. There's more than one that envies you your choice.'

'I don't think it was a choice, an act of will, I mean, for either of us. We both simply realised it.'

'Oh, my! Well, your realisation stole from us someone special, I'll have you know.'

'I'm realising it more and more every day. But I think the reason for your call is not just to hear our love story.'

'No. Will you be at home in about a quarter of an hour? I've just seen someone not too far away and could come if it suits.'

'You'll be most welcome, provided you call me Dee and I call you "sergeant"?'

She laughed.

'No chance, Lady Beeson!'

I knew I would like Abi and when she arrived, in far from plain clothes, I was not wrong. Armed with tea and a cake made by Nicola, we sat down to chat first about the morning's activity, with one part of my brain constantly trying to recall that I was with a highly skilled operator, who was also warm and friendly. I began by saying we had heard from Mark what Helen was requesting.

'It's more than a request. She has resolutely refused to say anything since she was taken to Plymouth and then transferred to Dawlish. She simply repeats the demand. Otherwise, nothing.

'The evidence from the recorded conversation and the fact that she had a knife in her handbag that she had already used to slash Mark's face implies a possibility that she intended it use it against you, either to disfigure you or worse. This has been reported to the magistrates, who will wait for a mental health assessment before proceeding further. Until the doctors make their report we cannot know if there is a serious mental health problem or she is adopting silence as a method of avoiding questioning. If it is the latter, she is doing so of her own volition. She won't speak to a solicitor or mental health legal advocate.'

'What do those caring for her think should happen?'

'They know that a willingness on your part to see her is accepting an encounter with someone who, when you last met, was threatening to kill you. That it is not a light matter, and which no police officer would recommend.

'So, what are you saying?'

'I'm in a multi-disciplinary team with skilled professionals *who* can't assess her if she continues to refuse to speak. But now we have reached an impasse. It will be perfectly understandable if you do not wish to see her, but at the present time, we are at something of an impasse. If this continues, she will have to come before the magistrates charged with grievous bodily harm and making threats with intent. These are serious charges, and she will be remanded in custody and sent for trial. With the evidence we have, she will go to prison.'

'Morally, I have no choice, so please inform the hospital that I will meet with Helen. I understand from Nicola that it would only take place in the presence of a third person, probably a nurse. Is that right?'

'You can take that as read, and you will also be observed on CCTV, which is essential for the doctors.'

'When?'

'It has been pencilled in for half past nine, if you can manage that.'

'Yes.'

'I'm sure the entire team caring for Helen would wish me to offer you their thanks for being willing to do this – not for their sake's but Helen's.'

Abi turned to Nicola.

'Once the wedding is behind you, might there be even a possibility that you would consider working part-time with me as a civilian observer? It would be more piecework than part time, in that sometimes I go into a family situation in which I should be accompanied by someone acting as advocate for the family who is not a police officer, there to see fair play, ensuring that the interests of those I am seeing are properly observed. It isn't every case by any means, but sometimes in a family court I have been accused of directing. Protecting the interests of a family is also a way of protecting me.'

'I'm not a lawyer, Abi.'

'Oh, we've got plenty of them, but I need someone as sensitive and aware as you to be present, watching. You would be paid of course, but no pressure. You have enough on your plate right now with your own family situation and the forthcoming wedding but give it some thought.'

'Tell me, Nicola,' I said, 'as a test, how do you think Abi's behaved with me?'

I was meaning it as a joke, but Nicola, I think, took it as a serious question.

'I've seen you in action before, Abi, so I know the ways you operate. If I had one anxiety about your conversation with my fiancée, it would be that you let yourself down by having shoes that don't match your handbag!'

'It ruined it for me too.' I added.

'H'm,' she said, 'perhaps you two deserve each other!'

15

I was asked to be at the Langdon Hospital by nine o'clock so those caring for Helen could meet me to "discuss parameters", whatever they might be. The place is modern and attractive, and I parked the car, fulfilling the obligation to tap in my car number once inside the reception area to avoid receiving a penalty ticket. I was feeling nervous, but I was met by someone called Ben, who described himself as Helen's designated nurse and he at once sensed my anxiety and took me into a room that was light and comfortable, explaining that this is where Helen would come to be with me.

'She'll come accompanied by Penny, also a nurse, who will remain with you throughout but won't interfere in such conversation as you can manage, unless it becomes obvious we should stop or that you wish to do so, which you can do by just saying so to Penny. You will also be observed and heard by Helen's doctor, using the camera over there on the wall above the picture. Helen has been told all this. Because she still hasn't said a word other than to ask to see you, we are taking the silence as consent. Dr Pilling will be here in a few moments to brief you. There's water on the table, but I can get you a cup of tea or coffee.'

'Water will be perfectly ok, thanks, Ben.'

He was a gentle person, which I assumed was essential for anyone working here. As a forensic hospital, it regularly received mostly men from prison with mental health problems, though there were also women patients other than Helen. I had read all this on the website the previous evening.

I stood and went to the window and looked out towards the sea, which was reflecting the sun in its ripples. The setting was delightful, and I could see people walking around engaged in a variety of tasks and pursuits. I turned round as I heard the door open and was greeted by the sight of an elderly lady, as I first thought, shuffling her way towards me and holding out her hand.

'Hello, I'm Lillian Pilling, Helen's consultant. Please let us sit down for a moment or two. Thank you for coming this morning. I hope your visit will enable us to make a proper assessment of Helen's state of mind. It has not been possible beyond recognising obvious disturbance. Something lies behind this aphasia, which we need to discover. Is there anything you wish to ask me?'

'The only question I have is to ask Helen why she needs to see me?'

'And that must be your starting point, but please, Dee, if I may call you that, be patient with her, no matter what she might say. As I'm sure Ben will have told you, you will be perfectly safe. Afterwards we can have a chat which will enable you to express your feelings and thoughts.'

Dr Pilling rose. She was perhaps a little older than I had imagined might be a consultant psychiatrist dealing with serious offenders, but I detected a mind that was as sharp as the knife that Helen had brought with her just four days earlier.

Shortly afterwards, the door opened again. Helen came in escorted by a young woman, presumably Penny, to a chair directly opposite me with our knees almost but not quite touching.

'Hello, Helen,' I began, 'it's not quite the *Cider Press Café*, but it will have to do.'

She looked awful, still wearing the clothes she had worn when she came to the house on Thursday. Her hair needed attention and there were bags under her eyes suggesting she wasn't sleeping too well.

'I was told you asked to see me.'

Her was face was expressionless, and she stared at me in a way I found unsettling.

'Of course, I wanted you,' she said. 'Who else? You and I are one, so nobody else would do. We haven't gone through a service of any kind, but neither have you and that bitch of a sister-in-law holding your son as a hostage. I imagine she's got him now, so she knows you will have to go back.'

'Don't you want to see Maisie and Angus? They're missing you, and Maisie doesn't understand why you're not there.'

'I meant what I told you about Mark having an affair. It's gone on for a long time. It's over, because we are the future, Dee.'

I sat there, my mind completely numb. Eventually I heard myself say, more than thought, 'I'm so glad you asked me to come, Helen, and it's so wonderful to see you. The important thing is that you talk about all this and explain everything to the doctors and nurses, and equally important that you keep up your creative writing. You'll need some for sending to the OU before the course starts.'

'Gosh, yes, I'd almost forgotten. I will, Dee. But your immediate task is to get Sam back from that cow. If need be, I'll take care of her for you permanently.'

'Of course'.

I looked at Penny.

'I need to leave.'

'Ok, Helen, we need to get you back to your room. Let's go.'

I don't think I would have argued with the tone of Penny's instruction and Helen didn't. She stood up, reached out and touched my hand.

'We're nearly there,' she said.'

'Yes,' I replied lamely, with no idea what else to say.

I sat down feeling strangely exhausted and immediately wishing I had not done this, feeling I had perhaps been manipulated not just by Helen, but by those hoping to achieve some sort of breakthrough with her, but at substantial cost to me.

Dr Pilling and Ben came into the room, and both sat down, and another person brought in a mug of tea for each of us, and then left.

'Thank you for doing that,' began Dr Pilling, 'which must have been so very difficult for you. We couldn't in advance know what she was going to say, and if we had, would not have let you be subjected to it. I apologise, even though it may be the only way we have made an inroad into understanding what is happening inside Helen. However, you handled it so very well and your mention that she should write more was inspired.'

'I completely agree with Lillian,' said Ben. 'I was impressed by the way you didn't outwardly react. Helen probably will think she was in charge, but you were.'

'It didn't feel like it. If I didn't show any reaction that was probably because as she spoke I froze, and I was utterly shocked by what she said about "taking care of" Nicola, which I took as a threat to kill her.'

'It was, and we are bound to inform the police of that. It will help them decide whether to charge her, but I think, Ben, we will proceed with a Section 3. What this means, Dee, is that the treatment Helen requires can only be given to her as an involuntary patient not well enough to make her own decisions about treatment. In the first place, Section 3 can last for up to six months then renewed. At this stage, we have no idea about a timeframe of treatment, other than knowing Helen needs help.'

I nodded.

'More important still, Dee, is whether we can be of help to you now. I really don't want you to leave with post-traumatic stress disorder. I can get someone to drive you home if it would help.'

'I think I will survive, Lillian.'

'Yes, but you've been recently bereaved.'

'My husband was forty years older than me, and he died exactly as he would have wished to, sitting next to me as I attended to our son. Although some people are shocked and say I shouldn't do anything like this after a loss, I'm getting married in two weeks' time to the wisest and best person I've ever known. I'll take my chances, and you underestimate the healing power of tea! I shall be fine.'

As soon as I set off, I called Nicola on the hands-free.

'I suppose, from the standpoint of the doctor, at least I got her talking, but she said enough to allow them to decide to section her, though they also have to let our friend Abi know, that she made a threat to kill you. Does that mean they will charge her?'

'Not if she's being sectioned, but it needs to be recorded all the same.'

'It's a nice modern place, but please promise me that when I have to be admitted, you will take me first to the seaside and drown me! I'm on my way back to you, my lovely, wonderful Nicola. When we pick Sam up, let's celebrate with a glass of cider.'

I knew, of course, that at some stage I would have to let Mark know how things had gone. He was taking the week off work, but I decided I would wait until he called me. He rang when I was still about a mile from home, and I said I would call him back when I got there.

'So how was Helen?' he asked. 'Was she able to speak?'

'She's able to speak, Mark, just refusing to do so, but, yes, she did, and I hope she will now continue to do so. They have decided, and I don't suppose you'll be surprised at this, to section her under the terms of the Mental Health Act. That means she will remain there and not be allowed to come home. This could be for six months, but even longer if need be.

'It wasn't easy, Mark. She shows no wish at the present time to want to see you or the children, but that will hopefully change with treatment.'

'Does this mean she won't be charged with assaulting me with a knife?'

'Remember, Mark, that she was intent on doing that or worse to me, and in theory could face a charge of intent to murder, but under the terms of the section, the police will not proceed.'

'I'm going to see a solicitor about divorce, Dee, and I shall seek custody of the children.'

'I'm sure a solicitor will guide you properly. The circumstances of her being an involuntary inpatient might affect the process of a divorce, but I know little about it how these things work. How are Maisie and Angus?'

Helen's mum has got Angus today and Maisie is now full-time

in school. At least I've got a bit of breathing space.'

'That's really important, Mark, and you know that Nicola and I are always here.'

'Thanks, Dee.'

I put my phone down. I had put it on speaker so Nicola could hear.

'I shouldn't think a divorce will be a problem but there's little hope of getting any sort of custody sorted for some time, though he will have to ensure that he can provide proper care for the children which won't be straightforward given his demanding job and a mortgage to maintain, especially given Angus still needs a lot of basic care. Oh, it's a colossal mess.'

'It is, but at least tomorrow we can have a day away and sample the delights of Salisbury.'

'I've been there before and the delights you describe are mostly just the Cathedral, but we might just be able to squeeze in a visit to dress shops. We're getting married 16 days from now and we've nothing to wear.'

'I like you when you wear nothing, but I'm not prepared to share that with our guests, so you're quite right,' I said.

It was almost time to collect Sam, who was for the first time sampling lunch in nursery, so would be a little later. Even so, as we left to collect him, I couldn't believe that it was not even one o'clock and I was already ready for bed.

16

Sam was excited to be at the Railway Station and to see the trains and all the people and was almost in ecstasy when we finally got into the carriage at Exeter St David's. The train was Waterloo bound but would stop everywhere it could manage in Devon and Dorset before our arrival in Wiltshire, though this only seemed to enhance Sam's enjoyment.

Just half an hour into the journey, we arrived in Honiton and Sam eagerly looked out of the window across to the platform on the other side.

'Uncle Mark,' he said suddenly and pointed.

His nephew, my son, was not mistaken. It was Mark, sitting on a bench with a woman, holding hands, which, as we looked, transformed into a long kiss. There was no chance that he would notice us, engrossed as he was, and soon our train pulled out. So far, neither of us had spoken as we stared goggle-eyed out of the window.

Finally, Nicola said, 'It looks like Helen was telling the truth. Those two hadn't just met accidentally on the platform.'

'Mark wouldn't be the first not to want to own up to that, and especially not to his sister.'

'That's true and I can't say I begrudge him some sort of attention given what he's been through, but I wonder if knowing about it as Helen does, or thinks she does, played some part in setting in motion her present troubles.'

'Do you think,' I asked, 'we should pass on this information to Dawlish? At least it might help them know everything Helen says isn't coming out of a disordered mind.'

'That would be risky, Dee. We don't know how long this has been in place or whether Helen really knows or merely suspects. In fact, unless we can learn more, interfering further would not be altogether sensible, and I don't want to be the person challenging Mark over this, and you're not.'

'I agree with that. But is there anything we can do? Is it something we ought to mention to Abi?'

'Having an affair, or a relationship I would prefer to call it, is not a crime. Mark remains the victim of a crime even though it's never likely to see the light of day in a courtroom. What Helen has been saying can't simply be the product of Mark seeing someone, can it?'

'I've no idea, but I still think it might help Helen if someone knew that whether she knew or simply had suspicions, Mark *is* in a relationship with another woman. I hate having to say this, my love, but the only person who can talk to him about this, and not in any accusatory sort of way, is his sister.'

'We should get Sam to do it. After all, it was you who saw Uncle Mark, you clever boy!'

Sam grinned in appreciation of the appreciation but diverted his attention to our pulling into the station at Axminster, where there was a train waiting to leave in the opposite direction. Sam was thrilled when it moved out.

I imagine that if you were to get lost in the back streets of Salisbury, you have a sure guide in the spire of the cathedral. Like the polestar it's visible for miles around and presumably no sat-nav is needed. Leaving the station, we followed the star to the cathedral, which is huge, bigger than that in Exeter though that may be the effect of the spire. The inside was disappointing in that there was so little colour, and although the architecture was wonderful to look up to, and I can't even begin to imagine how they built it back at the beginning of the thirteenth century, overall Exeter's much finer.

Worst of all were the huge dark blue windows at the East End. We looked at it in dismay. A guide with her green sash sidled up to us.

'It's the Prisoner of Conscience Window,' she said.

'It's hideous,' said Nicola. 'It cuts out all the light.'

'There's scaffolding behind at the moment.'

'That makes no difference. The glass is deep blue, and the rising sun ought to pour in. Does nobody here read George Herbert? It's a dated political posture. It truly is hideous.'

'It was the brainchild of our former Dean, Sydney Evans.'

'And so he inflicted on succeeding generations his own obsession. It truly is horrible.'

The guide backed off with a painful smile, no doubt relieved when we departed, as were we.

We had some lunch in something calling itself *The Boston Tea Party*, a name I recognised from Exeter, a café which served all-day breakfast with an excellent menu for children, so Sam tucked in to sausages, scrambled egg and mushrooms. Nicola and I had something called the West Country Breakfast, which was so good and filling, we agreed we would need little more that day.

After lunch, Nicola and Sam went to a playground we had passed earlier and I went to see Mr Gleadall, who came into the reception area of the offices I had entered, looking very smart indeed in his three-piece suit. It was the first time we had met face-to-face.

'Lady Beeson, thank you so much for coming here.'

'Please call me Dee,' I said.

'If you please, then, Dee.'

I followed him down a carpeted corridor and into a large room where he had a considerable number of files on his desk. He noticed my glance.

'Yes, this is my lot for the week. Hard to credit that a religious institution generates so much legal activity, but there we are. Now, let me get the papers we need to attend to. They're straightforward, authorising me to act now probate has been granted regarding the contents of Sir André's will.'

'Ok. Show me where to sign and then advise me what I should do next, as I can hardly walk into my bank in Exeter and ask to pay in two million pounds.'

'Oh, they wouldn't mind that; it's taking it out again that would trouble them. But I'm not the person to advise you. Do you know Jasper Ridley? He's the accountant Sir André has used for a good many years. He is an accountant but can also give good advice as to the best places to invest your money, and that of your son. With good investment ½ million pounds today will in 15 years' time be a substantial 18th birthday present.

'All the funds are now available to you, and notice will be given to the other recipients to arrange transfers, now you have released them. Once all that is completed, Sir André's account will be closed.'

He stood up showing that the affairs of the Cathedral now demanded his attention.

'We shall have further contact of course, Dee, once you have arranged for the legacies of yourself and Samuel, and can I recommend that your own will be updated once you have married and that you appoint a second trustee for Samuel's investment, but it should not be your future partner.

'I look forward to our further engagement, Mr Gleadall. I'm sure André would want me to continue with you. Might you be that second trustee and draw up the necessary deeds?'

'That would be a great honour, but I may telephone you and ask you to repeat your wish to continue with my services once you have received our final account!'

We laughed together as he led me out into the busy street. I was now a millionaire and thought it hilarious. I called Nicola and the three of us at once retreated into a different coffee shop for tea and a cake (for despite the earlier feast my contact with the law had made me hungry). Sam was asleep throughout, no doubt building up his strength to survive his mother, and second mother-to-be (for we had already decided that Nicola would adopt him) shopping for their wedding outfits!

The Salisbury shops were disappointing, for as with other city shopping areas, many had closed and lay empty. After traipsing round with little success, we abandoned the search, but then, unexpectedly, saw a shop that looked more hopeful. We had already decided that despite my now being a millionaire, we both wanted to wear something simple and lovely, and things we could wear again. We found them here. Nicola chose a lovely flowery tea dress and I a short sleeve midi dress which, with a couple of lovely scarves, came to under £200!

Sitting on the train, I had to make a sudden exit to the loo. My period had begun as I knew Nicola's had just the day before. We laughed to think we were now like nuns who, it is said, all menstruate at the same time – poor things, just imagine all that PMT! However, the curse was timely given the days left before the wedding and we were not nuns!

In bed that night, what exercised us was Mark and what we had seen that morning on the platform in Honiton (which we both thought a good title for a novel! After talking it through Nicola said: 'I can't go behind Mark's back. I'll talk to him.'

'Yes, I think that's best, provided he knows we are not expressing disapproval of any kind. We only saw him kissing a woman but know nothing more. He might have just met her, and whatever is the case, Helen's catastrophic mental health can't simply be caused by an affair begun fourteen months ago, as she claims.'

'Oh, my love, I am going to say something you might disagree with, but I think you should be the one to speak to him, not me. You've seen Helen and you're not his sister. I think he will be more open with you.'

'Gee, thanks,' I said, giving her a far from chaste kiss, though for the rest of the night we observed the proprieties of convent life.

'Mark, it's your sister-in-law to be here.'

'Hi Dee, I'm just about to take Angus to Ashburton for a day with his granny.'

'I won't keep you as I'm on the verge of taking Sam to nursery, but there's something I need to talk over with you since I saw Helen and would prefer to do it face-to-face. Might you be able to come here from Ashburton? It won't take long, but it's important. Nicola will be working, so it'll just be me.'

'Of course. I'll see you in about forty minutes' time.'

Mark is a little older than Nicola and has done well to become manager of a large franchise restaurant. He is slim and good-looking but still bearing on his face the plaster covering the wound of Helen's assault.

We chatted in the kitchen about the kids as I made coffee and then went through to the sitting room.'

'Nicola is in the study but will be listening to music through her headphones. I'm sure that won't prevent us from speaking openly, but I wanted you to know that.'

'I always assumed poets worked in silence.'

'I've only met a few, but they all seem to do their writing in different ways, sometimes even sitting in a coffee shop. Anyway, I went to Salisbury yesterday, well, the three of us did. I had to sign legal documents relating to André's will and we wanted to get some kit for our wedding day.'

'Successful?'

'I hope so, but not typical bridal outfits – pretty, but serviceable beyond the big day, and we hope you'll come wearing whatever you want. No formal wedding attire.'

'That's great. I hate dressing up in all that sort of palaver.'

'Whilst on our way, when the train stopped in Honiton, Sam pointed out the window and said "Uncle Mark".'

He gave a guilty smile.

'In which case, I suspect what might be about to follow.'

'Actually, Mark, you don't. Yes, we saw you holding hands and kissing, but we both more than understand that your marriage to Helen has probably been over even before Angus was born, and we'd be the first to recognise that you are free to discover love wherever and with whomsoever you choose. The only thing that troubles me is to know whether her suspicion of your new relationship might have set in motion, "triggered" is the in word, some of Helen's difficulties.'

'Amelia was staying at the Premier Inn overnight for a work event that was happening in our place. We were short-staffed that night (when are we not?) and I was helping with their table, and we fell for each other. She's a pharmacist in Honiton and we could only manage a short time together at the station.'

'Oh, Mark, don't you dare say that! One of the greatest love films ever made was called *Brief Encounter* and mostly set in a railway station.'

He laughed.

'You're very clever,'

'No, I'm not, Mark, trust me.'

'What you need to know is that I met Amelia just two months ago. I have never had any kind of relationship other than a working one with Amanda, my deputy, which is what Helen accused me of.'

'Are you hopeful of a future together with Amelia?'

'She's single and we love one another. I know there's Maisie's and Angus's needs to be agreed, but I am getting a divorce and I would love to marry Amelia.'

'Have you asked her?'

'Well, not yet.'

'Get on with it, Mark. Life is short, you know.'

'I can tell you and Nicola are made for each other.'

'Oh?'

'I couldn't exactly say why, and I've never even considered the thought of two people of the same sex, you know, being married, but you two fit together like pieces of a jigsaw.'

'If we avoid all conversation to do with what we've been talking about, would you like Nicola to come and join us?'

'I quite like my sister, so yes.'

I rose and knocked on the study door.

'Coffee or tea?'

'Definitely tea.'

She came over to Mark and gave him a hug and kiss, and I went into the kitchen. By the time I returned, Mark had told Nicola about Amelia.'

'Have Maisie and Angus met her?' asked their aunt.

'No. We both feel that until things have settled, and we know what's happening to Helen, that's quite enough for them to be handling. And this is something I forgot to tell you, Dee, Amelia has a son, Daniel, aged three. It was a silly mistake, she said, during a conference. He is a Ghanaian lecturer in pharmacy at

Sheffield University, so Daniel is a gorgeous shade of brown, and his biological father pays up each month.'

'The longer I live,' I said, 'the more wonderful I think life is in all its complexity.'

'You're right about waiting to introduce Amelia to the children,' said Nicola, 'but you don't need to hide her away from us. We'd love to meet her, though does she know about us?'

'Yes, and she would like to meet you.'

'It needs to be arranged then, like weddings need to be arranged, which is a far from subtle hint to my fiancée to make sure all the arrangements about food and drink are sorted.'

'Oh yes. In fact, I'll get on with it now and leave brother and sister to talk.'

17

We were now on the final run-up to the wedding day, finalising practicalities. However, trouble arrived in the form of a call from Hoddlesden.

'Hello, Dorothea. I've bought a new dress for the wedding and I'm wanting to check with you about times of train arrivals in Exeter so you can pick me up. I thought you'd probably need me for the best part of a week before the day itself – that's what mothers do.'

'I'm sorry, mum, but it's going to be a tiny affair for none but a few in a tiny location, and we've already arranged it.'

'You're turning me away from my daughter's wedding?'

'You had pride of place when I wed André, so you've done it for me once. This is a very different sort of wedding and it's best done quietly – not in the newspapers!'

'I'm disgusted, and I think what you're doing is disgusting. It's unnatural for two women to get married.'

'In which case, given that I'm disgusting and unnatural, it's a good job you won't be coming.'

'Who's giving you away?'

'No one. It doesn't work like that anymore, and we'll be spending the night together before the day. Things have changed.'

'I'm still your mother. That's not changed, even if you've clearly been poisoned against me by that woman. Just don't let her near any of your money because I bet that's what she's after.'

'What money?'

'You're not telling me André wasn't a wealthy man? It'll be all yours now.'

'André was a civil servant. His money, his savings if you like, are tied up in our house and he changed his will so that Sam will be properly provided for.'

'But doesn't Chloe earn a lot from her books?'

'Oh loads! It works out at about £1.75 per copy, before tax, and no poet sells many copies. You have to be Jeffrey Archer to make money from writing books.'

'Isn't he the one who went to prison?'

'And he's even made more money from writing about it!'

'Well, I'm not right pleased, Dorothea, and your sisters and brothers will feel the same.'

'Actually, they didn't attend last time.'

'Didn't they? Oh, I thought they had. It's different where you live. Any road, they're all moslems here now. Going into Darren's like entering Pakistan.'

'It's called Darwen, mother.'

'It might as well be called something foreign now as it's mostly foreigners who live there, even if most of them were born here. If they want to live here, they should all become Christians like the rest of us.'

Quite what made my mother count herself as a Christian I cannot even guess at, other than the certainty that God is white and English and guarantees her a seat in heaven, to which he would do us all a favour if he delivered her from us soon! It was a peevish thought, but before feeling guilty, I remembered in time that I meant it!

Abi called on Friday afternoon with a report from Dawlish. Mark had told her about Amelia, and she said that as this had no bearing on Helen's state of mind, she had not felt obliged to pass it on.

'I should have come earlier in the week, Dee, to see how you were after your meeting with Helen, and I gather it was not a pleasant experience.'

'In terms of content, it was almost identical to the original encounter here without the knife, with the addition of a nurse called Penny.'

'She's good – shares the care for Helen with Ben. We had a case conference this morning and Helen is speaking a little, but not saying a great deal. She's very withdrawn and keeps asking for you. Dr Pilling and her team will persist but suggest this may take a long time. There is no diagnosis at present, which makes beginning treatment difficult. She has been informed that Mark is seeking a divorce, but has shown no reaction, and still does not respond to any mention of Maisie and Angus.'

'This is awful, Abi,' said Nicola.

'Yes, and I shan't be taking part anymore, given that we shall not be pressing charges and Mark won't either, unless of course she were to be discharged soon, which will not happen. I regret to say that there's no shortage of other work to be done, and I am eager to know what you might have decided about the job offer I made to you on Monday.'

'So am I,' replied Nicola. 'We have had a full week and until after we get back from Italy, I can't give you an answer.'

'That's fine. It's good to know you haven't yet said no to the idea. It keeps my hope alive.'

That evening we talked about that job, as well as about money, for the time being assuming that I would remain as basic home maker and child carer, which I didn't mind.

'I want nothing financial to cause us difficulties, which I know can often be the case,' I said once Sam was asleep, though it had taken a little longer for him to settle than usual.

'I agree, but Dee, you now have over two million pounds in your account, and I have about eight thousand. There's a world of difference between the two and since we met, you've been paying for everything, even the dress I'm marrying you in.'

'It's not something I think about. What's mine is yours and if it means I'm sponsoring the arts, then fine. But you're right, we should get this on a proper footing.

'Mr Gleadall says I should deal with an accountant for advice on investment for both Sam and me, and I'll get round to it soon, but what might be best is that we have a joint account with, I don't know, say £10,000 in it, for our regular living, topped up when it falls below a certain level we can agree on.'

'Topped up how?'

'By courtesy of my late husband. We should invest most of the money from his will, but investments are locked away and mostly inaccessible, so we need to make sure at least £100,000 can be accessed. That should do us for a few years at least, but I've told you before you can't have a new car every year!'

Nicola laughed.

'I truly think.' I continued, 'that you should learn from Abi's offer of that job that she recognises qualities in you I know.'

She took my hand but then we heard a cry from Sam. I went to him and could tell at once that something was the matter. He clearly had a temperature, but I could see at once the cause: chickenpox. There was a rash round his neck and tiny spots showing. I wasn't totally surprised because it had been mentioned at nursery that it was doing the rounds, nor being a profound believer in Sod's Law, was I altogether surprised that this should happen in the week before our wedding!

How did parents manage before Calpol, I wondered, as Nicola brought some from the bathroom cabinet, together with a bottle of camomile lotion I hadn't even previously noticed?

'I got it in Boots when we were in Salisbury,' she said, answering my unasked question. 'Sam's at just the age, in contact with other children, when chickenpox is likely, so when I was buying things for you and me, I added it.'

I shook my head a little.

'You're quite amazing. Were you ever a girl guide?'

'I was, and then a Ranger, and got the Gold Award. I didn't go in for the Duke of Edinburgh's, however, because by then I knew I wanted to go into the police service.'

'And did you get the camomile buying badge?'

She stuck her tongue out at me.

By morning, Sam had turned into Spotty Muldoon and was clearly feeling poorly and striving to always scratch. I insisted Nicola continued her writing routine whilst I encouraged Sam to wear his gloves though that was going to be a day-long fight which I knew I might lose and, in the end, went for socks which could go up his arm and be harder to remove. I also had to convince him that as he was poorly, he couldn't go to nursery, but he wanted to see his friends and cried. The joys of parenthood!

Sam eventually fell asleep shortly before Nicola returned from the world of poesy to that of infectious diseases.

'I've looked chickenpox up on my phone,' I said, 'and it usually subsides within seven days. You'd better call your mum and let her know we shall have pot noodles for our Sunday lunch this weekend. Just imagine how it would be for Mark if Maisie and Angus became infected?'

Mr Jasper Ridley had been André's accountant, though I didn't even know he had one, something I concealed when I finally got through to him.

'Lady Beeson, I think this is the first time we've spoken, and please accept my sincere condolences on the loss of your husband. He was a lovely man, and although he would never speak about his work, the little I know suggests he did important things.'

'The most important of which, Mr Ridley, was marrying me, wouldn't you agree?'

He laughed.

'I gather from our mutual friend Mr Gleadall that you now own a sum of money, with which I might assist as you wonder how to make the best use of it, both for yourself and your son. Mr Gleadall has not told me the sums involved, but if I can be of assistance, then I will seek to do my best to advise you. The important thing will be to allow the investments to grow. So are you willing to tell me the sums involved?'

'Oh yes, it would be a pointless conversation otherwise. André has left Sam £500,000 which will be available to him on his 18th birthday though in the terms of the will, should he predecease me, and at the moment he has chickenpox, that sum will revert to me.'

'How old is Sam?'

'Three.'

'In fifteen years he will receive considerably more than that, considerably more. And what of your own legacy?'

'Mr Gleadall has completed probate, and I suspect you know full well how much I am talking about because he will have asked you to deal with taxation matters.'

'Oh dear, forgive my unsuccessful attempts at protecting confidentiality. Sir André once told me you were one of the cleverest people he had ever met, and it seems he was right. So, yes, I know he is holding for you a sum of £2,280,000 and one of our first acts must be to get it away from him as he will charge you a fee for that by the day. I say that as your accountant. I do not work for him but am happy to do so for you, should you require my services.'

'As you know already know everything, I think I will do so, though I bet you're not cheap either!'

'Lady Beeson, what an outrageous thing to say when you've never even once sat in my extremely plush suite of offices with every amenity and one or two more in Wandsworth.'

'Wandsworth?'

'Much cheaper than up west, as they say.'

I laughed.

'Your wealthy solicitor has informed that as from Thursday of next week, you will be Mrs Dorothea Fairchild, and that you are changing Sam's name to yours. I would recommend that we do nothing about investments until after these changes have taken place, because changing names after you have invested is always complex. I'll make some recommendations for you almost at once, but wait for you to let me know when Sam's name changes before I act on his behalf. In the meantime, may I suggest you arrange with Mr Gleadall to release to you £250,000 at once – spending money we might call it, but the important things is that it needs to be easily and almost immediately accessible should you need it. I would also recommend that if you are planning a joint account after your wedding, you should both also keep accounts in your own names. In that way, I can make even more money from dealing with them each year, though it is also a wise thing to do, both of you retaining £10,000 in those accounts. I will write all this down and send it by post. You have a lot to deal with in these next few days, wedding and chickenpox among them, so allow me to delay this until after the event has taken place. One other thing, you must both make new wills.'

'Yes, Mr Gleadall mentioned that.'

'So, when next we speak, you will be Mrs Fairchild. One of my sons is married to another man, and they are so happy together. At one time I was fearful, and I was wrong totally, so I wish you both much joy in your life together. And I want to thank you for retaining my services. It's tough here in Wandsworth and I need the work!'

I laughed.

'I think we shall get on well, Mr Ridley, with one proviso, and that it that when we speak next, you call me Dee.'

'Oh, but what of Dorothea Brooke?'

'She found happiness too and presumably changed her to Ladislaw. That's all that matters, isn't it?'

'Indeed, it is, Dee, and you can call me Bobby.'

'Bobby?'

'Jasper sound posh for business purposes, but it's been a horrible burden to have carry all these years, so those close to me know me be by second name, Robert – Bobby.'

'It's been lovely talking to you, Bobby.'

'And you, Dee.'

18

Our main concern in the days immediately prior to the wedding was ensuring enough food in the house for our visitors. After a week, Sam had recovered and enjoyed the attentions of Sharon, Kim, and Olivia, and much more alarmingly, Nicola was enjoying the attentions of Sharon!

Kim was keen to inspect the security provisions that had been installed two days earlier by the team she had sent from Bristol, led, bizarrely, by a woman who knew Emily and Alex in Derbyshire, though didn't say how, other than that she had done some work there.

Kim's job was extremely demanding, and she received security reports every few minutes.

'It's not my idea of a holiday, Kim. You might almost be in your office.'

'I'm leaving at the end of October. My great friend Martha, who was my boss and head of the service, has already retired. I was asked to take over, but I ask you, would you want to meet every morning with the Prime Minister and Home Secretary at 7:30? And there's a couple of big messes, not something I was part of, likely to do us harm, so I'm hoping we can leave London and allow me time for the two ladies in my life.'

'They look well,' I said.

'She won't tell you, but Sharon had a breast lump scare in the summer. It was nothing in the end but might account for why she was testy about Nicola at the time of André's funeral. We've also a friend in Scotland who's had to have breast surgery, and it scared Sharon.

For Nicola, the greatest joy was the presence of Viv and Emily (children left at home with husbands), though I too was so pleased to see them again. They went up on to Dartmoor to walk and talk, mostly not of poetry, Nicola reported, but of what they could see, from which poetry might later be made, "recollected in tranquility" as Viv said to laughter (a Wordsworth joke, that had to be explained to me by Nicola later), as all our visitors gathered for an outstanding supper made by me with due modesty!

On the eve of wedding day I had a call from my sister Hippolyta in Lancaster.

'Polly,' I said, 'how lovely to hear from you.'

'I'm calling for everyone, brothers, sisters, children, to say we'll be thinking of you tomorrow and hope it goes well. We're all very proud of you, Dee, and wish we could see more of you. Can't you bring Nicola (mother insists on calling her Chloe) and Sam to see the north?'

'Yes, Nicola's closest friend lives near Kendal, and we're been invited stay with her and her family, so it might happen. And about Medusa, how is she?'

'She's got t'vapours right now because she's missing t'wedding, but sadly I think she'll recover.'

'Polly, you're as bad as me.'

'I sometimes wish I was you, Dee. I'd give a lot to have a new life, but there's not a lot I can do with three boys to run after.'

'Two, you mean?'

'Oh no, I mean three, if you get my meaning.'

'You could always have an affair, Polly,' I said jokingly.

There was a moment of hesitation.

'It's not an affair, Dee, it's a lot more than that. I love him so much and he loves me, but I'm stuck.

'No Polly, you're not. Can you and he not actually start a new life together, even with the two lads?'

'I suppose.'

'Then what's holding you back?'

'Fear, I suppose.'

'Of what people might say?'

'No. Fuck the lot of them.'

'That would be exhausting.'

We both laughed.

'No, it's fear of leaving behind tedious but safe mediocrity for an unknown.'

'Why don't you have a few days away by yourself visiting your sister in Devon, plus one? You can stay with us. I mean it. Sam would love to meet his aunt Polly, and you and your friend could have a few days of normality together to give it all a think through. You would, of course, have to sleep in a locked room, and he outside in the garage.'

'Of course, you cheeky haperth. He's called Simon, unmarried and my age.'

'How did you meet?'

'He's my GP.'

'Polly, I love you. Look, your sister in Devon needs to talk to someone in the family. Fix it, lass!'

The forecast for the day hinted at showers, and none came. We'd been on the previous afternoon to run through using the words written by Nicola to express our love and commitment to one another, and we both cried at the rehearsal but not at the actual wedding. We travelled in the same car with Sam, driven by Mark, and were met at the door by the registrar who we had not previously met but for whom it was not his first same sex wedding. Then we entered the hall with the Bach Brandenburg Number Four playing, Nicola with her dad who looked as if he might burst with happiness, and myself with Sharon, the first woman who ever made me think I could be attracted to someone of my own sex.

For us both the highlights were a poem especially written by Olivia Doyle (aka Viv), and a tape of Maddy Prior singing *Lovely On the Water*, which had most of us present and even the Registrar wiping our eyes by the sheer beauty of the Steeleye Span performance. It was a song Nicola and I adored: "As I walked out one morning, in the Springtime of the year". It might have been October, but it was a Spring Day for us.

And almost before we knew, it was over. We had paid for the ceremony to be videod rather than endure the palaver of a photographer, though just about everyone produced phones to record the event.

As we ate lunch, Sharon made an impromptu speech that was hilarious, mainly at my expense, but said that no matter how lucky Nicola was to be marrying me, I was no less lucky to be marrying her. Typically, she stole the day looking glamorous, recalling for me the day I first met her, when the headteacher of a posh girl's school stunned everyone on the choral singing course wearing the sexiest attire imaginable! I looked at our friends and knew why I loved these women.

Fiona had made the most amazing wedding cake. She and Tom seemed so happy to be celebrating their daughter's wedding, perhaps more than ever given that Mark had informed them he was seeking a divorce, though whether they yet knew about Amelia, we didn't know. Mark had been back to work this week, and we had been absent on the Sunday in case Sam was still infectious.

We had specifically asked our guests for their presence and no presents. The exception to this was a railway set for I bought for Sam, which so delighted him and which he would take back with him to Ashburton and which his grandpa couldn't wait to set up and play with!

Shortly after six o'clock we set off for our wedding night at the 5 Star Lympstone Manor, across the Estuary and within easy reach of the airport for our early flight on the following morning. Nicola has told me again and again since that the hotel was superb and our room so lovely, but I remember only one thing – my poet, my own Nicola.

The wonders of a wedding night can quickly dissipate in an airport, even the relatively small one in Exeter, but by mid-morning we were on our way to Pisa. We took off over the sea and our landing was much the same; the runway requiring the pilot to approach at low level over the water and beach. I thought back a day to our wedding and decided it would not be quite so lovely *in* the water!

I loved Italy from the first moment I stood on the concourse walking to the terminal building, but most of all the sound of the spoken words, even banal instructions, which must have been uttered thousands of times, but sounded as poetry to me. I slept on Nicola's shoulder on the bus drive to Florence and woke to find myself in heaven!

I am not so daft as to confuse the amazing centre of the city with what lies outside it: a modern city with all its problems, but what a centre! Our hotel was beside the Ponte Vecchio at which tourists ogle in wonder (and are ripped off by the jewellery shopkeepers), near to where the poets Robert and Elizabeth Barrett Browning lived, opposite the Pitti Palace.

Nicola had pre-booked the Uffizi, so we avoided the queues. I had never previously wept before a painting, but as I stood looking at Botticelli's "Birth of Venus" I knew I was gazing at beauty, pure and simple, and I could not control the tears running down my cheeks. I think I could have stood there for hours feeding upon the work which was considerably larger than any painting I have had ever previously seen, and then, adjacent to it, the same model in his "Primavera", and here she is, more than 500 years old and still adored.

I was less enamoured of Botticelli's religious works, (which of course he did to earn his keep) and so many other virgins, assumptions (I had thought assumptions were something quite different) and crucifixions in one place, which made me feel somewhat nauseous after a while, but there were other works to restore my balance. We had some lunch on the roof but before we left to return to the marital bed in the heat of the October sun, I had to return to Venus, though as I undressed my wife that afternoon, I was once again in the presence of beauty. She laughed when I compared her to Simonetta Vespucci, Botticelli's model, but it is so.

We were in Florence for just a few days and had to make the most of it. The Duomo was like Salisbury Cathedral – impressive outside but dull within, though the doors of the Baptistry opposite (though only copies) made me realise I had been in this world 34 years and had known nothing of this burst of art in its many attires. Was that a failure of my education or my imagination?

I was a little surprised when Nicola wished to take me to a convent. There were frescoes to be seen as we walked around the garden, but then she took me up a long stone staircase that turned right at the top, and then...! However, could I find the words to describe what faced me? It was a large fresco of the Annunciation by a monk, Fra Angelico, completed around 1442, and embodies what I can only call perfection. He had done this simply for his fellow monks as a fresco, painted into the surface of a wall cannot be moved and never sold and bought. There was another which moved me greatly, a fresco in the cell of one of the monks showing Mary Magdalene and the risen Christ in a garden replete with flowers, called "Noli Me Tangere" – do not touch me. It was as if they were dancing. Much though the great Annunciation was perfect, it was this that produced my tears again.

We visited several churches but, much to the amusement of my wife, the one I most loved was the Basilica Santissima Annunziata, which she wanted to show me primarily because as she said, "it's totally over the top". I loved the colour and could feel why someone here might be catholic. I saw people praying and some coming to confession in the funny boxes and had a sense that although Florence is really just one big art gallery and museum, at the heart of it all was a way of thinking and living characterised by an ancient faith I did not possess but could not stop myself admiring and almost wishing I could share.

Nicola loved the art as much as me, but for her Florence would always be primarily the city of her beloved Dante, of whom in my ignorance I knew nothing. She told me she had read *The Divine Comedy* only in English but hoped one day to manage sufficient Italian to read the original for herself.

'It was the first great work of literature in the Middle Ages not to be written in Latin, but in the language of the people of Florence, which became the Italian we know. I've heard it being read, and it sounds as wonderful to my ears as Botticelli to our eyes, though appeared a hundred years before he painted.'

'A Comedy? Is it funny?'

'No. Commedia meant something quite different. It is an enormous poem of almost 15,000 lines, an account of the poet's journey through Hell and Purgatory to the heights of Heaven and the Divine. It reflects the worldview of 1321, quite different to our own, but is ultimately concerned with the triumph of love, human and divine, which are surely timeless.'

'We didn't do it at my school.'

'Nor at mine, but I spent most of my two years at Hendon learning to be a police officer reading it. The contrast each day could not have been greater and whilst of course we look at the world differently now, I sometimes wonder if the world that could produce such work and the others we have seen here, is not preferable to our own, though love has not changed, as I know for certain. For Beatrice, I read Dee.'

I didn't know what she was referring to but knew it must be good.

On our last day we visited the Academia. Once again, the foresight and planning of Nicola meant we could avoid the long queues. At the centre is the huge *David* by Michelangelo though I had seen the exact copy in the Piazza del Signore, but what I was much more taken by were the unfinished sculptures which give the appearance of men seeking to free themselves from the stone. They are known as The Slaves. I found them profoundly moving, and I gazed at them for ages, captivated by their captivation. What

an irony that we should be so moved by unfinished works, and because we were in Florence, I recall having a passing thought that perhaps that is how God sees us and still loves us.

Plans to visit other galleries and churches were abandoned, primarily because, and I was surprised it was possible, I was supersaturated by beauty and could take no more.

After our last breakfast we went out to do a little tourist shopping and then made our way back to the railway station in the shadow of Santa Maria Novella in which Nicola showed me the first ever art work portraying perspective, a massive fresco of the Trinity.

'It was done by a man called Masaccio, which is short for "mad Thomas" in 1427.'

'Well, he may have been mad, but the man was a genius,' I replied, awestruck.

'Next time we come, I'll also show you something he did in the Brancacci Chapel, a tiny work in a hideous church, which is astonishing.'

'Do you mean we haven't seen everything in Florence?'

'We would need many more visits to do that. Now, from the sublime to the ridiculous. Our bus to Pisa will be outside the back of the church by the railway station. We should go. Imagine missing it and having to remain here longer!'

'That would be so tragic,' I said, taking hold of her and kissing her in front of the Trinity that seemed unmoved by our love. A passing guide was not quite so enamoured by our embrace and told us to leave! Perhaps I wouldn't become a catholic after all!

Once we had landed, I couldn't wait to collect Sam. I had zoomed him each evening before his bedtime but was excited at the thought of holding him again. It was clear he was no less pleased to see Nicola and me, but we sensed at once in Fiona that something was wrong.

'Come on, mum,' said Nicola, 'what are you not telling us?'

'The hospital rang Mark to tell him Helen had attempted suicide.'

19

Our arrival home was subdued. The house felt empty, though Sam quickly filled it with his happiness, and it was difficult for us not to come to share that with him. Nicola searched the freezer and rustled up something for our supper. Since breakfast we had only had an excuse for a sandwich on the aeroplane, and we were both hungry.

Whilst I was attending to Sam, Nicola called Mark. He knew little more than Fiona had told us and had been informed as her next of kin. There was no explanation why she had done it. A little later, as we emptied one of the bottles of wine we had brought back, we received a call from Abi, who didn't know whether we knew about Helen.

'She slit her wrist on a sharp piece of metal she has noticed on a staircase,' she told me, 'having been told you and Nicola had married.'

'But why on earth was she told that?' I asked. 'The doctors must have been as mad as their patients to do such a thing.'

'They didn't. They held an immediate inquiry. It turns out that a ward orderly had overheard two of the staff mentioning the wedding, and whilst she was cleaning Helen's room, when Helen was going on and on about how she and you would soon be together, lost her patience and to shut her up, told her about your wedding.'

'Oh shit!'

'The orderly has been suspended and will almost certainly be fired, but Helen could have died had not another staff member looked into her room and seen fresh blood dripping under the chair in which Helen was sitting.'

'Mark doesn't know these details.'

'No, but he has been told her suicide predated his solicitor registering a divorce petition on Helen.'

'I thought you were not involved anymore.'

'The suicide attempt made that inevitable, I'm afraid.'

I put the phone down.

'It seems we may be stuck in Dante's Hell,' I said.

'We are not, my beloved, but Helen is, and we must hope she can be safely guided upwards. I sometimes wish I believed that praying for someone could do something, because just now I can't think of anything else, and that at least is something, if only to make me feel better.'

'I used to pray when I was a little girl. We were told we had to do so at school, though I noticed that nothing we prayed for ever happened. When I asked the vicar who came to do assembly once a week why this was, he said that our prayers didn't come from a pure heart, that we were being selfish in what we prayed for and that all prayers had to be in what he called "God's will". Even at ten, I knew that was a huge cop-out and I remember thinking that, therefore, almost everything else he told us might be rubbish. A right little devil I was.'

'You were courageous, as you always are. I've re-written Pope's words, which now read: "Courage rushes in where angels fear to tread!".'

I laughed and gave her a cuddle.

I spent much of the following morning attending to the dirty washing that inevitably follows even a brief holiday. With Sam at nursery and Nicola writing, I made myself a coffee as the washing machine continued its labours and sat down to think through my new life. An hour later, when I mentioned to Nicola my thoughts about my new life, she told me *La Vita Nuova*, Italian for "new life", was a work written by Dante before *The Divine Comedy*. She thought this highly propitious.

That afternoon I received a call from Hippolyta, my sister.

'Poppy!'

'Hi there. How was the honeymoon?'

'Wouldn't you like to know?'

'Well, to be honest, I would, as my imagination only stretches so far, but that's not why I've called. I've told my boys that their aunt Dorothea has important business, almost certainly to with our mother and finance, that she has to speak about, face to face, so I'm going to Devon to see her.'

'That sounds like a great idea. But less so if you're coming by yourself.'

'Ah well, it's funny you should mention that. I'm certainly getting the train from Preston by myself, though sadly my ticket will only take me as far as Wigan Westgate, and I'm very much hoping I might get a lift from there to Dartington.'

'Parking is available. So, when?'

'Simon's taking next week off, so can your b&b receive guests from Sunday evening?'

'That would be smashing, and I'll be able to shed my posh way of talking for a few days.'

'You've always talked posh, idiot. Mum sent you to elocution in Darwen every Saturday morning, if I remember aright. The teacher was called Joyce Stirrup.'

'She was too. She was lovely and taught me how to read poetry and entered me into competitions.'

'Mum was so proud of you. In fact, we all were, but you were the only one who stuck at it, and we envied seeing your name in the Darwen Advertiser.'

'It served me well when I got the job at Betty's, I can tell you.'

'And now?'

'I still read poetry aloud, but when I'm outside walking by myself. Nicola says it's by far the best way to enjoy poetry.'

'Is hers any good?'

'No.'

'But I thought she had books out.'

'I said it wasn't good because it's way better than good and I'm not just saying that because she's sitting beside me and it's her turn to make the tea.'

'Is she nice, Dee?'

'I refer the lady to my previous comment!'

'I'm looking forward to meeting her and Sam.'

'I'll warn them.'

'But seriously, Dee, thank you for this. It means a great deal, and you and me will have to do some talking. You're not just the posh member of the family, you've always been the most sensible.'

'Sometimes, though, we have to get beyond the sensible and do what's best for the sake of our soul.'

'You haven't got religion, have you?'

'What? A lesbian like me? No chance.'

Sharon telephoned to find out about our honeymoon.

'My darling Dee, how is married life?'

'Unexpectedly busy, running a family and a poet in residence.'

'And the situation with your sister-in-law?'

'Even if I brought you up to speed, as they say, there would be little to report. Following her suicide attempt, she has apparently reverted to silence again.'

'A suicide attempt? I didn't know about that.'

I recounted the circumstances.

'I'm sorry for anyone in her situation, but I worry for you. Nothing in this is your fault, but I can't imagine, knowing you, that it's not becoming something of a burden.'

'I suspect that my being called *Lady* played a part in the obsession, and I'm so glad now to be simply Mrs Fairchild.'

'I imagine there's been probate and death duties to sort.'

'It's all finished now, but Sharon, there's a huge mystery in André's will, of which I knew nothing in advance. He has left £100,000 to a man in Ballymena, Northern Ireland I've never heard of and know nothing about.'

'Do you know his name?'

'Michael Donahue.'

'And going through André's things, have you not found anything mentioning him?'

'There weren't many things left after Kim's crew arrived and took away his computer and most of his papers, none of which have yet been returned.'

'There was no mention of regular sums going out of his account.'

'I didn't need or want access to his accounts, so I've no idea.'

'Would you like me to mention it to Kim? She's leaving the service next week, but she might just run it through the computers to see if anything crops up.'

'Oh God, that could open a can of worms I don't want even to think about. André's will has left me a moderately wealthy woman and provided generously for Sam. Part of me thinks he did what he did for a reason that should perhaps be allowed to die with him.'

'And the other part of you?'

'Let's just say I'm curious.'

I had taken a step toward discovering something, anything, about Michael Donahue. I knew full well that even just, almost casually, mentioning his name, would be enough for the journalist in her to sniff out a mystery to be solved. I knew it might be risky. Something had been concealed from me, buried, and I only hoped it wasn't an unexploded bomb.

20

Of my four siblings, Polly was always my favourite, mainly because we were closest in age at just a year apart, and both went to Hoddlesden Church of England Primary School and Darwen Vale where there was no encouragement to make something of our lives. Poppy and I both left at sixteen. She learned secretarial skills in a FE College, and I went to the local Catering School. Of the other three, Oberon (Ron as we know him) studies drama (with such a name, what else?) and is assistant director of a travelling theatre company in Scotland. Hermione has kept her name and works for the ambulance service as a paramedic in Bolton, whilst Fyodor (whom we and everyone else call Fred) is a factory manager in Accrington. And I became a Lady and live in Devon but looking forward to welcoming Polly for her naughty days and nights away with Dr Simon Grantly.

Nicola smiled at me.

'Is he really called Dr Grantly?'

'Yes, why are you smiling?'

'It's the name of one of the leading characters in Trollope's six Barchester novels. I shall try not to confuse him with the Archdeacon.'

'You behave in the presence of my family,' I said as firmly as I could without grinning.

'I'm excited by the prospect of meeting them, and mum's invited us all to supper on Tuesday, hoping Polly's not like your mum who almost talked her into the ground when she was here after the funeral.'

'She's not. Polly's smashing, though it's been quite a while since I saw her last. Perhaps she's put on loads of weight and Simon is really her personal trainer.'

We heard a car stop outside.

'I think we're about to find out.'

I opened the door and fell into the arms of my sister, who was as slim and lovely as ever with her long russet hair.

'Oh, Dee, what a fabulous place to live and you're looking so great.'

Behind her was a tall and probably handsome man hidden behind a light brown beard.

'And you must be the chauffeur,' I said, advancing towards his outstretched hand, which I took in mine.

'Come in. Nicola has gone to put the kettle on and to bring Sam to meet his aunty Polly and uncle Simon.

Sam was suddenly shy, but Nicola was not and soon even Sam warmed up with cake and a drink.

'I hope you don't mind, but it's Yorkshire Tea.'

It's my second favourite tipple,' came the gentle Scottish voice.

'You're a Scot,' I said. 'That wonderful. You never said,' I addressed my sister accusingly.

'Don't fret, lass, he's house trained except when England play Scotland at rugby, and he bursts into a rendering of Flower of Scotland.'

'Does that come after your favourite tipple, which I presume is native to the land of your birth?' said Nicola.

'Might be,' said Simon with a grin.

We settled them in, and Sam was delighted to discover a new aunt and uncle, though was clearly a little bemused by the accents. Simon won his heart by wanting to play with the train set as Polly came into the kitchen with me.

'Does mother know you've come?' I asked.

'Oh dear, what a shame. I forgot to mention it.'

'She'll be furious when she finds out.'

'You know neither of us care.'

'Hey, I like your Simon. How did it happen?'

'I have a mole on my back and was allocated to him. I was in there for almost half an hour – I felt a bit guilty about t'poor sods waiting – but something clicked between us, and neither of us could stop it. The mole was fine, but I get him to check every Thursday just in case!'

'How long?'

'Just normal but I'm not complaining!'

'I didn't mean that, though don't tell him it's just normal. I mean, when did this begin?'

'In August, so three months ago now.'

'I know about something just clicking into place. That's how it happened for Nicola and me.'

'She's a lovely-looking lass.'

'I hope you'll get to know her. Have you finished those carrots yet?'

As we cooked together, Polly told me about the collapse of family life at home. It had started with the realisation that she had stopped even caring for Jim a long time before she met Simon. They were living in the same house but far apart, and even the boys had noticed. Jim seemed to look on her as the person who did everything – cleaning, washing, cooking, and all that went with these, as he might have done when he was a lad and his mum spoiled him rotten. Bed had also become at first difficult, and then for Polly impossible.

'He was never very good at it. It was the equivalent of an instant meal: pop it into the microwave for 3 minutes. But more than anything he just settled into the role of miserable and boring Lancashire man who showed absolutely no interest in me, or even the lads. All he wanted to do was to sit in front of the telly when he got home, and I think he cared more about the characters he watched than he did for us. He even used to talk about them to me.'

'So why are you still there?'

'Two reasons. The first is obviously for the lads. They're 12 and 11 and I want what will be best for them.'

'Of course, but that doesn't include Jim, surely.'

'The other reason will best explained by Simon, so I'll get him to tell you. But we're here with you because we want to make a choice and need time together to make it together, and because

I've told him how my little sister is so very wise.'

'Little sister? I'm only a year younger than you. Believe me, Nicola's the wise one, but whatever the problems you might have and divorce is always messy, Polly you should be able to be happy and fulfilled, and growing in an unhappy home will affect the lads considerably.'

Returning to the sitting room, Simon and Nicola were talking books and clearly getting on well. Sam kept interrupting them, bringing various of his "friends" to introduce them to him, but he seemed a natural with children. Whilst Sam was with us, we kept the conversation light, but after his aunty Polly had given him a bath and uncle Simon read him a story, we sat down to our meal, and had a chance to talk. I plunged straight in.

'I love my sister, Simon. We don't see one another as often as we'd both like to, but she is clearly living an unhappy life from which she needs to be freed. From the way you are with her and look at one another, I can recognise the signs of love, but she tells me of a problem of which she thinks you would be the one to explain.'

'Polly said you were direct,' he replied with a large smile, reaching for a sip of wine before he went on.

'The problem's not strictly mine, but Polly's. Having a relationship with a patient can be a serious matter and reportable to the BMA. Frankly, if Polly and I can establish a life together, and the boys with us, if that is what they want, I will risk the scrutiny of the BMA. I am not married, but I suspect they will say I would have to move from my current practice. Falling in love is not yet a capital offence, but finding ourselves in the local rag comes close. Polly doesn't want me to risk being struck off, which won't happen. I've already contacted my rep at the Medical Defence Union, and she's told me I've nothing to fear even if, and it's a big if, it even reached the BMA. Jim, if Polly leaves and wants a divorce, may well find out why and make a formal complaint, or be advised to do so by his solicitor.

'So (and I hate sentences that begin with so, but here it is appropriate) I think I should seek another practice well away from where I am. There's no shortage of jobs available and I've seen one in Somerset that would allow me to become a full partner, from which, most importantly, I could go to watch the Bears in Bristol or the Chiefs in Exeter.'

'You'll see that rugby comes before me on his list of priorities,' said Polly with a smile.

Simon turned and looked at her.

'There's nothing in this world I wouldn't sacrifice to spend the rest of my life with you.'

'Ok,' I said. 'That's everything solved. The rest is mere detail. Whereabouts in Somerset?'

'Crewkerne, and we're due to meet the present team on Tuesday afternoon. They know about Polly and ...'

'Oh, there's things about Polly I know even you might not, but if you take the job, then I'll spare her blushes,' I said interrupting Simon's flow, causing us all to laugh.

'You wouldn't dare,' she said.

I smiled enigmatically and shrugged.

'Perhaps, Dee,' said Simon, 'you and I should have a little chat. Anyway, if we like it, we'll look for somewhere to live and move without a word in the practice to anyone about Polly. I think they'd be expecting me to move to somewhere more secure, so they won't be surprised.'

'Once Simon's gone, I will set the divorce in motion and hope for a quick get out. To be honest, provided he pays properly for the boys, I'll let him have whatever he wants. It'll mean a period of separation for Simon and me, but it might stop tongues wagging and prevent any fuss for Simon with the BMA.'

'Can I say something,' said Nicola. 'I am, after all, your sister-in-law, Polly. I think you are being a word my wonderful wife often uses, usually and rightly of me: daft. Simon, you of all people as a doctor should know that life is precious and may be cut short unexpectedly. So, the pair of you need to stop faffing about. Dee and I knew at once, and so we acted straight away. We knew what people might say about doing so just days after André's death (though they were wrong about that, it was about ten minutes after he died) but the only thing that mattered was the love we immediately knew. What other point to living can there be?'

I could see tears in Polly's eyes, and Simon took hold of her hand.

'And,' I said, 'Crewkerne's much nearer the Exeter Chiefs than Bristol, and the rugby's better, but more especially you'd be near us, and that would be wonderful for me, being selfish. And now that's decided, pass me your plates and Nicola can bring the pudding she's made!'

Simon and Polly were planning a visit to the sea at Salcombe, but before they left and after I'd taken Sam to nursery, I sat down with them over coffee.

'Please don't be offended by what I'm going to say, and it's not as condescending as it might sound. I'm now what the solicitor describes as moderately wealthy and finding, with help, the best ways of investing for maximum return, both for Sam's legacy and my own.'

'What does moderately wealthy mean, Dee?' asked Polly.'

'Two million or thereabouts, and half a million invested for Sam until he's eighteen.'

'Jesus!' said my sister.

'Nicola and I spoke about this in bed last night. Most of our money is in my name, but as far as I'm concerned, it's hers as well. We both agreed that we want to make sure there are no financial obstacles to your being able to be together as soon as possible. I can hold back £500,000 for you if it would save the interest on a prohibitive banking bridging loan.'

'I don't know what to say,' said Simon. 'What you are suggesting is a generosity way beyond anything I've ever come across before, but there's no way either that we need it or would want to tie ourselves as a family into knots over money. I've been well paid with little in the way of outgoings since I qualified, and I also have some family money from when my parents died, and I've already given a lot of thought to this, but your kindness, Dee, is amazing.'

Polly was sitting next to me on the sofa and took my hand.

'What a sister,' she muttered, 'what a woman. I only hope

Nicola knows what she has.'
   'Trust me,' I said, 'I'm the lucky one.'

21

Polly and Simon returned from Crewkerne on the Tuesday in time for supper in Ashburton and for Sam's bath and story in his room at his granny's where he was staying overnight.

They announced to us all, included Tom and Fiona, that Simon had accepted the invitation to join the practice in Crewkerne from January1st, which was great, he explained, because it meant he was beginning with a bank holiday which made us all laugh. And to my delight, Polly said she would come with him from the start, and though they still needed to find somewhere to live, as far as she was concerned, her own new life was beginning now. Clearly Dante was catching!

On the following morning Nicola offered to take Simon to experience the delights of the Dartington Estate and the Cider Press Café, allowing time for Polly and me to talk over family business of various kinds, focussing mainly on what was to be done about mother when she moved south.

'I'm the only one who sees her regularly, and I can't see Ron in Scotland or Jim or Hermione, wanting to take up that mantle. They can't stand her any more than we can, but she is our mother, when all's said and done,' said Polly.

'I've sometimes thought I should have a DNA test just to make sure. I feel that I have no part in her, but are you suggesting you should bring her down to pollute the south?'

'Oh God, no, but I have worries about her. She can manage by herself now, but that won't necessarily last. What then?'

'If need be, she'd have to go into care, but let's cross that bridge when it arises. Like you, I couldn't stand her anywhere nearer than Lancashire. She put the most ridiculous announcement in *The Times* about our wedding.'

'Oh, she was so proud of that and took it to just about every house in Hoggy and has probably had it framed and hung in the Con Club. But you're right, let's wait and see, but there's something else I want to ask you about, not because I need to know, but because I'm just plain curious.'

'Go on,' I said, thinking I knew what was coming, knowing my sister of old.

'Well, you know when a man and woman have sex, you know what's involved, though most of it never was with Jim, and I think Simon must have gained his knowledge and abilities in medical school. But how do two women manage?'

I laughed.

'Oh, we manage alright and remember, I have something to compare it with having been married to André. He was keen but had little idea. Foreplay was mostly twoplay! Neither Nicola nor I had ever had a sexual relationship with a woman before and it was a bit of a voyage of discovery and I'm not intending to make you blush, but let's just say that women know more about their bodies than men do, except in your case because you've got a doctor.'

Polly giggled.

'I just wondered, you know, as you do.'

They were returning north on the Friday, but on the day before paid another visit to Crewkerne and found a house that would suit them and, hopefully, Polly's lads. That evening, Simon used his laptop to put in an offer.

At breakfast on the Friday, Sam said he didn't want Aunty Polly and Uncle Simon to go.

'Mummy doesn't either, darling, but soon we'll be seeing them lots more.'

'We'll miss you, Sam,' said Polly. 'In fact, we'll miss mummy and Nicola too.'

The car was already loaded, and they set off shortly after I had taken Sam to nursery, and Nicola returned to her writing, which she had not minded being interrupted during their visit. We had all enjoyed having them to stay.

It was on the following morning that I had a call from our other sister, Hermione.

'Something terrible's happened, Dee. Polly was in a car with one of the local GPs and they were involved in a major car smash on the M6 in Cheshire. I understand they were both declared dead at the scene.'

'Please tell me this is a joke. I can't believe it.'

'I wish it were, but we're all puzzled by what they were doing together and where they had been. Jim says she caught the train to come to you on Sunday.'

'I'm utterly shocked. I can't speak now, I really can't. I'll have to call you back.'

I dropped the phone onto the floor.

'Nicola!' I called out.

She came out of her workroom immediately.

'What is it, Dee? What's the matter?'

I told her.

'No, surely not, no. It can't be.'

'I think we should take Sam over to Ashburton if they can have him, and we'll pick him up at lunch tomorrow.'

She picked up my phone from the floor and used it to call Fiona, briefly explaining.

'Let's go now.'

I grabbed some things for Sam, and we set off, not daring to speak, nor did so on the return journey. Once home, we made some tea and sat together on the sofa and we both finally allowed ourselves to sob.

'It is just so unfair,' I said through my tears. 'They had just discovered the hope for a new life together and here it was, dashed away from them.'

'The only consolation I can feel is that they died when they were feeling good and happy together and now at least they're spared all the mess they had to face. A poet called Mordaunt in the 18th century wrote: "One crowded hour of glorious life / Is worth an age without a name"'.'

'I'm going to have to call Hermione and explain what was going on. Will it all have to come out at an inquest?'

'I can't see why it should. It played no part in the accident's cause, but locally I imagine there are bound to be questions. "GP and patient killed in car crash on way back from secret holiday" – you can imagine the headlines in the local rag, and it wouldn't surprise me if they get in touch with you. The people we most need to be concerned for are Peter and Colin. Nothing could be gained by them knowing that their mother died because she was having an affair, as they would be told it was, with her doctor. So, whilst you might tell Hermione the truth, I think we should think up a scenario which allows Polly to have met Simon for a shared journey back after they were both in the area.'

'How are we going to do that? Wouldn't it be dishonest, and what if this came out in court?'

'It wouldn't. Polly came to stay here and, having mentioned it in passing to her doctor, learned he was coming to see a practice in the Southwest somewhere, so he offered to collect her to travel back north together. In that way, no reporters will poke their noses into Crewkerne, and I'd better contact the practice and let them know, and the estate agents.'

I called my sister.

'There's two stories to tell, Hermione.'

'Two?'

I told her first the official version created by Nicola, and then I told her the truth. There was silence at the other end.

'That means at least she died happier than she has been for years, but it's also tragic.'

'I know.'

'But you should be proud of your part in her newfound happiness, Dee, but your Nicola is quite right that we have to do what's most right for her boys. Look, I've got to get to work and then I'll have to go to Hoddlesden and see mother, I suppose.'

'Good luck with that. We both know that she'll make a huge drama out of this. Let me know when you learn details of the funeral. I want to be there.'

'Will you be bringing Nicola? I hope so.'

We both wanted to go down to the seat on the river where André had died, and we sat and held hands and wept a little but still enjoyed the sight of the Dart which exercised its customary soothing balm.

As I look back on Polly's death, now over six months ago, I realise I was much more affected by it than ever I had been over the loss of André. I have without a doubt learned a great deal about the ambivalence I lived with in my marriage which, when he died, protected me from the sort of painful grieving the death of my sister gave birth to. Nicola says maybe some of the depth of pain I have felt over Polly's death has allowed more of my painful feelings about André's death to emerge. I think it says a great deal about her that she can say such things with no worry that my love for her, and hers for me, could be diminished by being able to express such thoughts and feelings.

Nicola called her friend Viv to ask whether, when we had a date, we might use our trip north for the funerals (and I was determined to attend Simon's too, though in the end we couldn't go, as it took place in Aberdeen) to come and stay with them in the Dales, which she was delighted to welcome. She had put together a new collection and wanted Nicola's opinion before she risked sending it off to her publisher.

'It's not an easy time to get published,' Nicola explained, 'even if you are Olivia Doyle. Poetry does not sell. The Poets Laureate have an advantage in that their names are better known, but great work is being passed by, simply for financial reasons, though that's not new. The great composers often struggled and were as dependent on patronage as I am on you.'

'But did the patrons love and adore their court composers as I do you? I hope you know that if you asked, I would happily give you my millions, because I have happiness beyond all the gold in the world with you.'

'My darling, you say all the right things, and even when we're trying to cope with such a terrible loss to the world of two people who have could have shared the fruits of their love with others, my love for you grows even stronger.'

I burst into tears again.

Nicola made phone calls to Crewkerne and delivered the news to the senior partner, who was profoundly shocked. The estate agent was much more matter of fact about losing a sale and required no explanation.

Over the next few days, we received bits and pieces of information but as the only ones (together with Hermione in Bolton) who knew the complete story, we were left grieving, and frequently giving expression to anger about what had happened. We learned, however, that the inquest had been opened and adjourned, allowing the funerals to take place. Nicola found a report online from a newspaper in Chester reporting the incident in which four people lost their lives. The report mentioned thick fog and the involvement of lorries but was careful not to say more until the full inquest. It gave the names of those who had died and seeing it there on a computer screen brought home the terrible finality that death is – the end of possibility, the end of love other than as a feeling the living might have within themselves but without the physical reality of a presence. Just names on a screen like those on war memorials.

'Do you believe in life after death?' I asked Nicola as we ate breakfast one morning in the week after Polly's and Simon's death.

'If what I think you mean by that, and which millions unquestionably claim to do so, a kind of continuation of this life but in a different realm, then the answer is an unequivocal no. Of course not, though I can understand the dynamic that leads people to hope for that.

'Believing anything is no more than that – more wishing and hoping than knowledge. People believe all sorts of nonsense mostly because it's what they want to believe. But my love for you will live for ever because it emanates outwards, in my poetry which affects people, and in the way we are with others. It is released into the world. It is quite likely that, and hopefully many years hence, one of us will predecease the other, but our love can never die whilst the other remains.'

'And what about God? Do you believe in God?'

'How ever could anyone believe in the sort of gods any of the religions have produced unless dire necessity drove them to it, psychological need, I mean? More than that I can only say I don't know anything much other than to echo Hamlet: "There are more things in heaven and Earth ... Than are dreamt of in your philosophy". Perhaps he wrote those words in the light of the death of his young son Hamlet, and they might comfort us after Polly's and Simon's death, but I will choose to live with the love I know, not the fanciful love of a supposed God of love that Christians in particular sentimentalise but contradicts the evidence of suffering and pain. For me it is enough to know that Polly and Simon died in love together, though that won't be mentioned at the funeral which no doubt will be one big sentimental lie.'

'Do tell me, my darling,' I said, taking her hand, 'what you added to your cereal this morning, and whatever it was, can I have   some,   please?'

22

As now sadly seems to be the norm, the funeral would not be taking place for another two weeks, and inevitably the undertakers gained from the delay by charging for storage of the deceased. I booked the three of us into a family room at a hotel for one night. The funeral was to take place at Blackburn Crematorium in the afternoon, which would allow me to take Nicola and Sam with me to show the delights of my home village, and the even lesser delight of my mother, on the morning of the funeral. After the funeral, we would continue up the M6 to Viv in the Cumbrian Dales.

I telephoned Sharon and told her about the deaths of my sister. She was typically kind and understanding on the phone. I told her I felt guilty, as had I not invited them to come, and this had led to their deaths. As gently as possible, but firmly, she said that in this world, things happen all the time and that we are all part of the crisscrossing of the good and the tragic in ways we can never foresee. I should focus, she said, as had Nicola, on the good I had enabled them to know.

'Dee, quality of love is not the same as quantity. They were returning full of hope and no doubt full of joy, even if they also knew there were complexities before them. If something terrible were to happen to you today, you have lived love with Nicola and André. Length of days, when you continue to know and experience that love is, of course, to be desired, but as Tennyson wrote: "Tis better to have loved and lost than never to have loved at all." You won't, and I hope you don't – what Kim calls a recommendation – say anything of this at the funeral, but you,

Nicola and your other sister know. You can both rejoice at that inside yourselves, even in Blackburn Crematorium!'

In the next few days, I also received several calls from my mother, mostly wanting to know why I had needed Polly to come. I tried fending her off, but her persistence eventually wore me down.

'Polly was extremely unhappy and wanting to leave Jim, and I offered her the chance to get away to talk it through.'

'Oh, but Jim says they were a happy couple.'

'Mother, I've told you why Polly came. There's no more to say.'

'But what about the doctor she was with? That's very odd.'

'She said when she got here that she was hoping to get a lift back because her GP was somewhere down here looking at a new job and had offered to meet her and drive her back.'

'Were they having an affair?'

'What a horrible mind you must have, and a terrible thing to say about your daughter who's just been killed. I've told you how it was they were travelling together. I thought he was being kind and you might just consider why if such an eligible bachelor at his age was not married. Gay men don't have affairs with women.' (Sorry, ghost of Simon, though I didn't actually say you were gay!)

'Oh!'

'We'll come and see you on the morning of the funeral. Sam will want to see his Lancashire grandma, and I want to show Hoddlesden off to Nicola.'

'Won't you be staying?'

'No. We'll be leaving after the funeral to stay with one of Nicola's friends.'

'Abandoning me.'

'You have the three others.'

'They come no more often than you do. Hippolyta was the only one who bothered with me and now she's dead. Jim and the boys will get all the fuss, but I'm her mother. I gave birth to her.'

'Yes, and that's truly terrible to live with. Whenever anyone loses a child, at whatever stage in life, it's always a tragedy. You lost dad when he wasn't so very old and you survived because you are a survivor, and I think you know that. Bad things are happening all the time, but I think you can be proud of your daughter because when we were together in the last few days she was determined in a way I have never seen before, and which I think she got from you, to live her own life with the boys, even though she knew she would have to go through a messy divorce. I think you should be proud of her. I really do, and proud of who you are, even if you might need to tone that down with the rest of your children and show gentleness rather than your normal aggresion which prevents the others wanting to be with you because they're intimidated by it.'

I turned to Nicola, who was sitting next to me, and putting my hand over the phone, whispered, 'Am I laying it on too thick?'

She shook her head, smiled, and took my hand.

'Anyroad,' I said, lapsing into Lancashire speak, 'we'll be with you first thing on the morning of the funeral.'

'I'll make sandwiches for dinner.'

'Thanks, mum. Now, you take good care of yourself.'

'Thanks, love, I will.'

I can't remember when she would have last used any word of affection to me, and I hoped Polly's death might bring about a change for the better in my mum. Well, I can always hope!

I put my arm around Nicola's shoulder and drew her to me.

'You are the very best of friends, the best of people, and the very best poet I know.'

'Thank you, my love, for most of that, but of course you don't know many poets and I can tell you without selling myself short, that I envy the poetry of Olivia Doyle because I know it's better than mine, and it's the same with Emily's.'

'Alright, will it be enough then, to say you're the best poet I ever make love with?'

'I don't think that can be disputed, though it will be an unusual addition to the blurb on the back cover of my next book!"

As I had found when André died, life goes on regardless. The clocks cannot be stopped as Auden desired. Even on the wrist of the dead, the second hand continues to make its way relentlessly. I reflected on this as I was loading the washing machine on the following morning. Polly had been killed – a massive tragedy – and here I was doing the washing as normal.

Sharon telephoned a couple of days later.

'I want you to know as much as I know about Michael Donahue to whom André left £100,000 in his will. Are you sitting comfortably? Then I'll begin.

'Michael Donahue was born in Dundalk in County Louth, in the Irish Republic, on September 29th, 1992, and baptised just four days later, and given the name of the saint on whose day he was born.'

'He is a catholic then,' said Nicola.

'Yes, and Dundalk is near the border with the North and in the Troubles, was labelled "El Paso", a place where hard men of the republican movement were supposed to hang out waiting for their next foray and killing spree across the border.

'His mother is called Brighid, as many Irish women are, and lives in Ballymena in the North with her son. Michael was educated locally, and then entered St. Patrick's Seminary, Maynooth, Co. Kildare, to train for the priesthood. He is currently a curate at St Patrick's Church in the parish of Kirkinriola. His mother serves as his housekeeper, I imagine. He is, however, not an only child, because he has a brother, though I suspect he doesn't know that any more than does the brother, your son, Sam.'

'What?' I burst out. 'You mean André was his father, and I never knew?'

'I mean exactly that.'

'But why was I never told this?' my voice rising, reflecting my shock.

'Oh, Dee, as I know from Kim, who has always been tight-lipped about anything to do with Northern Ireland, anyone involved in the Troubles never speaks about it. And that included André.'

'But I was his wife.'

'And I have been married to Kim for years and know next to

nothing about her work.'

'But do you know any more? In 1993 Dundalk cannot possibly have been a safe place for André to be there, so how on earth did it happen that he could have had a relationship with a catholic woman there?'

'Honestly, Dee, Kim could not tell me more though whether she knew no more or because that information can't ever be released, I don't know and she wouldn't say.'

'Oh my God,' I said, putting hands to my mouth. 'This is completely bizarre. My former husband had a son, who is almost the same age as me and a catholic priest, and I knew nothing about it. In just a few days, I've lost a sister and gained a sort of stepson whom I suppose I would have to call "Father". What is going on in my world?'

23

It was hard to know whether to laugh or cry. As we went to bed, I could say little, as I was totally wrapped up in what I had heard from Sharon. And what I heard was a story of a double betrayal, possibly of his own country's armed forces, but more especially of me.

For what seemed like forever, I found sleep impossible, going over and over Sharon's words. At about 3:00, I got up and made myself a cup of Rooibos tea and sat on the sofa.

In a matter of days, Helen had first announced the intent of a sexual assault on me and was prepared to murder me with the knife she had brought if I didn't do as she wished; then my sister and I, who had drawn close in a way that we had not known for years had been sent off by me to her death; and, now, I had discovered that my late husband had lived a massive lie and had another family of which he had told me nothing, and of which I would never have known had he not died. As I sat there, getting cold, my mind could take nothing of it in other than to think that André had taken me up primarily as his comfort blanket as old age came upon him, and my chief value to him was in bed, in the kitchen and to decorate his life. He had shared none of his ongoing historical research with me, though it took him away from me for hours each day behind the closed door of his study. And for a moment, I wondered if this wasn't being repeated each day when Nicola closed the door on me to do her writing. Wasn't I just a dupe, a simpleton?

I didn't hear Nicola approach until she sat down next to me and placed her arm around my shoulder.

'Come back to bed,' she said. 'If you want to talk, it will be warmer and comfier, and you might even get some sleep.'

I turned to look at her beautiful face.

'Tell me you love me,' I said.

'You know I love you.'

'No, please, tell me.'

'I love you, Dee, from the depths of my being, and I promise I will withhold nothing from you – ever.'

It sounds a ridiculous thing to report, but I simply collapsed into her and allowed myself, body and soul, to be subsumed within her. I cannot say how long this lasted – it might have been a few seconds or even a year, because it was an experience of eternity, like when I had stood before Venus in Florence. Back in time, I gazed at her.

'Ok. Bed it is.'

When I eventually dragged myself from bed, I found Nicola had already taken Sam to nursery but had left breakfast ready for me with the addition of clotted cream to place over the marmalade over the butter over the toast! I'm sure every doctor in the world would have advised me against but on this morning, I needed comfort food.

On her return she joined me at the table and herself had an extra slice of toast with all the bad goodies!

'Darling,' I said, 'when you do your writing, is it possible, at least on the days that Sam is at school, that you leave the door of the study even a tiny bit ajar, as a sign to me I am not closed out of any part of your life? You understand why I ask, don't you? André closed the door to his study, sometimes for hours, and I knew nothing of what he did, or with whom he might be corresponding.'

'I hope I might keep my earphones on when I need the sound of music to keep me focussed on my writing. It cuts out the silly chatter of those parts of my brain that I don't need for my writing.'

'Of course, and when Sam is here, the door needs to be closed or he will be in there disturbing you. You know he loves to be in the study because he knows it is so special to you, and he adores you and everything you do.'

'And he is my own special boyfriend. But you must be exhausted.'

I was, and throughout the day would find myself unexpectedly waking up having drifted off and then having to endure that awful physical feeling that follows an unplanned daytime doze. I'm not sure of the precise mental state I was in when I received a phone call from Abi.

'Unexpectedly, yesterday I was invited to a further case conference about Helen. They are working towards a diagnosis of what is called Borderline Personality Disorder. Since the failed suicide attempt, she has at last talked to the doctors. They reported that you are no longer at the forefront of her thinking, which I'm sure you are pleased to know.'

'Yes, I am, but can you tell me more about the diagnosis?'

'It's obviously a serious psychiatric condition and may well have been triggered by serious hormonal changes in the last months of her pregnancy, releasing powerful and potentially dangerous symptoms which you know only too well. However, the tone of the meeting, to which I contributed nothing, was that they should look to set up a package of care for Helen at home, which will include the use of a drug called Queliapine and something I've never heard of, a psychotherapy known as Dialectical Behaviour Therapy, DBT with, of course, close and regular monitoring.'

'That seems a genuine breakthrough.'

'Ah, yes, well, I was coming to that. The breakthrough was your visit and since her suicide attempt, she's no longer preoccupied with you and has apparently said that the reason she became obsessed was because you were the first person she could relate to naturally, the first to see something in her that was good. So, and this is the tough part, Dee, I have been asked to see if you will meet with her again in the hospital before she is discharged, which they wish to happen before too long, to see if there is any possibility that she can now relate to you properly and then become a sort of haven for her.'

'To live with us?'

'No. The police would not sanction that, and, anyway, it's not what they want, nor what you would want either. They are hoping for a normal friendship with her and someone to whom she could turn for support when, say, needing a doctor's visit or as she goes through the divorce.'

'That's asking a huge amount, Abi.'

'Yes, I know and the staff at the hospital know it too. I and they will also fully understand if you simply want to refuse. Nothing had been said to Helen about this, by the way.'

'Where would she go to live if she comes out?'

'That would need to be thought through carefully given the divorce proceedings begun by Mark, as will the conditions for her involvement with the children, whom she hasn't seen since her hospitalisation, so this will not happen in a hurry.

'What the team is asking is whether you would see how it might go, though they would like to talk it through with you unless, of course, your response is an absolute refusal.'

'Oh Abi, you cannot know, but my sister has just been killed in a car crash, and I discovered only last night that my late husband has another family in Ireland, including a half-brother to Sam. This is not the best time for me to think about what you are asking, however much I want Helen able to live as full a life as possible once again.'

'Dee, I'm so sorry to have inflicted this on you. You must be doubly devastated.'

'I've known better times.'

'Look, I will report this back to the hospital, and they will have to think again about a plan for Helen's rehab. Try to forget my call and give yourself completely to these other things which matter so much and require your undivided attention.'

'Abi, it's the weekend. Please don't reply to the hospital until Monday. Instead, could you manage a cup of tea and a piece of one of Nicola's cakes tomorrow afternoon? It would be lovely to see you, and the two of you can discuss how you want to work together.'

'You mean she's willing to do so?'

'I suppose I must, if that's what I said.'

I had another call to make that evening, to Brendan O'Callaghan.

'Hello Mary, it's Dee here, is it possible to have a word with Brendan. It's important.'

'I'll fetch him.'

'Dee, hello.'

'I need to hear from you, Brendan, about something extremely important that I've learned from my friends who worked for the security service, something best not spoken over the telephone.'

'We have a friend over from Ireland with us just now who flies back tomorrow evening. Could you come here on Sunday afternoon. It's obviously important and in the light of what you said last time I want to help as best I can. Otherwise, how are things?'

'Just great. My sister was killed last week in a car crash and now it seems that the person who threatened to kill me with a knife she brought to the house, is going to be released from the unit where has been detained. So, yeah, just great!'

24

As I played with Sam on the floor of the sitting room, I wondered how much sleep I might get tonight after that latest phone call from Abi, and I eagerly awaited Nicola's return from Ashburton where she had gone to collect our supper, of which one of Fiona's students had produced an excess at the college, and which she had offered to Nicola. She called on the car phone as she left her mum's to let me know.

Once back, I poured out to her the contents of Abi's call.'

'OMG', she said. 'Troubles clearly do come in threes.'

'Abi said to put it from my mind, but that's a bit like being told your house is on fire, but to put it out of your mind because you're busy.'

'And you've invited her to tea tomorrow, so that means it's far from your mind, but how else could it be? The only good thing is that at least there may be a way forward for Helen. I've heard of BPD but have no idea what it involves, either for the person with it or those around them.'

'But who *is* there around her? I imagine she will have to go to live with her mum and dad, but what's going to happen about the children?'

'This is going to be very difficult for Mark with a divorce pending and wishing to marry Amelia.'

'Life, it would seem, is awash with complexity.'

'*Ours* though, Dee, for they are ours and not yours, which we shall face with love together.'

'Ah, the joy of being married to a poet!'

I managed to sleep that night and surfaced even later than usual on the Saturday morning, when Nicola finally woke me at nine o'clock with croissants and apricot conserve, our usual Saturday morning bed treat with Sam sitting between us as we ate.

Once up, showered and dressed, I was most surprised to receive a phone call from Polly's husband, Jim.

'Why did Polly come to see you?'

'I needed to talk over with her, before I spoke to our other siblings, my concern for our mother, and to share what thoughts she might have about the future.'

'Couldn't you have done that on the phone?'

'We agreed it would be lovely for us to spend a few days together, and I was pleased to welcome her here.'

'She came by train?'

'From Preston she told me.'

'But what did she say about the return trip? Had she bought a return ticket?'

'Jim, I've no idea what sort of ticket she bought. But when she got here, she said she might get a lift back as her GP had told her he was down here somewhere looking at a new job. She was pleased to take up the offer.'

'Didn't you think it was odd?'

'It never occurred to me. It was the sort of opportunity anyone might prefer to having to endure the train and the many changes that have to be made between here and Preston.'

'And whilst she was with you, did she have contact with him?'

'Yes, of course. She spoke on the phone to confirm the arrangement. But Jim, I don't understand what you're suggesting. Are you suggesting there was something going on between them? All I can tell you is that there was no evidence of anything like that whilst she was here, and as we are talking about my sister and the mother of my nephews, I find your suggestion offensive.'

'I still think it odd.'

'Jim, I can't control your suspicions, but if that's the story you want to tell Colin and Peter, then you should think again. They have lost their mother. Tarnishing her name will not help them cope. They need your total support, not silly thoughts without foundation. You've got to make Colin and Peter the centre of your concerns now and that's going to demand all your energies. Condemning Polly falsely will not help.'

I ended the call feeling as politicians must when they answer questions on television, but it was not a pleasant feeling. Telling him the truth would not serve Polly's concern for her boys, or at least that's what I consoled myself with for engaging in such a deceit.

I spent the rest of the morning baking for Abi's visit in the afternoon, whilst Nicola and Sam went into Totnes to do some shopping. On Saturdays we usually went up the road for a light lunch at the *Green Table*, and being November, it was quieter than it is sometimes in the summer months. Sam always had the same Peanut Butter and Jam sandwich which he loved, and we most definitely did not!

Abi arrived just after four o'clock. Nicola and I had not much time to talk over my conversation with her of the previous afternoon, and I was still a mass of pain and contradiction.

'Tell us, first,' I said, 'exactly what the staff are saying about Helen.'

'I can't add anything more to what I told you yesterday. Their diagnosis is Borderline Personality Disorder, or as it's sometimes called Emotionally Unstable Personality Disorder. Dr Pilling reported that her symptoms were entirely characteristic of this.'

What does borderline mean?' asked Nicola.

'As far as I know, it's the border between neurosis and psychosis, but I can't really explain what means.'

'Isn't it really just a case of wanting to get her out?'

'The medical staff never want to keep anyone hospitalised longer than necessary, unless they are prisoners.'

'But Helen attacked Mark and brought a knife here and threatened both Nicola and me. I understand no one should be in hospital longer than necessary, but what about those occurrences? Does it mean she's got off scot-free? Has it been considered that she is playing a part to avoid any charges being brought?'

'You're right to ask these things, and I'm exactly the wrong person to attempt an answer. From the police point of view, the charges have been withdrawn from the magistrates' court, but if she is really playing a clever game, I can't myself see how that would have included an almost successful suicide attempt.'

'Nor me,' added Nicola. 'I think that if you will speak with the doctors, these questions can be answered better by them than Abi, but even that, Dee, would be a giant step to take. If you then said you could not go any further, at least you would have better knowledge on which to base your decision. Either way, it has to be your decision, but you know that whoever choice you make, I will support you wholeheartedly.'

'This is not a good time to think this through, but I can't simply abandon our sister-in-law as she still is, without having listened to how it is. However, I have a condition. I'll only agree to meet the doctors if I can be accompanied by Nicola.'

'Dr Pilling had expected that and has already agreed.'

'So, has it already been assumed and decided?'

'On Monday she has patients to see in Plymouth and said she would be happy to come here and see you on her way home.'

'In which case, the answer has to be "yes but ...".'

'I'm sure she will understand that.'

'Let's go out for a meal,' said Nicola, after Abi had left.

'It's a bit late to get somewhere on a Saturday evening.'

'It's not what you know, you know! The owner of the Union Inn at Denbury has said he can always find me a table – in return for sorting something for him. It's basic pub food but I think we need to get out, provided Sam's happy to stay with his granny and grandpa tonight and come back after lunch tomorrow.'

'Oh yes, please,' came a little voice.

'Ok,' I said, 'but check with your mum and dad first.'

The evening was exactly what I needed and with Nicola driving, I availed myself of several cocktails and, later, enjoyed passion without the constraints of having to be quiet so as not to wake Sam!

At Sunday lunch, we could talk to Mark. Helen's mother had informed him that the hope was to discharge her home, about which he was in a total panic.

'The house is in both our names so I presume she has a legal right to return but the simple fact is I don't want her near my children, and surely the threats she made to you both, which might have been backed up with the knife she had with her, are more than enough to make a case against allowing her home. Apparently, she's got some of mental illness, which when I looked it up on the internet makes me even more even determined to stop this.'

'You need to speak to your solicitor as a matter of urgency, Mark,' said Nicola. 'This sort of matter is wholly beyond my experience and knowledge. But I'm certain that nothing can happen without you hearing directly from the hospital and not just through Helen's mother.'

'Why can't things just be straightforward? All these complications and all caused by me or because I'm me if you take my meaning.'

I was driving us to Bovey Tracey.

'Surely all lives are complex simply because we live with others. We're not hermits living in isolation, but people inevitably caught up in webs we need for living. Lovers might have a fantasy of wanting to be alone on a desert island, but it's only a fantasy.'

I pulled into the drive of the O'Callaghans.

'Now for further complications,' I said.

Mary opened the door, as Brendan advanced towards us to hug and kiss, and lead us into their sitting room.

'Dee, we're so sorry to hear about your sister's death.'

'Thank you, but that's not what I want to talk about. When we spoke the other day, you broke the Official Secrets Act about my part on the arrest of a Moslem terrorist in Yorkshire, which you had learned from André. What I now know has come from an MI5 source, but I suspect you may already know it, and that you know considerably more than I know, and the time has come for you to reveal the extent of your knowledge.'

'You need to tell me just what it is you think I might know, and what you say you now know, otherwise I'm at a loss.'

I told him what Sharon had told me, and how it linked with the considerable legacy left to Michael Donahue in André's will.

I went on, 'If André could tell you something contrary to the Act about me, I find it hard to believe that being Irish and having a small involvement with republican groups, he didn't tell you about this.'

'Please understand, Dee, that my involvement with any republican groups was more by accident than design and I know nothing more than you of their activities either now or back then in Dundalk. Had it been otherwise, do you really think the security service would let me function here in England?'

'No, but what were you told by André about his son?'

'Again, I know nothing about that time and his part in it. That, I imagine, is information that will never be released, and he did not tell me, and to be honest, I didn't want to know, because that knowledge would be dangerous. And I imagine he would never have spoken of it to you either, for the same reasons of national security and your own safety.

'However, in the days after your life had just been saved André told me he had a son, a priest in Ireland, born during the Troubles, and he swore me to secrecy.'

'I knew nothing about this, Dee,' said Mary, 'and I'm as flabbergasted as you, just as I was at what you told us the other day.'

'What did he say about Brighid, Michael's mother?' asked Nicola.

'I didn't know her name or anything about her. But as I have thought about this, he said something when we all thought an assault was being made on his life. It was also in your post-operative period. He said. "I knew I was perfectly safe, Brendan, I'm off limits".'

'What did he mean by that?' I asked.

'I have no idea, but if MI5 does, you can bet your bottom

dollar you will never find out.'

25

As I had noticed before, even when we feel things are falling apart, the washing and shopping still have to be done, and the house doesn't clean itself, though Nicola is a dab hand with the vacuum. Only after lunch when Sam still needed a sleep did we have the chance to talk about the forthcoming visit of Dr Pilling, having for now let Brendan's words of the previous afternoon sink into the unconscious part of our minds, until we could think of how we could explore them further, if it all.

Sam woke up as Dr Pilling arrived, which delayed our ability to talk, but a DVD eventually allowed us a measure of peace.

'I am delighted to meet you, Nicola. Abi Molloy has spoken highly of your work as a police officer and says she hopes to work with you alongside her in a new capacity. But I know you better as Chloe Thomas, whose collections I continue to enjoy, and can I look forward in the next to a work celebrating love?'

'How on earth do you know that? Abi doesn't know, and the point of a pen name is to protect a writer's wish for anonymity.'

'I was told by your sister-in-law. She is very proud of you.'

'Helen? That is is a surprise, though I can't imagine she has read my work.'

'I gather from Abi that you've expressed a willingness to allow me to explain where we are at with Helen and our hopes for a better future for her, so thank you for that.

'Your visit, Dee, which you found alarming, began releasing her speech, though we have had the setback of her self-harm. However, she has made progress such as to allow us to make a tentative diagnosis of Borderline Personality Disorder. This is serious, but is, most of us believe, best dealt with outside the confines of a hospital.

'Its causes are unclear and can involve genetic, neurological, environmental, and social factors. In Helen's case, the hormonal shift in the latter stages of her pregnancy may have also played a part, but we suspect there may be other factors which therapy might explore, and we will treat her also with medication. But we can't consider discharge until there is somewhere safe for her, and people to be there for her.'

'And you want me to be one of them,' I said, 'despite being the intended victim of a potentially murderous obsession? *She* might be in a safe place, but would I? And this when I am having to cope with the death of my sister in a car crash which will mean a trip to the north, and the shock of discovering my late husband had a second family hidden away somewhere. So, Lillian, please explain where I can place a further encounter with Helen in all this?'

'I am sorry to hear of your sister's death, which is terrible. As for the discovery of your late husband's betrayal, which is not too strong a word, I cannot even imagine the pain you must be feeling.'

I told her briefly of Polly's visit, her discovery of hope and sudden death, and I could see how moved she was.

'I long since gave up any pretensions to belief in God, which is sad, because it deprives me of the hope I might have had to spit in his face.'

She smiled.

'Your sister died with love and hope in her heart. For her I am glad, strange to say, if that does not offend you. I see so many with neither hope nor love, and even without the slightest trace of love for themselves. That is where Helen is now, not least because she now knows what a terrible thing she did towards the one person who accepted and encouraged her. It is little wonder she should fall in love with you. I accept there is no way right now that we can include you in our hopes for Helen's discharge, which will be difficult enough given that her husband is seeking a divorce, but even to see her again would I am certain, not place you at any risk, but might help her considerably. I even feel she could receive your own troubles with care and sympathy. But, Dee, I will not ask the impossible.'

'My husband, Lillian,' I said, 'worked for the security services engaged in what is perhaps best described as debriefing those with sometimes less than good intent. One of those who worked with him, now a senior police officer in Exeter, told me he worked without coercion but with understanding and gentle warmth, and accomplished so much in that way. Perhaps you and he were trained together! You too have a way with words, so I will give it one more go.'

'When is your sister's funeral?'

'In a fortnight's time.'

'Would you be willing to come and see Helen on Wednesday afternoon? We have a small house, away from the hospital where this could take place, but you will be perfectly safe as a nurse will be in an adjacent room, watching and listening. If this goes well, and I think it will, perhaps you, Nicola, could see her with Dee on a subsequent occasion?'

'That has to be Dee's decision, Dr Pilling, not mine. My only reservation is a fear that you might be rushing. Borderline Personality Disorder, from what I have been reading, is a serious mental health condition from which up to 10% of sufferers eventually take their own lives, and that there may well recurrent episodes in which others are potentially at risk.'

'The internet no doubt brings richness in so many ways, which as a writer you know. But I think it more like Pandora's box. GPs are now invited often simply to confirm a patient's own internet-derived diagnosis, and it can make psychiatrists of all who read its mental health pages, many of which are, in any case, rarely updated.

'Psychiatric diagnoses are models constructed to assist our attention to a patient, but they are only models and need constant amendment for each person, all of whom differ. I imagine you rarely produce a finished work at one sitting, and the published work will be considerably different from your first draft.'

'As sure as eggs is eggs. Second editions of books

characteristically read considerably differently from the first.'

'So do my diagnoses – frequently. We don't have the advantages of some of my medical colleagues, even the neurologists. We can't accurately discover what's happening in the brain in ways they can, say, diagnose a tumour in the brain. by scans. Neither, however, is it merely trial and error, though of course sometimes we get it wrong. Maybe you discard or delete some of your own work.'

'That happens a great deal, believe you me, but with considerably less at stake for me than for your patients and those with whom they come into contact.'

'BPD is only a model, open to change, and no two patients are alike. I see something positive in Helen, and you, Dee, have seen it too. There are, I suspect, hidden happenings in her past that will need skilled and assiduous therapy to unearth, but Dee, I share what you have seen, and that's why you hold an important key, though not the only certainly, but one that may enable her to recover.

'Do you read much poetry? Very few have ever come across Chloe Thomas.'

'When I can, between writing endless reports and trying to put together broken lives. I read poetry before breakfast and I try to range widely, but it is essential for me as a priest might feel his morning prayers. But now I must go. A woman's work is never done, and it is my turn to cook.'

'In which case, your husband is a fortunate man,' I said.

She smiled.

'I'm sure I mentioned neither word.'

She stood and as I was helping her on with her coat, Nicola disappeared into the study and returned with some papers, thrusting them into Lillian's hand.

'Just some models, Dr Pilling, for morning!' she said with a huge smile.

After Lillian had left, I said, to Nicola, 'Well, it's all straightforward now: Polly's death, André's betrayal, and Helen's discharge. I do so wish it was in a novel so I could turn over the pages and see how things work out.'

'If it's any help, you are my heroine, and we're going to do all this together. In stories, though rarely in life, there are usually happy endings. In life we simply have to muddle through and make the most of it, and we shall, Dee, my beloved, we shall.'

'That sounds like a good ending to a chapter in our story, though I wish I knew what might happen next.'

26

Turning over a page just brings another page, as every day after a death is just another day. This one began with a phone call from Hermione.

'Has Jim called you?'

'Yes. Wanting to discover the extent of his own failures as a husband, but do you know anything about how Colin and Peter are?'

'No. I spoke to Jim, but he said nothing other than continually going on about why Polly was with her GP when they died.'

'I've spoken to mum and told her we'll come to see her on the morning on the morning of the funeral and we'll take her to the Crem, but she'll need someone to take her home afterwards. We are going straight on up to Cumbria.'

'I'll do that.'

'But tell me about you, Hermione. I feel it's such a shame that circumstances have taken me away from you, as they did Polly.'

'It happens, Dee, especially in an age when we're all so much more mobile than we were in Hoddlesden days, but I'm ok, drifting into middle age but never bored in my work or with my friends. Two kids in their teens are almost as exacting at home as my patients are at work. I mostly do nights now and try to sleep during the day. It pays more and is also an effective contraception.'

I laughed.

'I can imagine, but otherwise is Graham ok?'

'Boring, but that seems to happen, but at least he's only boring, not like Jim, who was dead from the neck up for years. Poor

Polly.'

With a considerable measure of trepidation, I made my way to Dawlish after lunch on Wednesday. I accepted all the reassurances given by Lillian but given my previous experiences, I was apprehensive as I knocked on the door. It was opened by someone who announced herself as Sylvia, a reassuringly large lady of West Indian origin.

'You must be Dee', she said. 'Helen's been telling me about you, and she's very much looking forward to seeing you. I will monitor you throughout and the decision when to end the session is wholly yours. I'll bring you in a cup of tea as it will remind Helen I'm here.'

'Thank you. Milk, no sugar.'

Sylvia opened the door into a spacious room decorated in gentle pastel colours with a sofa and two comfortable armchairs, in one of which sat Helen, smiling at me.

'Hi Dee, come and join me.'

I sat in the other armchair.

'You're looking much better than when I saw you last, Helen.'

'It's amazing what a hairdresser and some makeup can do.'

'I hear it might be possible for you to be discharged soon.'

'Strictly it's called "discharged into the community", meaning there will still be people checking up and reporting on me.'

I noticed her wrist still bandaged but said nothing, and Sylvia came in with the cup of tea.

'I was told about your sister's death. I gather she had been down to stay with you.'

'Yes, but such things happen.'

She smiled.

'I have a hope, however, Dee, that once I've been discharged, I can take up your suggestion that I enrol on a creative writing course. My stay in hospital will provide me with lots of material, I can tell you.'

I nodded encouragingly.

'I'm sure. But what are you thinking about where you will go?'

I sensed an immediate change of manner.

'Home, of course. Where else? I assume you know your brother-in-law wants a divorce. That is hardly a surprise given his record with the women working for him. I have known for ages, long before I first got ill, that he looked on the girls he employed as fair game. That's how he got me, remember? His sister and her thieving parents won't want to acknowledge that, Dee, and it wouldn't surprise me to know that he has already someone lined up to take my place. But he's in for one hell of a surprise when this comes to court, and I've been assured by my solicitor that there is ample evidence of his repeated adulteries, and when it comes out, it's the sort of repeat behaviour the company he works for won't tolerate and neither will I. Haha. I hope his face is recovering. He'll not be so handsome now.'

I listened with mounting concern, but what, I wondered, if it was true and that Nicola and I had been lied to by Mark? What if Amelia was just the latest and, as Helen had said, being prepared to replace her?

'I can see from your face, Dee, that what I'm saying is conflicting with what Mark might have told you. All I can say is that I am not making this up.'

'What about Maisie and Angus?'

'They're Mark's problem. He started this. I need to get out of here.'

'There's no rush.'

'Well, actually there is, Dee. Don't forget, you're the reason I'm being held here against my will!'

Her tone was angrier now, but I resolved not to rise to the bait.

'I'm hoping to get back into my ordinary life as soon as possible, too. You are not the only one having to deal with major personal issues, though I can appreciate that given your present circumstances, all you have to think about are your own concerns.'

'I thought you came today to concern yourself with me, not for me to have to be bored stiff listening to your moans. Perhaps you should go.'

'As I understand it, Helen, I am the one who decides when we end our time together. I shan't forget what happened at our house. You need to be clear about that.'

'Are you saying you're refusing to help me, being the one who got me in here? Because that's what it sounds like.'

'Yes, that's exactly what I am saying. I've come today because I've been asked to. But you are not my priority at the present time.'

'In which case, Dee, there's no point in my seeing you or relying on you. I gather you are now married to Mark's sister, though the idea of two women in bed together disgusts me. I bet she's as sex mad as he is, and I happen to know you're not the first poor bitch she has forced into her bed. Well, good luck and watch your bank account. I've told you before about that fucking family. I should have stopped you when I had the chance – to protect you from them. But now I see you are just the same as them and next time I won't fail.'

She was shouting by now.

I stood, and as I did so, the door opened and Sylvia came in, indicating with an outstretched arm that Helen was not to move.

'I'll show you out,' she said to me.

'This has been a dreadful mistake,' she said, shaking her head, as I stepped outside the front door. 'I am so sorry and I shall make my report as soon as possible. This should never have been allowed.'

She reached out a hand to take mine.

'I need to call for backup to get Helen back.'

I mumbled something or other in reply and turned to walk down the road towards my car. I was shaking and not sure how I was ever going to drive home safely. Once in the car, I immediately burst into tears. What I had just experienced was a form of dreadful abuse, not just from Helen, which was bad enough, but from those who should have been as concerned with my mental well-being, no less than hers, and here I was, abandoned and feeling ravaged.

I called Nicola, who was with Sam in a children's playground in Totnes.

'Oh God, no! Why ever did I let you agree? Please don't drive. I'm going to call Abi and ask her to get someone to drive you home. Just get out of the car and walk in the fresh air. If you can find a café, get a cup of tea.'

'I'm desperate for a pee.'

'In which case, make sure it's a café with a loo. I'll get someone to call you, so they know where you are. You'll soon be here safe with me, my darling.'

I walked down towards the Front where there were several potential places where I could go for a drink, and happily the second I tried showed me to the loo as they made my drink. I had been there only a few minutes when I received a call from Abi asking me where I was and saying she was already on her way.

'You would be impressed by the flashing blue lights, Dee. I get little chance to use them nowadays. I'll be with you soon.'

About fifteen minutes later, I heard an approaching siren as an unmarked car with cleverly concealed flashing lights stopped outside the café, and Abi came in to find me.

'Come on, lovely lady, let's get you home,' she said, raising me from my seat.

Silence had fallen in the café, and they probably assumed I was some kind of mass murderer being arrested to protect them. The thought made me smile. Abi placed me in the passenger seat. In the back there was a uniformed constable who smiled at me.

'I'll drive your car home,' he said. 'Just show us where it is.'

Abi drove to the car, and I handed over the keys. As yet she had said nothing about what happened, but immediately pressed me to tell my story as soon as we set off, still with lights flashing but no siren.

I eventually managed to describe the events of my visit.

'I will make a full report of this, Dee,' she said, as she made our way along the coast road, through Teignmouth and Newton Abbot, and on to the A38, travelling at speeds I could hardly believe, with total control.

'There has been a serious failure of professional judgement resulting in you being placed in a position of considerable risk. As I initially passed on to you the message, I must accept a measure of responsibility, but the whole senior management team that agreed to the decision will now be under scrutiny. The

Prison Service and we have to rely on skilled practitioners providing a place of safety not just for patients but even more for someone brought in to test out a belief that Helen was showing signs of being no longer a danger. Clearly, they were wrong. I think they have been guilty of criminal neglect as well as professional misjudgement. It is a serious matter.'

We arrived home, and I had still barely stopped shaking. Nicola had sensibly dropped Sam off at her mum's, and came out to the car to bring me in. Abi followed us.

'What do you need, my love?'

'I need your love, and another visit to the loo. But cups of tea for Abi and myself will, I'm sure, be welcome.'

When I returned, Abi and Nicola were discussing what might have to follow.

'I was just saying to Nicola tthe whole encounter will have been recorded so it won't be necessary for you to go through it, but, once I've spoken to my Inspector, I may have to return to take a full statement on what preceded the visit, when Dr Pilling came to see you. In the light of your sister's tragic death, and the matter to do with your late husband, at the very least, someone should be for the chop.'

Having collected him from Ashburton in time for supper and his bath, I was reading Sam a story when Nicola called me to say Dr Pilling was on the phone.

'I'm so sorry, Dee. Sylvia urgently wanted me to see the recording of your session with Helen, and I have just done so here at home. I subjected you to something you should never had been asked to endure, but more importantly, how are you now?'

'I was badly shaken, Lillian, and can't deny how badly I feel let down. The truth emerged quickly, did it? How could you have missed it, and allowed yourselves to be taken in by her?'

'It was professional negligence on my part, no more, no less. In the morning I shall meet with my colleagues and inform them of my resignation with immediate effect.'

'Doing that will help neither me nor Helen. You made a mistake, from which I will recover, but doesn't Helen now need you more than ever?

'My professional skills were seriously askew. As a psychiatrist I persuaded you, against your better judgement, to place yourself, primarily for our needs, into a position which ignored yours completely, and may well have made them worse. My colleagues will know that I must resign before an enquiry forces it. Her care will be taken over by another doctor and I can assure you there will no further discussion of discharge. She deceived us and I fell for it.'

'And what am I to make of the things she said about Mark?'

'You can discount them completely. Accusations and lying are part and parcel of daily work in Langdon House. I at least can derive some comfort from knowing how you, Nicola and Sam supply the mutual love you can rely on.'

27

Shortly after Nicola had completed her morning work, and I had returned from taking Sam to his nursery, we had a visit from Inspector Annie Hill, Abi's senior officer, and head of family liaison in the county.

'I've just come from the Langdon and seen a run-through of the recording made yesterday of your visit to Helen Fairchild, held in what they, laughingly in the circumstances, call their "safe house". I want above all to apologise to you that my sergeant was the person to raise this is as a possibility with you. You have personal links with her, Nicola, so it's understandable that she should have offered to do this, but it was inappropriate. She maintains her visit was only to ask you to consider a meeting with one of the professional staff from the hospital. Is that correct?'

'Yes,' I replied. 'I can assure you she applied no coercion, especially knowing that I am handling other issues at the present time.'

'I am hardly an independent witness, Annie,' added Nicola, 'because Abi is a friend, a former and, maybe also, future colleague, but I could not fault what she said to Dee. Whether it was appropriate for her to do that is not for me to say, but I can understand why she thought it was.'

'I need to hear your account of the visit of Dr Pilling to consider a meeting with Helen Fairchild.'

To the best of my ability, with some prompting from Nicola, I sought to recall all that Lillian had said, but emphasising the promised safety which I now felt had been absent.

'I need you to be clear about one thing above all. "You will be perfectly safe" were the words you have just reported. I need you to be certain about that.'

'I am.'

'I was present, Annie. They were the exact words, not least because having looked up Borderline Personality Disorder on the internet I wanted for Dee something that would protect her against the possibility of what in fact took place.'

'I was informed when I arrived at the hospital this morning that Dr Pilling had been at first suspended, but has now resigned from her position. There will be an enquiry for what is a serious breach of protocol. The new acting senior psychiatrist, Dr Greene, told me that the circumstances are such that it is likely Dr Pilling will be struck off should you wish to make a formal complaint both to the hospital and of course, to us, on the grounds of criminal neglect. I can only advise you to consult a lawyer specialising in medical neglect if that is how you decide to proceed.'

'I can tell you now, Inspector, that I shall do neither. I have enough in my in-tray without wishing for any involvement with lawyers, official enquiries or even police officers. I am sure Dr Pilling acted in the best interests of her patient but underestimated the extent of the cunning and deceit Helen has shown and has already made a personal apology.'

'When was that?' she asked, altering her tone.

'She called me last night after she had seen the recording herself, to apologise and ask how I was.'

'There is no way she should have done that, as she will know. Did she put any pressure on you not to make a formal complaint?'

'No.'

'And did you tell her that you do not wish to do so.'

'No.'

'Dee, I'm sorry but I must ask again to be absolutely clear. Did Dr Pilling make even the slightest suggestion that you should not make a formal complaint.'

'No, she didn't.'

'Thank you. If you continue to decide not to do so, the hospital will deal with the matter internally and sweep the whole thing under the carpet. Dr Pilling will leave but others included in the decision-making will allow her to be the fall guy for what was a team decision and may yet have unknown consequences for your own mental state. This took place just yesterday and your life was being threatened.'

'Inspector, I feel under considerably more pressure from you than anything said to me by Dr Pilling. In a very long career, she has almost certainly made the right decisions most of the time. I respect her, not least because she recognises that this was not her finest moment. Well, I think we're all allowed one of them from time to time, and I'm not intending to make it worse for her, mainly because although it was traumatic yesterday afternoon – look, I've survived!'

'We all make mistakes, yes, we do, and I have done so. The higher up you are the more significant the consequences, however, and that increases the extent of responsibility and answerability.'

'I wish, Inspector, no further involvement with Helen Fairchild. Perhaps you can understand that. Dr Pilling has resigned from her position. In one sense, at least, justice is satisfied.'

'I do understand, Dee, but I have to ask these questions as I'm sure Nicola will acknowledge.'

'Helen said things about Mark. Will he be informed about her accusations, and about the implication that she intended doing him more harm?'

'His lawyer will have access to them. Because Helen is subject to a section order, and therefore wholly unreliable, he will be better off ignoring them. His difficulty will be in his care for their children. But now, I shall leave you. However, Nicola,' she added, turning towards my wife, 'I very much hope you will work with Abi. You were stolen from us by this woman here, and I can more than appreciate why you might have allowed yourself to be captured, but we'd welcome just a part of you back.'

'We've not really been able to give a great deal of thought to it, but Abi knows I'm not against the idea.'

That evening I had a thought.

'We need to get right away for a while. Do you think Viv might cope with us before the funeral for a day or two, so we could leave Sam with them on the day of the funeral. I'm only taking you as a necessary part of your education which has hitherto been sadly lacking.'

'Weren't we in the north when we visited Derbyshire?'

'Anywhere south of Manchester or Sheffield is in the Midlands, and I even have my doubts about Manchester!'

'You are an inverted snob,' replied Nicola. 'But is there a hope that you might to take me to Ilkley and experience for myself your former domain at *Betty's*?'

'I'd love to take you. I haven't been back since I left and I would love to see if it's up to scratch.'

'And will you start talking northern if we do?'

'I thought I'd never actually stopped.'

'Oh, you've definitely "poshed up", but I'll give Viv a call. I'm sure she'll do what she can, especially when I describe recent happenings.'

'"Poshed up", my arse!'

'Ooh, I love it when you talk dirty!'

Nicola set about planning our trip north for Monday to stay with Viv, Eamonn and their two children in Dentdale, in the Cumbrian Dales.

'Did you mention that we might want to stay for at least a month?' I asked Nicola.

'When I told her something of what you are facing, she offered that anyway. She was so pleased we are coming.'

'I know how delighted you will be to spend time with Viv again, but so will I. In my poetry walks, I've been reading some of her work. She's very good. I hope we can get to Grasmere and see where Dorothy Wordsworth lived – oh, and her brother, whoever he might have been, but mainly Dorothy.'

'I approve,' she said with a smile.

28

I had dreaded passing the site of Poppy's death on the M6, but there was no indication of where it had taken place. The M5, and M6 as far as Preston was busy, but after that it felt like the open road, though we needed the sat nav to direct us as dusk fell to Viv's house in deepest Dentdale.

'"And arrived at evening, not a moment too soon finding the place",' Nicola said, quoting T S Eliot, as Viv came towards us.

'"It was, you may say, satisfactory",' came the reply.

However was I going to cope with two poets? I wondered.

'Eamonn apologises for not being here to welcome you,' said Viv, as she gave us a hug and kiss, 'but in these wonderfully unenlightened parts there is still an early evening surgery – so he's just next door but will be here soon, but come in, and Sam, you have two people waiting to meet you.'

Sam looked up at me, and I gave him a measuring smile.

'It will be just like nursery,' I said.

Ursula was a gorgeous little girl, the same age as Sam, and her brother, Greg, a year older, and shyly they hid behind Viv's legs until they realised Sam was not a monster to be feared! In minutes, they were playing together happily.

The house was solid, stone-built, and spacious. Pete and Ed, Eamonn's adopted sons, had flown the nest, but had still left their mark in their former rooms, as Viv explained as she showed me into what had been Ed's room.

'They're smashing young men. Ed studied agronomy, and lives with his girlfriend, Sam, in Berwick. They've been together since they were in their teens here. Pete's in his final year at

Cambridge doing archaeology. Technically, he's still based at home, but uses every holiday to go on digs in different parts of the world.'

'It sounds as if they're both down to earth,' I said.

Viv smiled at my little joke.

'You've had a pretty grim time, Dee, since we met at Emily's. I hope the funeral won't spoil the chance to unwind, and please stay as long as you wish.'

'Funerals are always awful and this one particularly so because of the lost opportunities that seemed at last to be in place for Polly, but you know that, I'm sure. There must be people here too who die before their time.'

'Of course, but living in a deeply rural community, we're more used to life and death around us all the time. This is livestock country. There is no arable. People are more accustomed to the inevitability of death.'

'What I feel already is the relief of being away. '

'Good, and don't forget that when Nicola and I are in full poetic flow, you can't tell us to belt up.'

'I wouldn't do that. Under guidance from your friend, I'm learning the difference between good poetry and bad, and that good poets can also write bad poems, not all of which go into the wastepaper bin as soon as they might, but your published works are good. Thank you for them.'

'When I met you, Dee, I had a strong sense that you are someone who always strives to speak your mind without favour. I will therefore take your "good" as praise indeed.

'Now I must return to the kitchen and most likely find your wife fast asleep in the armchair in front of the fire. The children seem happy together, and Eamonn should be here in a matter of minutes as his last scheduled patient was half an hour ago, though that's quite normal for a consultation.'

'Seriously?'

'Yes. That's why I know we'll be living here a long time. This is what the practice of medicine should be like everywhere.'

Eamonn was some years older than Viv and a very good

looking man with lots of hair, greying nicely and the sort of GP I could open up to easily. In a short while we got on well, lamenting our poetic inadequacies, but glad each to live with the sources of such inspiration. As I shared with him the complexities of my present concerns, he told of his own scapes of the past. He had once been sentenced to five years in prison on a trumped-up charge of assisted suicide overturned by the Appeal Court after three months incarceration. After this, he had received significant support from a PC Young who had followed him to the north when he had moved to his practice here, though at the time he was living with an Indian woman and her two sons. She had died of sepsis following an ectopic pregnancy. Only then did he and Viv come together, and she revealed herself as Olivia Doyle. That much we had in common, as I had discovered my own new partner, also a police officer, was Chloe Thomas.

'Mind you,' said Eamonn, 'I had no idea who Olivia Doyle was, even when Viv informed me.'

'In which case, welcome me to the club!' I said, as we laughed together.

On the following morning, after Viv had taken Greg to school and Eamonn departed for a surgery in nearby Sedbergh, we went with Viv out for a coffee and toasted teacake to the town of Kirkby Stephen, a few miles to the north, where the Settle to Carlisle railway line runs, which I knew from my time in Ilkley, as it stopped there on its way towards the most scenic route in England.

I felt immediately at home in the countryside. It's quite different to Dartmoor, strangely wilder and more appealing. The town was small and relatively quiet as it was now late autumn and containing very few visitors. It's exactly the sort of place I might choose to live. And of course, it's in the north, where I belong.

Viv amused us by recounting an arrest she had made on her first ever visit to the café, since which occasion, she was well-known to the staff who greeted her warmly. Sam and Ursula had brought fur animals with them and played with them and each other as we chatted.

'We're pressing ahead with my adoption of Sam,' Nicola told Viv. 'We've waited until all the legalities surrounding his dad's death have been sorted, so can now get that under way.'

'And what about his newly discovered brother? Are you going to make contact?'

'I think we owe it to both Michael Donahue and Sam to let them know they have a sibling, though it's possible that he knows already. We don't know what André communicated, either to him or his mother.'

'He lived in a world of secrets,' continued Nicola. 'We can only assume that this liaison infringed some sort of protocol, but other than confirming that Michael is André's son, MI5 has told us nothing. You and I, Viv, as former police officers, are bound by the Official Secrets Act, so we know that although someone somewhere knows something, they aren't telling!'

'What are you intending to do?' Viv asked me.

'One possibility is to attend Mass in Dundalk and surprise Fr Michael and all the congregation, though that would be less than kind, but given that there is government secrecy involved and Dundalk is in Northern Ireland and not in the Republic, I'm not sure we want to advertise our visit more than necessary. It might be better to fly to Dublin and drive across the Border rather than have our names appear on a manifold checked by a government computer. Or do you think that's being paranoid?'

'Anything to do with Northern Ireland commands attention, especially if André's involvement was secret, so going via Dublin might make a great deal of sense. But you will need to know that Michael and his mother are going to be there. It would be a regrettable irony if they chose that time to be on holiday in, say, Devon!'

'They are citizens of the Republic, so I would imagine they will not be bound to maintain official secrets, but well ... all we can do is telephone and find out if they would be willing for us to come and meet them. Presumably Michael has accepted the £100,000 left to him.'

Early on Thursday morning, Nicola and I journeyed the short distance down the M6 to the exit for Blackburn and then on to Hoddlesden and my mother.

29

This was going to be a tough day for all of us and I wanted above all to try to extend compassion to my mother, for she was that day attending the funeral of her daughter. But quickly I realised that it might have been easier hitting my head against a brick wall. Everything I had done was wrong: her non-invite to our wedding, not bringing Sam to see her, inviting Polly to Devon and causing her death, not staying with her for the funeral and, almost certainly the rain that was falling, though my memory was that it always rained in Hoddlesden.

She lived in a somewhat poky terraced house in a street that would not have been out of place in an original Coronation St set from the 1960s, with extraordinarily steep stairs and paper thin walls.

'Your address is almost famous,' said Nicola, '10 Browning Street – not where the Prime Minister lives, but named, I imagine, after Robert and Elizabeth Barrett Browning, the poets, whose home Dee and I visited in Florence on our honeymoon.'

'I have your books,' she said. 'Will you sign them with a personal message, perhaps even "to a special mother-in-law".'

We avoided eye contact, and Nicola responded, 'I would love to.'

Oh, the joyous art of hypocrisy! But as I led her out for the grand tour, we could barely contain our amusement.

There is nothing to see in Hoddlesden, erected to house workers for the local cotton mill. Its setting is bleak on one side of a descending hill facing Pickup Bank, locally known as "Pickabonk" at the top of which, in the graveyard of an abandoned chapel, lie the mortal remains of my dad. I also showed her Hargreaves St, always known as "Top Row" with its exotic view across the ruins of the former Pipe Works in the hollow below. We went past The Ranken pub into Baynes St to see my old school, before returning to my mother's lair. I had lived here for years, but only after having gone away did I notice on my return how forbidding and bleak the place was.

The funeral was set for 1:30 and my mother had made us sandwiches, allowing time to get to the Crem (the Lancashire pronunciation of which always being *Cream*atorium) perched on its hill, passing Ewood Park, the home of Blackburn Rovers FC.

'Dad used to take me there to watch Rovers. He could remember the glory days, when they won the Premier League under Kenny Dalglish with Alan Shearer scoring all the goals. Tragically, they were relegated four years later, but I loved my Saturday afternoons with dad.'

'I can always encourage you to take Sam to watch Plymouth Argyle,' said Nicola.'

'I would rather attend a funeral!' I replied.

'How would you know the difference?' she said with a grin.

'We are on our way to mark a tragedy,' said my mother, sternly. 'Levity is entirely inappropriate.'

Nicola's eyes caught my own in the rear-view mirror, and our eyes smiled!

After we had parked and made our way towards the building, I was determined not to fall into conversation with Jim, but made at once for Peter and Colin who were looking forlorn.

'You can be proud of your mum,' I said, 'and she was so proud of you. When she left me to come home to you, the thought of your happiness was at the forefront of her mind. She wanted you to have a good quality of life. I know I live a long way off, but don't hesitate ever to call me.'

'I'm not sure quite what they made of that,' said Nicola, as I made my way to speak to my two brothers, both of whom were ashen-faced.

'This is Nicola, my wife,' I said pointedly. 'And these are my brothers, Oberon and Fyodor.'

'Hello Ron, hello Fred,' said Nicola, shaking hands. 'I've heard so much about you.'

Whatever replies they made were mumbled, perhaps stunned to be in the presence of their sister and her wife, a manner of life perhaps less well taken for granted in East Lancashire., though Oberon worked in the world of theatre and must have been more accustomed.

Out of the corner of my eye, I could see Jim was making his way towards me and I turned to face him head on.

'Oh Jim, what a terrible day for you and the boys,' I said, desperately hoping that the hearse would soon appear.

'I'm far from convinced that I've been told the truth about Polly's death, Dee.'

'This is my wife Nicola, Jim.'

'Oh yes, pleased to meet you,' he said, ignoring her completely. 'I think you're not telling me everything.'

I suddenly lost it, days of grief and anger saved up for this moment.

'Alright,' I said, 'though this is neither the time nor the place, but I *will* tell you everything Polly told me. She said that life with you had become utterly mind-numbing and soul-destroying, and that she longed for something and someone quite different. The doctor who offered to give her a lift and died with her was someone she could talk to, not least about how appalling a husband and father you are.'

My voice was rising in volume.

'And I can tell you for certain that he was gay and she knew that. So, if anyone is responsible for Polly's death, Jim, it was you. You weren't in the car on that day, but you drove her to her death!'

Conversations around us had stopped, and people stared.

'Now you have been told the truth, Jim, and you need to live with it. There is no one to blame for this day, Jim, but you.'

Hearing an approaching vehicle, everyone turned to look. Coming towards us was a young woman in a black top hat, black jacket and a remarkably short black skirt, wielding a silver-topped mace, followed by the hearse, and together they stopped in front of the doors to the crem, where a gawky vicar, who like everyone else had heard what I had said to Jim was clearly struggling to take everything in. I decided there and then not to join the procession into the chapel, took Nicola's hand and headed towards the car park.

'Oh dear,' I said, as Nicola drove owards the motorway. 'I fear I might have spoiled the occasion.'

'I was extremely proud of you, my darling, and so would Polly have been. I bet you were a vociferous supporter watching Blackburn Rovers! Now, let's get back to Sam.'

Nicola's account of the day, with appropriate poetic observations, brought merriment to the table as we ate that evening.

'The thing I've noticed about you, Dee,' she added, 'is that since we've been together, and remembering that correlation is not causation, you've become remarkably stroppy, and I love it. You would never have said what you did to Jim at the funeral of his wife and your sister, even months ago.'

'I'm not sure I agree,' said Viv. 'When we were at Emily's, I was sometimes taken aback by the honesty of what you said, and more than a little grateful you're not a poetry critic.'

We laughed.

'I've seen one or two commentaries on Nicola's shelves – Auden and Emily Dickinson spring to mind, though I've opened neither,' I said, 'and perhaps I'm showing how little I understand poetry, but surely the significance has to be in the poem itself as I read it aloud. What would be the point of writing something for others to read so obscure or deeply personal that it requires explanation? Doesn't the meaning belong entirely within the words? And sometimes as I read them aloud, the meaning of the words emerges differently on a second or third reading. That probably means I'm producing my own inner commentary as I walk along.'

'I think we should change the subject away from poetry,' said Viv. 'You are much too disconcerting!'

Perhaps it was the effect of the wine, but once again we

laughed.

'The only thing I can add, Dee,' said Eamonn, 'is to remark on the courage with which you handled all that stuff to do with your sister-in-law back in Devon. You might have refused to see her, but although what you described from that last meeting was pretty awful, you let them know how much they had failed you (and her), by not recognising just how manipulative those with BPD can be.'

'On the subject of manipulation by institutions,' said Viv. 'I've had a thought following on from what you've said about the possibility of visiting Northern Ireland. Paranoia aside, it's not impossible that whatever happened all those years ago whereby your late husband fathered a child in a deeply Republican area and about which you are not being told, contacts might be still monitored, but a phone call to Fr Michael Donahue from someone living in Cumbria might pass unnoticed.'

'You mean Dee should call whilst we are here? That's not a bad idea. But Dee, it has to be up to you,' said Nicola.

'No. It doesn't. I have pledged myself to you, my beloved, and whatever we do, we do together. My marriage to André was not a marriage of equals - ours is.'

On the following morning, Viv suggested we take Eamonn's Range Rover, pile Ursula and Sam into the back and pay a visit to Grasmere and Rydal, the realm of the Wordsworths, but I decided I couldn't face a trip in a car today and offered instead to stay back with the two children, allowing the poets to spend time with Dorothy, William and one another. I had missed Sam in the previous couple of days and wanted to get to know Ursula better, plus enjoying my time with Eamonn. I enjoy male company, especially as warm and intelligent as his. He came in for lunch after a morning doing house calls, mostly to farmhouse and with nothing before his evening surgery, it provided us with the opportunity to share our thoughts and feelings.

'What an extraordinary time you have had since your husband died,' said Eamonn as I returned from encouraging Ursula and Sam to have a post-lunch rest.

'Extraordinary might also describe your own experience. Your partner Bobbie died suddenly, not just carrying your child, but *because* she was carrying your child, if I understand correctly what an ectopic pregnancy is, though at the time you were also in love with a police officer. Eamonn, if I can say this, I'm truly impressed by how you dealt with uncovering all your contradictions.'

'Viv was quite right. She warned me before you came that you are direct.'

'She flatters me. I spent six years in a marriage being anything other than direct. His death has freed me to be me. And like you, I have been released from the constraints of pretension by a police officer!'

He laughed.

'But do tell me, if you dare, which of the two you prefer in bed – the poet or the policewoman?'

Now we both laughed.

'I am so happy living and working here and for Viv it's a perfect place for writing and being a mum, both of which she loves. That is has happened results from terrible events but had I not been in prison, had Bobbie not died – well, who knows how my life would have been? By accepting the bad and not allowing it to destroy me, here I am with Viv and our two children. Thankfully, neither of us lives in those previous generations of hypocritical morality endorsed by an unforgiving religion.'

'Though that unforgiving religion still looks on my love as sinful though I couldn't give a shit what it thinks, not least because the Church prefers to endorse hypocrisy rather than admit how many gay and lesbian priests it has who just get on with life. But isn't that like the entire issue of assisted suicide in your own profession? You went to prison because of that.'

'In caring for the dying in great pain and distress, good doctors know what they are doing to treat those symptoms even though they know the means we use may suppress breathing and possibly hasten death. Religious nuts don't seem able to recognise that.'

'How do you define a religious nut?'

'Anyone who believes in God! I'm always wary of religion in patients, and that's not an ideal way to function as a physician. I genuinely believe the people in our practice trust my colleague and me, not least because we don't charge, and the vets do!'

'Do you have a good colleague?'

Claire and I have a strong relationship, and the people here appreciate her. She also knows a lot about a lot of things, so she and Viv can easily fill any space with conversation – trust me!'

'Presumably she knows who Olivia is?'

'Yes, but her identity is otherwise not known, even among the poetry readers of Dentdale.'

'Are there many?'

'At a rough estimate, I would say none!'

30

On Saturday morning, as I sat next to her in the surgery, away from the children playing noisily, Viv telephoned the Presbytery in Dundalk, and turned on the speakerphone.

'Fr Michael,' said the voice, a lovely gentle southern Irish accent.

'Hello Father Michael. My name is Viv Manville and I'm calling you from Cumbria, and I'm doing so on behalf of someone sitting next to me who can hear our conversation.'

'That sounds most intriguing.'

'It might get even more intriguing if I tell you that in an adjacent room playing with my own two small children is a three-year-old boy called Sam, who is your half-brother.'

There was silence for a few seconds.

'Is the person listening called Dorothea by any chance?'

'She prefers to be called Dee, but it is. Would you like to speak to her?'

'I need to sit down. I didn't know I had a brother, but yes, please.'

Viv handed me the phone and left. I turned off the speaker.

'Hello, Fr Michael, this is the mother of your wonderful half-brother.'

'It's Michael, and he's my whole brother, and my Saturday morning, and in fact my whole universe, has just been turned upside down.'

'You don't mind me calling?'

'Mind? I'm overjoyed to hear from you. How? What? – heck, I don't know what questions to ask. All I knew was that I'd been left a huge amount of money in a will. I only know your name because it was mentioned in the solicitor's letter as the other executor, so it is just a guess that you might be Sir André's wife or widow I should say.'

'Michael, I didn't know Michael Donahue existed until the will was shown me, other than that he had an address in Ballymena. And to be honest, I didn't even know where Ballymena was. I eventually found out the little I now know from someone probably even then shouldn't have told me.'

'And you live in Cumbria?'

'No, in Devon, but we're staying here with friends, and she had the idea that just in case my contacts with Northern Ireland were monitored, a call from Cumbria wouldn't attract attention. Your father worked for MI5.'

'Then it wouldn't surprise me if any contacts with Ireland were being monitored. There's still a huge amount of suspicion towards a priest from the Republic working in the North.'

'Michael, could you bear meeting your brother and me? I am, and clearly you are too, in a state of almost total ignorance.'

'Dee, that would be more wonderful than I could say.'

'I wondered if we might fly to Dublin and then hire a car and meet up with you somewhere you might suggest in the Republic.'

'That would be a great idea. The Longford Arms Hotel in Longford is just off the N4, straight out of Dublin. I can bring my mother down and we could all stay for a couple of days. I imagine there's a huge amount to talk about!'

'Oh yes. However, you need to know that I have married again, and I have a wife, called Nicola, whom I will also want to come. She will adopt Sam soon. She is a poet published as Chloe Thomas. Do you have objections to a same sex marriage?'

'I'm not likely ever to be allowed to conduct one, but I'm already excited at the prospect of meeting my family, which until less than a quarter of an hour ago, I didn't even know I had. When can you come?'

'Doesn't that depend on when you can manage it?'

'I work here with another priest who won't miss me.'

'We're heading back to Devon where we live on Monday, but I

can see what might be possible regarding flights and let you know. As far as I'm concerned, we can come as soon as there's room in the hotel and on the aeroplanes.'

We swapped mobile numbers.

'Oh Dee, you can't know what this might mean for me.'

'And no less for me, believe me.'

'Dee, I'm a catholic priest, I can believe anything.'

For a moment I thought I might explode, but somehow managed not to do so, and made my way back into the main part of the house where expectant faces greeted me.

'There's a priest in Ireland reeling in both senses of the word.'

I told them at once how the call had gone, and immediately they shared my excitement.

'I've had a thought,' said Eamonn. 'If this can happen soon, why not fly from Manchester, leaving your car there, and breaking your long journey home? You could even meet Sam's brother and his mum on Monday if we can find flights for you. And if the security service is keeping half an eye on you, which I doubt, they wouldn't expect you to be flying from Manchester.'

Manchester was fully booked on both Monday and Tuesday, and Exeter was little better, but we managed to find a flight to Dublin from Bristol on Tuesday. We would drive there on Monday and leave the car at the airport and stay overnight in a hotel at the airport. Within an hour, it was fixed up. We would be in our Family Room in Longford by early-afternoon. I sent a text to Michael, and he replied immediately confirming that he would be there waiting for us. Sam was more excited by the thought that we were going to be going into an aeroplane than meeting his brother for the first time!

After lunch Nicola and I drove down the Lune Valley, past Kirkby Lonsdale, Settle and Skipton on the A65 to have coffee and a cake in *Betty's* in Ilkley. The shop had hardly changed but I was amused to be kept waiting for a table by a lass who would still have been at primary school when I was first there. However, our stay in the queue was short-lived and interrupted by a shriek of recognition by the new manager with whom I had worked in the Harrogate branch some years earlier.

'For heaven's sake, lass,' she said to the bewildered girl, 'that's Lady Beeson. Come on in, Dee.'

She showed us to a table still in the process of being prepared.

'Just wait while I tell everyone you're here.'

In a few moments, cooks and all the other kitchen staff showed up, and I was causing quite a commotion, but it was tremendous to be back. Nicola looked in amazement, wondering how long it would be before the requested drink and food would take to come given that all the cooks were gathered round our table! But in time the new manager sent them back to work, and we received our order, though I was refused when I asked for the bill. At the front of the café in the splendid bread and cake shop, I eagerly bought bread and cakes in abundance to shower the doctors, poets and those who live with them as gifts with which to say thank you for our wonderful stay.

I gave Nicola a trip round the town, showing her the flat above the shop where I had lived and taking her down to the bridge over the river. Ilkley is a delightful dales town ruined only by the sheer volume of traffic passing through towards Bradford and Leeds, and then returning. As we headed back to Dent, however, already my mind was turning towards the following days and the discoveries to be unearthed in a hotel in Ireland.

We met Claire, Eamonn's partner when she handed over to him at 6:00pm. She was a countrywoman by upbringing and clearly enjoyed the practice of medicine here, ably supported by her mother, also a doctor, though retired.

'I am so pleased to meet you, Chloe,' she said after having been introduced to Nicola. 'Olivia kindly loaned me two of your books. I have taken them with me in the car and read them aloud to the sheep and they seem to like them, as I do.'

'Thank you,' said Nicola. 'What the sheep think matters to me, though I fear they buy few copies, having to rely instead on passing physicians to amuse and entertain them.'

'Ah well, all we like sheep, as I gather from Viv sales of top-class poetry to humans, is not great.'

'Poets are better valued when dead, as sheep I should imagine.'
Claire laughed.

'Here's not a place to profess being veggie or a vegan, that's for
certain, and by sheer coincidence, did you know you're all
joining us for Sunday lunch tomorrow when my mother will do
wonders with lamb?'

'I forgot to mention it,' said Viv, 'but I've had Claire's mother's
lamb before and though you two are good cooks, you're in for a
treat!'

Claire's mother was multi-talented. Not only did she cook
well, but also worked as the Practice Manager and even did the
occasional surgery when called upon. She and her daughter were
obviously very close and seeing them together, I felt pangs of
envy. I might as well not have had a mother, and I had not heard
from her since the funeral, though on the Sunday afternoon,
Hermione called to report how dire the ceremony had been given
what had preceded it. Her primary concern was for Peter and
Colin and felt that although I had put a stop to Jim's endless
suspicions, perhaps my timing might have been better.

'I know you're right and for the lads' sake I regret it, but it was
the convergence of my grief and that horrible man wanting to
claim the moral high ground, and I simply let it all out. My only
consolation is that the lads already knew how useless a father and
husband he was, so that wasn't something new, and at least I
covered up the genuine nature of the tragedy, that she had found
love at the last.'

'You pushed truth away when you maintained Simon was gay.'

'But he was. When we left us on that fateful morning, he was
merry and gay. It's not my fault the English language is
sometimes ambiguous.'

She laughed.

The two poets disappeared in the afternoon into nearby
Barbondale, prefaced by a visit to the Quaker Meeting House at
Briggflats, dating from 1675, more interesting because of its link

with the poem of the same name written by Basil Bunting, apparently one of the leading 20th century Modernists. In the dale they parked and climbed Barbon High Fell and with its views over Lunesdale, and no doubt, talked endlessly.

I had a lovely afternoon with the three children and Eamonn. I really liked him and could imagine his patients did too and could easily imagine why he had attracted women in the past.

'I totally messed up my first marriage and then my relationship with Bonnie was wholly compromised by my involvement with Viv. When she died, Viv was there – loving, caring, and making no demands. Now I have a measure of security, wholly thanks to her.'

'No, Eamonn, it's wholly thanks to you. Being an outstanding and clearly much-loved doctor (which is what Claire told me) comes from within you. I notice you've put stabilisers on Bonnie's bike. Viv did that for you, but she knew that once you were being and doing what you were capable of, they could come off.'

'Gosh, I wish I could be a fly on the wall when you meet your new family. Viv says you always tell how it is. I hope they're ready   for   you.   '

31

As we arrived at Bristol airport after what had seemed an endless motorway trudge from Cumbria, it felt odd to be so near home and now heading off in the opposite direction, though first we had a night in the nearby hotel, and fortified ourselves with "as much breakfast as you can eat"!

We found the long-term car park with ease and made our way to the check-in desk and Passport Control. I had brought our passports with us because it was something I always did when I travelled on the grounds of "You never know when you might have to prove your identity". Although I had a document signed by the registrar at our wedding, it was still bearing my Beeson name, as was Sam's. This had not been a problem at check-in, nor when we had flown to Italy, but the officer at the Passport Control indicated I should wait until he had checked something, for which he picked up his phone and spoke. Nicola had already gone through and looked back anxiously. The officer put down his phone and wished us a pleasant stay in Ireland but provided no explanation for the delay.

'Thank you, André Beeson,' I murmured crossly, as Sam and I caught up with Nicola.

'Did you say something?' she asked.

'A message for the dead!'

'I did wonder.'

Through the departure lounge window Sam watched aeroplanes landing and taking off as we had ridiculously expensive drinks.

'It's been quite a trip,' said Nicola.

'Congratulations madam, I said. 'You win the prize for the understatement of the year! But that aside, have you enjoyed our days in the North? I hope you feel you had enough time with Viv.'

'It's been tremendous and provided us with a chance to share recent work. We speak often enough on Zoom, but it's not the same as being there with her.'

'I can see what drove her to choose Eamonn,' I said. 'We say "good" too often, but he seemed like a genuinely good man, despite his colourful past. I think he's trustworthy, and has in Viv a terrific partner. The people they serve should count their blessings as well as their sheep.'

Once on the plane, with Sam on the aisle seat next to me and Nicola across from him, we climbed and banked over the Irish Sea. Sam was anxious at first but soon settled and swapped seats with me so he could look out of the window.

There was a hiatus at the car hire desk as, despite being clear about the order in advance, one without a child seat had been brought and we had a tiresome wait before the vehicle we had ordered arrived. The airport lies to the north of the city, but the route to the N4 was straightforward, with much less traffic than around Exeter. Ahead lay a journey of about 80 miles and no matter what might await us, I hoped it would bring light.

The hotel was in the centre of the town and very grand, boasting a gym and, oddly, a saltwater swimming pool as part of its status as a Spa Hotel, but I thought the mental gymnastics of the next 48 hours would be more than enough. As we approached Reception there before us stood a good-looking young man who could almost have been an earlier version of André, and with him a nice-looking lady in, perhaps, her mid-sixties, both with wide smiles and open arms.

'Hello and welcome to Ireland, the home of good rugby,' said Michael (for it was he).

Immediately I laughed.

'Hey, we come from Exeter, so be careful what you say,' I replied, accepting his arms around me. 'I'm hoping you are Michael, or this is most strange.'

'Dee, please meet my mum, Brighid.'

We shook hands.

'Michael's way more effusive than me, at least when greeting ladies I've noticed,' she said.

'And this is my wife Nicola and peeping out from behind her legs is your brother.'

Michael hugged and kissed Nicola and then went down onto his knees.

'Hello Sam, I'm Michael, and we are going to be great friends.' He reached into his inside pocket and produced a book which he showed Sam. Would like me to read you a story on that sofa over there, just us two men together, and leave these terrible women to unpack their bags?'

Sam looked up at me with eager eyes.

'Of course, you can, though let me give you a drink to take with you.'

I produced his drink container from my bag and handed it to him, and he handed it to Michael and then reached for his hand.

'That wasn't much of a battle,' said Nicola, laughing. 'Well done, Michael!'

With them settled on the sofa, Brighid guided us to our room, and helped us hang our clothes.

'They have a grand laundry service here, Dee,' said Brighid.

Nicola and I both laughed.

'I think what you mean is that having been away from home for over a week, our clothes could do with some attention.'

Clearly, André's former lover had a sharp eye.

Sam had an early supper, and one attraction of the hotel was a babysitting service, allowing the four of us to have dinner in the restaurant.

'First to discover I have a brother, and then to find how wonderful a brother, has made this such a special day for me.'

'He was quite impressed, too. Your choice of story enthralled him, and he hasn't been able to stop talking about the promised swim tomorrow. Thank you, Michael.'

Once we had ordered, we realised that the time had come to talk and, more importantly, listen.

'Until the contents of André's will were revealed, I knew nothing of its contents nor of the existence of either of you,' I began. 'Not only before he and I married, but throughout our short time together, his life was shrouded in secrecy. It was a sort of unwritten rule that I did not ask, and I imagined I did not need to do so, that I knew all that I needed to know.

'His will named Michael Donahue, but that meant nothing at all and the security service had removed all his papers and computer within a day of his death, none of which has since been returned. In the UK there is what's known as the Official Secrets Act, used to conceal almost anything those in power choose, and sometimes it appears, they do so because they can.'

'We have one too,' said Brighid, 'but Freedom of Information legislation has largely restricted it to civil servants.'

'Anything more I know was revealed in an almost certain breach of the Act by a close friend who is married to someone with access to secret files, and you can imagine the shock of discovering that my husband had another family of which I knew nothing.'

'I can't understand what this must have been like for you,' said Brighid.

'I have only been able to deal with it because I have Nicola with me.' I looked at Michael, so like André. 'Your father died a peaceful death, Michael. We were sitting on a bench by his favourite stretch of the river Dart, he to one side of me and Sam on the other. I was giving him a drink and when I turned back, I could see at once that he had died. I made a call and ten minutes later, a police constable arrived, and I knew at once that she was something special.'

'You're a police officer?' said Michael to Nicola, his eyes widening.

'I was then, but my Chief Constable asked to me to stay and look after Dee. The Chief had been a good friend of your father and thought it would be useful for me to support Dee until the funeral. And then I stayed on and resigned from the force and have been concentrating on writing poetry, caring for Sam, of whom I'm soon legally adopting as his other mother, and above all being there in every way for my new wife.'

'All I know,' I continued, 'or all I have been allowed to know, is that André came to Belfast to work in some capacity for the UK government during the worst of the Troubles, engaged primarily in the work of interrogation. He then spent time in the Middle East and learned Arabic, which I suspect proved useful in his work with Islamic terrorists and others once he returned to London, which he continued until his retirement.

'For a short while I worked at the interrogation centre in charge of the canteen and then he sweet-talked me into marrying him!'

'That rings bells,' said Brighid with an enigmatic smile.

'We were married for just six years. I did sometimes ask about his past, but he insisted ignorance was my best protection. Then an attempt was made by an IRA splinter group to murder a woman who had been responsible for murders of republicans in the Troubles who had come to our house to see André.'

'Nancy Carmichael,' said Brighid.

I paused, wondering how she knew.

'The attempt was foiled, but Nancy committed suicide at our house with a gun provided by André, during the following night. Because of the trauma of the event I had a massive uterine haemorrhage and rushed into hospital where a brilliant doctor saved my life though I lost the twins I was carrying.'

'That's terrible,' said Michael. 'two more victims of the civil war.'

'How amazing that after such a happening you went on to give birth to Sam,' said Brighid.

'I told you he is a brilliant doctor. He was from Galway and is still a friend as he works as a consultant in Exeter. But when I saw him last, he told me something André had begged him to keep secret. His actual words were, "I knew I was perfectly safe, Brendan, I'm off limits", but gave Brendan no explanation. Nicola and I concluded the only explanation for what he said to Brendan must lie here!'

We sat in silence for a little while, Brighid and Michael both studiously attending to their food.

'Dee, I will tell you everything I know, but would prefer to do so by daylight rather that at a meal table,' said Brighid. 'Might you and I go for a walk tomorrow, outside the town? I'm not wanting to exclude you, Nicola, and of course, Dee will later tell you everything there is to know, but it would be easier for just the two of us to talk together.'

'I think that's sensible,' said Nicola, 'but you ought to know that Dee is also having to handle other matters just now.'

Nicola briefly told of Poppy's death and about Helen.

'I haven't told you these things,' continued Nicola,' to suggest Dee is not up to whatever it is you need to say tomorrow, Brighid, for the precise opposite is the case. I want you to know that the woman I have pledged myself to for life is unbelievably tough so be sure, Brigid, that you tell her everything.'

Brighid smiled.

'You're pretty tough yourself, dear poet,' she replied.

'Is Sam named after Samuel, his mighty namesake in the Old Testament?' asked Michael.

'Trust me,' I said with a broad grin, 'it really would be a shock if you tell me in the morning that André was more religious than I ever knew, but no. He is named after Samuel Pepys, the man whose diaries André read frequently and who, of course, coined the phrase "and so to bed". Perhaps we should heed his words!'

32

Brighid drove three or four miles out of the town where we left the car and began a gentle uphill walk.

'You know, Dee, it's extremely disconcerting that when I look at my son, I can see so clearly the version of your husband that I knew many years earlier.'

'The likeness had struck me too, though André was much older when I met him, perhaps how Michael will look when he's a bishop.'

'Ah, you must tell him that. He's got a great sense of humour! But I must now tell you how his father entered my life.'

'Even in the darkest days of the Troubles in the North, both sides wanted peace even while they went on killing. Dundalk is close to the border. Some of the most violent members of the IRA, men who would kill without compunction, and women too, used it as their base. Nancy Carmichael was well known there as an executioner of touts, as they were called, catholics who betrayed the cause. I can tell you she killed more than a few, among them two Americans and captured members of the SAS, but also girls who might have had even the slightest dalliance with a Prod or a soldier. She put a bullet in the back of the head of each one, "nutting" it was called. She wasn't the only one, but she was widely feared within the movement.

'As you may know, after the civil war ended (and for republicans that is what it was, not the prissy "Troubles") she left the country and went to live in London. The Irish government did not want her back as it would stir up all sorts of hatred and a public trial that would do no one any favours. I learned that she was always under the scrutiny of the UK secret services though not actually protected by them. As far as I know she remained staunchly republican to the end and those seeking her death were family members of those she nutted in conjunction with a splinter group, not former provos. She had never turned tout herself.

'Occasionally back then, by secret agreement, an unofficial attempt was made to secure a ceasefire. Arrangements were made for a meeting of someone from the High Command to meet a representative of the UK government. The Command agreed they would allow André Beeson to come to Dundalk under escort, to meet whoever the Council agreed on, probably McGuiness himself. He was more trusted than others having secured more releases of catholics than other interrogators, and those returning reported that he seemed not unsympathetic to the republican cause.

'It was an extremely dangerous game he was playing. I was on the fringe of the Council. I knew them all and sometimes when I learned what some of them did on active service, I felt a tremor of horror. I took him a message to him where he was staying from the High Command for relay to London and he used his incredible charm to seduce me, though I was a more than willing victim. I wasn't executed by Nancy, because they could use me to spy on the spy, and I did so, though, of course, André knew this.

'I fell in love with him, but we both knew that were we to disappear to a life together away from the civil war, we would be hunted down and killed, because we knew too much. We also knew that our liaison could not last. Peace was not breaking out soon, and he discussed this with the highest level of Command who agreed that he should be returned to the North, but without me. I was a sort of hostage.

'Our parting was the very worst day of my life. That was when I told him I was pregnant. He tried to urge the Council to let him stay, but personal concerns were wholly subordinate to those of the cause, and they still had plans for me. He was escorted to the border and secretly handed over. Technically, he was now the enemy again, though told he would not be a target, and I guess that is what he meant when he spoke to your doctor friend.

'London withdrew him at once sent him to Cairo. He was compromised up to his eyeballs. I have to tell you, Dee, that I never stopped loving him, but secret details in the Good Friday Concordat meant that whilst he remained a serving officer in the service we were never to meet again.'

'So, you never saw each other again?'

'Whilst he was in the Middle East he began supporting me financially and we regularly wrote to one another, and occasionally spoke.'

'But did you ever see each other again?'

Brighid hesitated before speaking further.

'André was a clever man and secured for us both second passports with different names. With them we met in Boston, Massachusetts on a number of occasions, though in that American-Irish city I could have walked the streets with my original name and be regarded as a hero by many.'

'Was Michael with you?'

'No. My own mother was still alive, and we have an extended family, so Michael got used to my being away. As far as everyone was concerned it was my television work that took me to America. He knows no different to this day.'

'How recently did this happen?'

She hesitated again before speaking.

'Do you recall André receiving an invitation to a History Conference in Phildalephia about 18 months ago? Sam was small and André knew you would not be able to accompany him though the invitation was deliberately addressed to you both, knowing that there was no chance of you attending. He told me that he told you that because you couldn't come with him, he wouldn't attend, but that you urged him to do so, and he did. Exactly as planned. There was no such a conference but I put a webpage up in case you looked it up on the internet and saw that Sir André Beeson was listed among the speakers. In fact, he flew to be with me in Michigan for ten days.'

I suddenly felt as if I was going to very sick.

'So how recently were you in touch?' I asked.

'I last spoke with André on June 15th this year, just two weeks before he died.'

My stomach continued churning.

'He told me then that he'd had some chest pain but thought it nothing to worry about and we were begin to plan another meeting.'

'Michael said you and he knew nothing about me or Sam.'

'I told Michael nothing,'

'But you knew?'

'Nicola impressed on me last the night the necessity of telling you everything and I assume that is indeed your wish?'

'It is.'

'André had known a fair few ladies over the years with whom he shared whatever he chose, and never elaborated but I assumed he meant sex, but told me that now he had met a woman in Yorkshire he thought would provide him with such care as he might need as he became older. He told me of your miscarriage and later, of your second, successful pregnancy. He also became fearful, almost paranoid, that being so very much younger, you might find someone of your own age. I didn't know everything, but I knew a huge amount about you and your life with him.

'He continued to send me more than €1,700 a month, that's £1,500. I had assumed, mistakenly, that I would be a beneficiary in his will, but I was overjoyed to learn that Michael received a large sum.'

We walked in silence, my mind completely numb. Finally, I stopped walking and stood still, looking at Brighid.

'Are you still tied up with the republican cause? Are you one of those who sought to kill Nancy Carmichael, and inadvertently, as Michael pointed out, also cause the deaths of my never-to-be-born twins?'

'Carmichael was vile in every way, wholly devoid of conscience, and I certainly cannot mourn her, but I have had no contacts with any of the remaining republican groups since the Good Friday Agreement was made. Do you really think the UK government would have let you come here if I had?'

I thought back to the pause at Bristol Airport.

'And what do you think of it now? I don't mean André's part, which as far as I'm concerned was absolute betrayal, but your own?'

'I don't think *I* have ever done you any harm, Dee. It was only when Michael received the legacy that I learned of André's death, though the silence had led me to think it might be so, though I searched in vain for notices or obituaries.

'They were not allowed.'

'And even if I had known these things, why would I have wanted to contact you? He had told me that you knew nothing about me or Michael. That you have had to learn all this today from me is to have learned of a great betrayal, not just by André but those in MI5 who have always known this, and kept it from you, allegedly your friends.'

'I hardly know what to think, let alone know what to say. Yes, it's true you have done me no harm but, Brighid, haven't you betrayed Michael?'

'The civil war, what are called the Troubles, reaches deep still, and Michael has enough to deal with as a catholic priest in Northern Ireland as it is, without burdening him with knowledge that might threaten him. André's legacy now allows him some choices.'

'It's odd he left nothing to you.'

'I don't have a small child to house and care for, and I have worked, so over the years, having saved André's monthly money for 25 years, I have a considerable amount on which to live.'

'Tell me, Brighid, if you can, who did André really serve here on this island?'

'The UK government, which continued to employ him, will tell you he served them. Republicans here will tell you he served them, and perhaps both are correct. André survived where few others did. He was what I suppose spy writers would describe as a double agent, but I believe myself he was on our side more than yours.'

'Well, it is abundantly clear he wasn't on my side! He was more than happy to have sex with me regularly though he wasn't especially good at it, as perhaps you know, but I can't ever recall him saying he loved me. Did he ever say to you that he loved me?'

'I think you know the answer to that, Dee, as I do. We could have made a life together had he wished, and I said so. We could have made that life in America without difficulty. I'm not sure André knew what love demanded, and given his upbringing, how could he?'

'You know about that?'

'Oh yes. He was so proud of his mother, and maybe she was the only one he ever loved. I'm afraid, Dee,' she gave a laugh and took my arm, holding me close, 'we lost out to a whore.'

I have her a wry smile.

'His will has made me moderately wealthy, or so my solicitor informed me, and clearly, he has done the same for you. Do you have any idea where his money came from?'

'Are you wondering whether some of it might have come from the IRA here or supporters in Boston?'

'It's a reasonable supposition.'

'I honestly don't think he received a cent. Most of their money went to the purchase of guns from North Africa. I think the answer must lie in his involvements in the Middle East. André, as we both now know, had the knack of riding two horses at the same time, even when they were moving in opposite directions. He travelled extensively in Moslem lands, which at the time was a relatively safe thing to do and he became fluent in Arabic. He came back, and my regular payments increased significantly, which is most likely where our moderate wealth, as your lawyer put it, originated.

'Islamic money I can live with!'

'Me too.'

We turned back towards the car.

'What work did you do, apart that is, from being Fr Donahue's housekeeper?'

'I worked for RTÉ, first as a dogsbody or runner as they call it, and gradually made my way up to being an assistant producer.'

'Wow!'

'I was only an *assistant* producer, Dee! But it was fun and I was based in Cork, which is a grand place to live and far from the Border.

'Have there been other men in your life?'

'One or two, you know, over the years, but as André provided me with financial security, I didn't need a husband.'

'Nor me, it now seems. I'm happier with a wife.'

'Working in television, I've long since known same-sex couples and rejoice that they can now marry, even here in Ireland, and who would ever have thought that? But you have a special lady there, Dee.'

'I know.'

'And what I know, Brighid, is that although you have revealed what are to me devastating things about that man, you've told me almost nothing about you and your part in the life of Dundalk. You've said you were close to the inner circle of the high command of the IRA, so tell me what it was that enabled you and André to live after your liaison with him. Why were you both spared a nutting from Carmichael?'

She stopped, clearly thinking hard.

'IRA men were soldiers in a war. But they were also men with normal needs whichmeant from time to time they needed women, and the women needed looking after and defending.'

'Prostitutes, you mean?'

'Look, it's more complicated than it sounds. Although there were a few women participating in active service with guns and grenades, not all the women who had relationships with the enemy were traitors. We sent them out, sometimes to trap men who were captured, tortured and killed, but also to provide information. You would be surprised by just how many SAS soldiers who could resist torture and were trained to the highest level, spilled out their secrets in bed. It was almost a service to let them meet that need as much as their sexual needs.'

'And?'

'I oversaw these women, their recruitment and training. They were as committed as the men to our cause and ready to serve in this way. So, prostitutes doesn't actually describe them.'

'And you were allocated to André, I suppose.'

'It wasn't like that. It wasn't meant to happen, but I fell for him, and when I reported it the High Command, instead of a bullet I was asked to continue and get out of him whatever I could. What followed was a cat-and-mouse game. I produced goods to satisfy, but provided him with considerable misinformation with an occasional goody thrown in. What he threw in of course became Michael.

'I misled André and held him emotionally dependent upon me. As far as the war effort was concerned, I was regarded highly, and once it had become clear the UK cottoned on to what André was revealing, he was no longer any use to us and he was sent back. In me the interrogator became the interrogated, and I was very good at it. I interrogated captured soldiers and touts, and I suppose what I learned sometimes led to their deaths, but I killed none directly. And once I was pregnant I was sent away, like village girls were in those days, but in my case to a life in the far south financed by André. Now, I have told you everything.'

It was my turn to be silent and I was so for about five minutes as we walked back towards the car. Eventually I stopped, and to hers and my own surprise, I took Brighid by the hand.

'You've done a fabulous job bringing up Michael. Did André not want to meet him?'

'He did and I always refused. I have never wanted Michael to know the part played in the civil war by either André or myself. And I've hardly ever spoken to him of André other than as the man who impregnated me back in 1992. If he has ever been curious, it has never been obvious to me, until out of the blue £100,000 arrived in his account, and then he received your phone call. You now know it all and I cannot of course stop you telling him everything I have told you.'

'But you would prefer me not to do so?'

She shrugged.

'Michael knows his father supported me whilst he was a child, but once he entered the Seminary, we never spoke of it again and ignorance is his best protection.'

'Are you sure about that. Look, Brighid, I am neither judge nor jury about any aspect of the Troubles including the parts you both played. But I imagine many are. Were you happy moving back north of the border? Doesn't that pose risks for you, and for Michael too?'

'I took voluntary redundancy when Michael moved to Ballymena to be there to support him. I despise living in the North, and so does he. I imagine that in England, people don't spit at you in the name of Jesus as you pass them on the street. And I am constantly looking over my shoulder and always must check under my car before I drive anywhere.'

'But can't he leave and come south?'

'Michael goes where he's sent.'

'Oh, what a fucking mess the British have made here!' I suddenly burst out, 'I don't just mean the Troubles, but the entire history from that bastard Oliver Cromwell onwards. It's the same everywhere: India, Israel, Rhodesia. Wherever the British flag has flown, catastrophe has been left behind. But must it be so for Michael and you for ever?'

'You need to talk with him, Dee. He needs to talk to someone right out of all this. And I think you are the right person at the right time. I would say it's not a moment too soon.'

33

It was clear when we arrived back at the hotel that Sam had been spoiled rotten by his brother and was desperate to report on everything they had done. Michael was proposing a trip out for a burger and fries to a place called *Jac O Bites Café*, and without knowing what a burger was, Sam was eager to try. How could we resist joining them? I did, however, ensure we had Sam's buggy with us, assuming, correctly as it turned out, that whilst he wanted to walk to Chapel Lane with Michael, by the end of lunch he would be tired.'

Nicola and I lagged a little behind the others as we made our way across the busy main road into the plethora of side streets.

'How was it?' asked Nicola.

'I've uncovered at least some of the reasons MI5 has withheld information from me. I was married to a double agent in the Troubles, and how he survived. I'll never know. And he's been a double agent ever since: two families, two children, and buying off the two women involved, one of whom he wanted mainly as a cross between skivvy and whore, and the other he's been seeing regularly, even during the time of my marriage.'

'Dee, that's simply horrendous. Do you think you've been given the truth?'

'About the lies and deceit I've been given, yes I do, and also perhaps about what happened back then, of which I'll tell you later, but I suspect she may still have links with republicanism for which André regarded her as some kind of insurance policy, so that if he kept paying, she would protect him from those who might still want to kill him.

'More than anything she fears for Michael and herself both becoming sectarian targets, not necessarily because of André, but because of her own involvement with the republican cause back then, but possibly, now as well. And ask yourself where we're going for lunch – a café called *Jac O Bites*. It would be hard to find a clearer sign of political affiliation than that. Anyway, she wants me to talk with Michael.'

'Michael's been wonderful with Sam, and here we are: *Jac O Bites*! Burgers and 17th century politics remembered, and both served with fries!'

Once back at the hotel, Nicola took Sam up to our room for a rest, whilst Brigid said she would do the same, leaving Michael and me together in the hotel lounge, which we had to ourselves.

'I've been on a very steep learning curve this morning with your mother. I now know lots of things which make sense but hurt a very great deal, and they are all about your father.'

'Your arrival in our life was bound to do that, Dee. But this has all had to come out and I can hope that the hurts you have received will recover now that you have that wonderful poet and my little brother in your life. You've also recently had the death of your sister to deal with and a tough time with Nicola's sister-in-law. That's more than enough for anyone. You could do without this.'

'Ah well, all three are family matters. We don't choose them, they choose us.

'Michael, how much do you know about your mother's involvement in the Troubles and her meeting with André?'

'Nothing. She says we have to move on, that it's over and done with, except of course it's not. Not if you're a catholic in Ballymena it's not, and certainly not if you're a catholic priest.'

'Why did you become a priest, may I ask?'

'You can ask me anything, Dee. In fact, I need you to. There were two reasons I became a priest. The first is that I was drawn by the hope of something larger, a universe of meaning where there was little else of meaning around me. Growing up, I longed for that, and the church claimed to offer exactly what I longed for, and when I was 18, I was persuaded that this could best be found in the priesthood, offering meaning to others. It's largely been a disappointing non-starter, because in the main they don't want that – all they want is cheap reassurance that all they are about can be safe, in this life and the next. I wanted to offer God, they wanted religion, a very poor second best.

'The second, and perhaps the real reason I became a priest, was the same as that of my parishioners: fear of life. Perhaps it was the absence of a father, but I was also running away from myself and chose apparent certainty over the risk of growing up and living with uncertainty and ambivalence. And yes, before you ask, I sensed my mother had involvements in the past, not just with André, but with the IRA, and I felt fear about the possibility that this might one day rebound and hit her and me.'

'That makes perfect sense and being sent to Ballymena must have heightened that sense of anxiety.'

'I tried to refuse, but I was under canonical obligation to obey the bishop. I would give anything to get away.'

'Would that include chucking it all in – the priesthood, I mean?'

'There is another aspect to be considered.'

'Go on.'

'Even when I was in my previous parish in the South, I had a sense that I needed to seek my deepest self, my true self, as the psychologists call it. Occasionally it emerged when I wasn't looking but did so one morning in a sermon I gave to a convent of nuns when their chaplain had developed Covid. I hadn't time to prepare anything and spoke off the cuff. I said something to the effect that beliefs that make up the faith of the church are only beliefs and not the reality of God, and that the poet John Donne had said: "Oh, to vex me, contraryes meet in one", and that we had to live with those contraries in ourselves and in the life of faith.

'Two things followed. Almost immediately, the Mother Superior made a complaint to the bishop that I was undermining the church's teaching, and in the light of the recent controversies about marriage and abortion, she urged I be disciplined. She also reported to him that one of her novices had already indicated to her that because of what she had heard in the sermon, she was leaving. It's amazing. I thought nobody listened to sermons. Anyway, early the next morning the bishop telephoned and told me I was beginning work in Ballymena on the following day, and that I should move with immediate effect. A telephone call! Imagine that.

'But another thing happened as I was packing my things and getting ready to leave. My doorbell rang, and the housekeeper said a young woman called Caoimhe Kelly was asking to meet me. I received her in the Parlour, of which the door had to remain open when a woman called. As she walked in, I thought she was the loveliest creature on God's earth, and having sat down, told me I had caused her to leave the convent that morning! I didn't recognise her because she had been wearing a habit on the previous morning, and immediately I suggested we went out for a walk where we could speak unheard by a housekeeper.

'It's not a long story, Dee, but I'll cut it short anyway. She agreed to drive me to Ballymena – as a novice her car had remained her property until she took vows – and we talked and laughed together all the way. She's 26, and after graduating from Trinity College, Dublin, had taught English in a school before becoming a novice. – "testing her vocation" as it is known. I had mentioned John Donne in my sermon and that was enough for her to know she couldn't stay in the convent any longer, denied access to poetry and secular literature. By the time we arrived in Ballymena, we were in love with one another, but there was a problem. I was expected to be saying mass on the following morning for my new parishioners. I arranged for her to stay in a small hotel for a few nights, before she then found a flat, and I was able to get her work as a teaching assistant in the parish school. I called on her every evening and, in the meantime, my mother had come from Cork.

'All three of us hated Ballymena from the very start, and Ballymena felt much the same about us. This was all just before I received the information from your solicitor of my legacy. We have the means now, but not the how, to get away. And then you phoned on Saturday morning, instinctively I knew he time had come. I told Caoimhe that the time of passing from Mt Purgatory into Paradise was now, if you will excuse the Dante she has been trying to educate me with, and that I was coming here yesterday and didn't think I would be back.'

'It isn't just the North though, is it, Michael? Since you became a priest, the Catholic Church, its priests and nuns, have undergone transformation right across Ireland. I would imagine, but correct me if I'm wrong, that no one is likely to spit at you in Longford, but that some might do so metaphorically if they knew you were a priest? This country has undergone a revolution, and although I only see what I read in the papers, young people have grown up without the desperate longing for security that allowed people to become so tied up in a religion that contained terrible excesses, and in the astonishing referendums on marriage equality and abortion, have given voice to the new reality they take for granted. That must be difficult for you as a priest.

'However, it's only fair to we should, perhaps, stop our conversation now.'

'What? Why?'

'Because you've told all this to the wrong person, but you can decide whether we go on or not.

'My sister Polly was desperately unhappy, living with a horrible man who cared nothing for her or their two boys. She met a truly lovely man, her GP, with whom she discovered love, so I invited them to come and stay, to see if their love was more than a transitory affair. They departed from us full of joy, intent on making the changes necessary as soon as they got back. They were killed on the way. As a priest, I'm sure you know such things happen all the time. I fear I ruined the funeral by loudly telling the husband what a scumbag he was, just as the coffin was arriving. I couldn't bear the thought that he would receive undeserved sympathy, so I'm afraid I let rip before all the mourners and told them what Polly was intent on telling him had she lived.'

'Jeez, I wish I could have been there.'

'Well, I did feel sorry for the poor sod who had to take the funeral.'

'Don't worry about that. He'll add it to the fund of stories he'll pass on to his colleagues over a well-deserved beer. But what has this to do with a decision I might need to end our conversation?'

'Because life is too short not to act now. When I say *now*, that is exactly what I mean – today. If that is not possible for you, then you should go back to the misery of Ballymena. We'll keep in touch, so you know how Sam's getting on, but that's all.

'And will you let rip at me if I make the wrong decision?'

'I prefer an audience, and there's only you and me.'

Michael laughed.

'My gifts are mostly limited to hindsight,' he said. 'But for once, this time, I was granted foresight. When you called last Saturday morning, I had an immediate sense that what you call the "now" was here, that your visit was going to make it happen.'

'When you told Caoimhe, what did she say?'

'She said she was sure she was getting Covid and that the best thing would be for her to pack her bags and leave at once to stay with her mother in Ballyboran, a village close to Athlone.'

'Which is where?'

'About 25 miles from here.'

'Might her Covid be better, such as to allow her to join us here tonight for dinner? I honestly and truly want the best for you, Michael, and I'm convinced that returning to Ballymena ever again, is not that. I think a conversation with Caoimhe tonight is very important, but now I must see Nicola, and tell her all about my conversation with your mother which was devastating, and then, just in passing of course, mention we might be joined by someone at dinner tonight.'

'I mentioned Caoimhe is an English graduate. She had read a collection by Chloe before going into the convent and thinks her work superb. Even if she doesn't want to come and see you or me, Dee, just the name of Chloe will make her come.'

'Well, she has much the same effect on me! Or is that too naughty a thing to say? See you later.'

To his credit, he blushed.

34

We took Sam out in his buggy. The weather was mild, and we probably had an hour of daylight left in the afternoon. I began by going over everything Brighit had told me. Nicola was appalled.

'He was using you. You know that, Dee? Using you and lying. I know he's Sam's father, and Michael's, but he has been a traitor, a deceiver from top to bottom, who has betrayed you, his two sons and his own country and there is someone you need to talk about this to – Sharon Atwood, married to Colonel Kim Atwood of MI5, who will have known all this and more. You need to know much your best friend knew and said nothing, to find out whether she has betrayed you, too. For heaven's sake, it's just a few months since she and Kim stayed with us for the funeral, when they wanted me to be kept out of your life.'

'I will talk to Sharon. However, that's not the only thing I need to tell you!'

I recounted the parts of my talk with Brighit, in which she referred to living in Ballymena, and then pointedly suggested I should speak with Michael. I then told her what he had told me.

'O Bejaysus! Isn't that what they say here when they are stunned? What are you like? I let you go for a walk and now you're on the verge of getting a catholic priest to break his vows.'

'If so, it's with a former nun, an English graduate who's a fan of Chloe Thomas.'

'Why didn't you say so? Obviously, a woman of some discernment then, but do you know what? Your mother got it wrong. You're not so much Dorothea Brooke as Emma Woodhouse.'

'Who?'

'I'll tell you in bed tonight.'

Arriving back at the hotel, we made a cup of tea in our room, before I shared with her an idea that was forming in my mind.

'O Bejaysus!' she said again in response.

I hugged and kissed her.

Michael called to take Sam for his tea, providing me with a chance for a shower and a change into the clothes the hotel laundry had washed and ironed for me. I then made a call to meet Brighid in her room. Less than an hour later, she checked out of the hotel, took Michael's car and drove off into the November darkness.

Sam was back in time for a bath and a story from me, and I prepared him for bed before the hotel babysitter arrived. Nicola, in the meantime, was busy on the internet.

When we arrived at the bar, Michael was sitting hand in hand with an attractive young woman wearing a simple but lovely flowery dress. They stood to greet us.

'Hello Caoimhe,' I said, 'I'm so pleased to meet you, and this is my wife Nicola, or as you know her, Chloe Thomas, and we hope you're fully recovered from your terrible Covid bout that came on so suddenly.'

'And disappeared just as suddenly,' she replied with an enormous smile.

The Head Waiter came with the menus, and we ordered.

'What was it like leaving your community? I've never spoken to a former nun before,' I began.

'I was only a novice, not an actual nun who's taken vows, so it was straightforward, if not exactly warmly received. It happened when some priest or other deputising for the regular chaplain turned up to say mass and in his sermon mentioned the name of John Donne. In a flash, I knew I must leave and return to the literature I loved. I then decided before I returned to living with my mother that I should thank the priest and tell him, only to find that he was on his way out for having said what he had. He told me he was having to get the train to Belfast and on to Ballymena, so I offered to drive him. I believe you know the rest.'

'Not completely,' I said. 'To spare the blushes of his ancient stepmother, he didn't say whether you became lovers, you know in the sort of sense even I gather John Donne would have understood.'

Caoimhe smiled.

'Of course we did, though it took us a wee while to get the hang of it – well, at least five minutes!' she added, to which we laughed.

The waiter came to take us through to the restaurant. As we sat down to the first course, I said, 'Your mother has gone back to clear out your things, Michael, and will load up her own car with them and intends then staying overnight with a cousin across the border, awaiting further orders. When everyone gets up in the morning, they will find that Fr Michael has done, what in Lancashire, we call "a moonlit flit", and Miss Kelly won't be helping in school again.

'Your father took enormous risks when he and your mother came together, and although she never told you, he continued to provide her with monthly payments of €1,700 right up to June of this year.'

'Surely you're kidding me.'

'It was his version of the substitute for the real thing, the love Brighid wanted from him and which he could never give. Your mother's a wealthy woman thanks to the man I was married to.'

'But you must have known about this? That's a lot of money going out.'

'I knew nothing. I didn't know you or she even existed. Earlier today, however, I learned she knew everything about me, where I came from, what work I did, our marriage, my miscarriage and the eventual birth of Sam. They saw each other regularly, mostly in America, even after he and I were married. I was told of a conference in Philadelphia set up by your very clever mother on a webpage, so that when André showed me it proudly as one of the keynote speakers, I was taken in. Their deceit allowed them 10 days together somewhere in Michigan, and more fool me, I sat at home with a small baby thinking he was away doing important things. She also confirmed what I had been suspecting that he saw me primarily as his chosen carer for the autumn days of his life: housekeeper and mistress.'

'My mother regularly went to America in connection with her work. Is that when they met up?'

'I don't think her work ever required those visits. And to cap it all, he told her just two weeks before he died on one of their regular phone calls that he had been having chest pain. He said nothing to me.'

'Oh, Dee, this is a dreadful story.'

'There are things about André's involvement in the Troubles, not to mention whatever he did in the Middle East, about which we shall never know and I am glad, but I regret having to tell you, Michael, that my husband, your father and Sam's father, almost certainly betrayed his country, betrayed me and that he and your mother have betrayed you.'

Michael's eyes were full of tears as he reached for the hand of Caoimhe.

'I have known nothing about the man who fathered me because that was all he did until the money from his will arrived out of the blue. But what he did to you was far worse than any consequences there have been for me.'

'That's not necessarily the case. Brighid admitted this to me this morning, that her involvement in the Troubles was such that she had to get as far away from Dundalk as possible once the Good Friday Agreement was signed. That was why she's been living in Cork.'

'But she always told me that was because she took a job there.'

'Moving to Cork preceded the job. No doubt in her mind to protect you, she has lied to you, Michael, never telling you about your father, the details of his other family, including the fact that you have a brother, nor about the considerable amounts of his money she has received over the past 25 years.

'Nor has she said anything to you about her involvement with the IRA at the time of the Troubles, though from that she told me it was, and I'm sorry to put it this way, clearly not inconsiderable. There can be other plausible explanation why she did not receive a bullet in the back of her head from Nancy Carmichael, which was usually what happened with any catholic girl sexually involved with a member of the UK security forces.'

Michael looked completely shaken by my words.

'I told her before she left late this afternoon, she should now pay into your account at least an amount equal to what André's will provided – as a reparation. She did not demur.'

'You both, your mother, Sam and we now have available the means with which to shape and fashion our lives, and of those we love. I made her laugh when I told her my solicitor said I was now moderately wealthy, but what I didn't tell her is that is that I have riches beyond measure in Nicola, riches beyond measure, and I might hazard a guess that you would say the same.'

'Oh yes I would,' he replied, looking at Caoimhe, smiling.

'I think, Michael,' said Nicola, that you are going to need time, space and a lot of love to work all this through. Caoimhe will provide the love, I'm sure, but the Emma Woodhouse in my life has a plan for the time and space.'

'Emma who?' asked a puzzled Michael.

'I'll tell you later,' said Caoimhe, laughing.

'You do not want to be fodder for headlines such as "Priest runs away with ex-nun" with the hounds of the press on your tail, so I've booked you on a flight from Belfast to Exeter tomorrow at 3:30, and your mother will meet you at 2:00pm and bring to the airport what you will need until the rest can be sent on.

'Early breakfast for you, Caoimhe, I'm afraid. You two can lie cuddling each other as late as you want on Friday morning, but tomorrow it's an early start. An Irish citizen called Caoimhe Kelly is booked of a flight with us from Dublin to Bristol, where we left our car. We need to be on our way by 6:30am. You, Michael, should take Caoilhme's car to Belfast and your mum will return it to her mum's on Friday."

You've set this up like spies,' said Michael.

'It's being close to you and Sam that does it. Subterfuge is in the genes,' I said, 'and it's catching.'

We all laughed, and I noticed the hands of former nun and priest squeeze together tightly.

I could hardly believe the price I had to pay for the car parking, almost as much as the cost of the flight! In Dublin, Caoimhe had been quiet, but seemed much more relaxed once we had landed and set off towards the Southwest on the M5.

'How is your mum feeling about this?' I asked from the rear seat, with Nicola driving alongside Caoimhe.

'She's thrilled. She never wanted me to be a nun and the thought that I am getting married excites her beyond belief when I called after our dinner last night.'

'You're getting married? Congratulations. I didn't know.'

He asked me as soon as we got back to the room.

'My stepson is a delightful man. You deserve one another – you're overdue a reward for hard labour!'

She laughed.

'It wasn't hard labour, you know, and in many ways, I enjoyed the convent, especially the silences, but I am excited about once again being able to read and write what I like.'

'Who do you go home to?' Nicola asked.

'You mean?'

'When I go home, it's to be with Donne, Dante, and Dee, plus Olivia Doyle and Emily Cunningham.'

'Well, Nicola, it would appear you and I are going to have to agree to share the former Dean of St Paul's, and not just his love poetry, and I already love you, Dee and Sam, but I'll now want to go home to Michael too.'

'Not an unsatisfactory answer, I suppose, though you might just have added Chloe Thomas!'

'I would have said that, but I thought it might just be a bit too creepy to say so!'

We were home shortly after lunch and went to *The Green Table* to eat, before Nicola and I left Caoimhe in charge of Sam to do a big shop in Totnes. Later Caoimhe and Nicola drove to the airport to collect Michael, whilst I made their beds and prepared "ready meals" from the freezer. Shame on me! By nine o'clock, we were all exhausted and in bed.

To his great disappointment, on his first morning back, Sam discovered that in his absence in the nursery Nativity Tableau (presumably a play was too much for tiny people), he had been cast as a sheep, though, to my slight alarm, he protested he wanted to be Mary! All the same, he was delighted to be back with his friends. Caoimhe, an early riser, had left Michael asleep, and came with me to take Sam.

'It's really strange,' she said on our way back, 'marrying Michael will make me Sam's sister-in-law. Is he ready for such a responsibility?'

'I shouldn't worry about that. As you heard when we took him in, he wanted to be the Virgin Mary!'

'Ah, well, not a role I would want myself and besides, it's no longer an appropriate role for me!'

We both laughed.

'The Catholic Church in Totnes operates as part of three parishes with a polish priest. I can find details for you about mass times if you like.'

'Thanks, Dee, now we are cohabiting, he and I are automatically excluded from receiving Holy Communion, and canonically we won't be allowed marriage in a Catholic Church because he has not been laicised.'

'Is that a bit like circumcision?'

'Too late if it is,' said Caoimhe with a laugh.

'I'm profoundly shocked, and you an ex-novice!'

'Oh, I'm still very much of a novice, but learning's proving great fun!'

We laughed most of the way back.

By the time Nicola emerged from the study and Michael from his bed, we sat together over coffee and tea in our sitting room.

'My mother texted me to say she's safely back in Cork. She had never put her house on the market, assuming she would be back sometime soon.'

'Good,' I said. 'However, the primary concern here is, "Where do we go from here?". Last Friday, you were both working, one a teaching assistant and the other a parish priest, and today you've woken up in South Devon. Soon, if not already, Michael's absence will have been informed to his bishop and I imagine the school will put two and two together and get the right answer. Now we must put our own two and two together and consider what happens next.'

'I think the answer is that nothing should happen next,' said Nicola. 'When I read a new poet, I need to read and re-read, to feel the heart of the one who has written. I think of every poem I read as written just for me to read. You need to do that, to do nothing but learn how to live and to love one another, and unless you cannot abide us, we would welcome you living with us as long as you need to and certainly at least until Christmas and preferably beyond. There will be seasonal work available on the Estate if you're interested and that will be a good way to meet people other than us. But not too much busyness. Only then, when you've read and re-read each other's hearts, should you make plans.'

'Nicola's right, though there are some immediate practicalities. You will need to register with a doctor, and I imagine you will want a car. And that leads me to the question of money. For easy access, consider opening a bank account here. If she's true to her word to me and doubles the amount from André, it would still only be a small proportion of what she received from him in the past five years and withheld from you. With that, you can make proper choices. Once you make them, you will be able to buy somewhere to live.'

'Why are doing this for us, Dee?' asked Michael.

'For three reasons. First, you are Sam's brother, and we are in every way members of one family. The second is that you and I, Michael, are victims of André Beeson and, to a lesser extent, Brighid Donahue. The third is that within a short time I've realised how much I love you two and long for your happiness. If I can help in that, I will have done what I can to help you recover from the things done to you, and I hope that might also help ameliorate the great pain with which I have returned. My sister is newly dead, my sister-in-law is in hell, and I have learned terrible things about the six years I spent being made a fool of before I met Nicola, and not just by André, but by some I thought were friends. That's proving tough to live with.

'If I have a healer, it is love's constancy, which I derive from Nicola, and the time I spend each day with my wonderful son, and now with two of the loveliest people it is our privilege to know.'

Caoimhe had tears running down her face.

'A medieval mystic said God may be caught by love but by thought never. I would change it to "by religion never", but Dorothea and Nicola, you have it in abundance and thank you for sharing it with us. We will strive to discover a love like yours and be there for you.'

We sat together in silence for a little while.

'And,' I said, 'alongside all this talk of love, there is a child to be collected and a dishwasher to be loaded. That's another thing I've been learning. Things happen and then there is the day after.'

35

After lunch, as Nicola and Caoimhe departed to collect Sam, I suggested Michael and I go out for a walk.

'How was your time at the airport yesterday?'

'I asked my mother if she could tell me more about any part she had in the Troubles, whether by herself or with André, but she said Belfast was no place to have such a conversation, and her chief longing once I had departed was to return to the relative safety south of the border. That didn't exactly increase my sense that she has nothing to hide.'

'She has a great deal to hide. Can you live without knowing it? You've done so until André's money came, but now something has emerged. A republican splinter group once came to Devon to kill Nancy Carmichael, so no one is ever likely to be wholly safe from idiots. I do not know if the name of Donahue will continue to be a potential source of danger to you, but you should contemplate the possibility of changing your surname. I am no longer Lady Beeson, but plain Mrs Fairchild and your brother is Sam Fairchild, or will be so legally soon.'

'You will never be plain, Dee.'

'What a smooth-talker you are, and for that you can buy me a coffee and cake ahead. In the meantime, Michael, I am not your bishop. You and Caoimhe are completely free to do whatever you wish and go anywhere, including leaving here, though I very much hope you won't. In the meantime, until you get your money sorted, I will give you what you need so you're free to act.'

'Caoimhe and I have been overwhelmed by your love and kindness. It's true we both need to do some clothes shopping and

I will begin opening an account here online with which I will need some help from Nicola, but otherwise what we most need is stability. I expect you've already realised that in just about every way that matters, Caoimhe is much older and wiser than me.'

'I know she loves you, and that's all that matters, but remember that in just about every way that matters, all women are older and wiser than men. You're going to be living with three of us for now, so get used to it!'

'Don't worry, my brother and I are up to the task.'

On Saturday morning, Michael and Caoimhe caught the number 7 bus from Totnes into Exeter. I warned them it would be a highly circuitous route round South Devon, but they seemed happy to sightsee.

Whilst I was out delivering them to the bus stop, Abi had called Nicola, but without news of Helen. As I knew in advance, Nicola informed Abi that she was ready to begin work with her. I knew she was feeling guilty about being a "kept woman", as she said jokingly, but I also knew that the time had come for her to do more than simply being at home, and I was feeling something of the same itch myself, despite the last couple of weeks' feverish activity, after which I needed a time to recover.

We had taken Sam to a birthday party after lunch, and I now made the call I wasn't exactly looking forward to.

'Hello, Sharon, it's Dee.'

'Hello. We think we may have found somewhere to live in Gloucestershire. We went to see it on Monday and we've put in an offer the Estate Agent thinks is likely to be accepted later today, so we're quite delighted. And how is life in Dartington and, more especially, how was your sister's funeral in Blackburn?'

When I told her how I had turned it into a disaster, albeit in Polly's name, she bestowed her approval!

'After a few days with a close friend of Nicola's and her husband, we went to Ireland.'

'Oh!'

'I felt it was right that Sam should meet his brother Michael,

and we also met his mother Brighid Donahue, with whom André
had a liaison back in the bad old days of the Troubles. I could not
have done this without the information you gave me, but as I was
to discover, your information led to considerably more than I had
expected, a great deal more.'

I told her everything I had discovered, other than mentioning
that Michael Donahue was now living here with us.

There was silence for at least thirty seconds, but I could hear
her breathing hard.

'I'll call you back,' she said and put her phone down.

Twenty minutes passed before my phone rang.

'Kim warned me before I passed on the little I did, that it might
be dangerous to do so, that you would work at it as a terrier. I'm
as shocked as you to learn what you have told me, truly shocked,
Dee. I knew nothing of André's curious arrangements with his
other family and the considerable amounts of money he was
obviously paying Brighid Donahue each month, perhaps as a sort
of insurance. Nor did I know anything about his clandestine
activities in Northern Ireland, but whatever they were, I urge you
to make no further effort to find out. Leave it be, not least,
because you might get into serious trouble. It is double plus
double O B: Out Of Bounds, and honestly, if I had known your
intentions to visit I would have stopped you going, taking
enormous risks, not just with your own safety but of Sam's and
Nicola's too.'

'In which case, I should mention that we have not returned
from Ireland empty-handed. Michael Donahue has left the
priesthood and he and his fiancée are now living with us. He flew
out of Belfast on Thursday afternoon, and we collected him at
the airport here.'

'What? Please, for mercy's sake, tell me you are kidding.'

'Brighid had told him nothing about her past and nothing about
André. However, yesterday afternoon he set about trying to open
a bank account here in the UK for which he will require certain
documents to be sent from his present bank in Dublin, and he
was redirected to a particular government department. He has his
birth certificate with him, but an official let slip that there was an

anomaly, that when Brighid left Dundalk after the Good Friday Agreement, a second birth certificate for Michael had been issued in the name of Donahue, and that the original named his mother as Bernadette Murphy, a name which he and I both realise will be highly significant to MI5 and the Irish government.'

'Holy shit, Dee, what have you done?'

'What I have done, Sharon, is simply pass on the baton you handed me. Michael is a citizen of the Irish Republic and not covered by the terms of the UK Official Secrets Act. We should not be having this conversation any more than you should have passed on to me the limited information you did. It has come as a shocking revelation to him with the realisation that his mother's name ties her more closely than he had realised to involvement with the IRA and therefore a strong link to whatever André was doing there, and I dread to think what might have befallen his mother in Ballymena had this ever emerged, but at least she is now safely back in the Republic.'

The phone had been passed over and the speakerphone obviously operating.

'Dee, this is Kim. I no longer work for the security service as you know, and no longer have access to any files relating to André's time in Belfast nor anything relating to his subsequent activities in the Middle East. The service operates according to sections, of which Northern Ireland is one – you can read that in any book about the work of MI5. I was never part of that section and as deputy director, my knowledge of the activities of each section was limited on a "need to know" basis. I did not need to know about things back then.'

'You're being disingenuous, Colonel Atwood. At the time of the attack on Nancy Carmichael, you were heavily involved, and there is simply no way that, as deputy director of MI5, you were unaware of the past and present activities of your senior interrogator. Doing so must have been a key aspect of your responsibilities. I can understand that you believed you could not reveal these things, but you can't convince me of your ignorance, Kim, and the one who has paid the heaviest price for your alleged confidentiality is me.'

'The name you have mentioned is in the public domain,' she responded, 'as it has been for over 25 years. An alternative identity is a concern only for the Irish government under the terms of the Belfast Agreement. I passed on information that I thought would be helpful to a friend, though that would be no defence should it come to court. But in telling you, I never imagined you might go to Ireland and place yourself at any kind of risk, but as Sharon said earlier, I should have known better that you would not let it lie.'

'You mean you were perfectly happy for me to marry a man with another family to which he was giving away a fortune, and ultimately bringing about an involvement with Nancy Carmichael which caused me to miscarry twins and almost die. I can't believe you've just said that.'

'The information to which you now have access is covered by the terms of the UK Official Secrets Act, but as you pointed out, it does not cover Michael Donahue. Please, Dee, be careful. My judgement is that you are not especially at risk, but if there is no noise, no one can hear it.'

'Kim, I feel extremely let down by you and Sharon because no matter what you may deny, I cannot trust the word of either of you to tell me the truth again. What I have learned about André has been devastating, and it might have been very different had those I thought loved me prevented me from being so badly betrayed by the man I married. In fact, betrayal is the word, isn't it, Kim?'

I ended the call.

I was feeling angry and very hurt. Kim was not being disingenuous, as I had said, – she had lied with her "If there is no noise, no one can hear it" – but the initial noise was hers. In effect, she had put into my hand an explosive device and was now blaming me for the resulting explosion. What on earth did she think I would do with this information, not least, because she knew where it would lead if I explored further?

Nicola was with me as I made the call, but had not heard the content, and I now explained to her all that first Sharon, and then

Kim, had said to me by way of an explanation of her conduct. It remained a fact, however, that Kim was herself now in breach of the Official Secrets Act, of which, until recently, she had been the guardian, much more seriously than I might have done, and the consequences therefore much further reaching.

'Wow,' said Nicola, 'no wonder they were in something of a panic, and urging you to do nothing further, because this could really have serious consequences for Kim, and for Sharon too, and I suppose also technically, for you and me.'

'I don't suppose you or I would want to take this any further, but I don't know if that is the same for Michael. I'm certain he wouldn't want to attract attention as his wretched mother's son, but how determined do you think he might be to explore further and find out what it was she did?'

'This all goes back to André and whatever it was he was doing in Dundalk in the Troubles. Has it occurred to you, Dee, that just possibly Brighid or Bernadette, as we must assume she was then, was an IRA setup, what is now known as a honey trap, to gain a hold over him? That would account for them allowing it to happen without the typically fatal consequences for her.

'On the other hand, if I might lapse into the words of our friend Mr Eliot: "All this was a long time ago". Shouldn't we be encouraging Michael to think forwards rather than back as Biighid maintained?'

'Oh my darling, you've taught me too well. That was from "The Journey of the Magi", yes?'

'Yes.'

'Well. Isn't the poem about an event long ago but very much alive to the speaker's present concerns? That could almost be a definition of the Troubles.'

My phone sounded again. It was Caoimhe to say that their bus would be back in Totnes at 16:07.

'I've got to pick Sam up from his party about then, so I'll be there,' I said to her. 'I hope you've had a good shopping trip.'

'We got everything we wanted in M&S including lunch. The good news is that my bank card worked, and maybe Michael's existing card would have done, but he chose not to try it, fearing it might be traced.'

'Ok, enjoy the scenery.'

Sam was over the moon that his brother collected him from the party and told everyone the identity of this handsome young man with the Irish accent. Siblings were normally a handful of years apart, so mothers collecting children were taken aback.

'It's true,' Michael told them. 'Sam is my brother, but don't worry how it's come to be. Dee's my stepmother, not my birth mother, given that she's only three years older than me. Sure, you know how these things are.'

As I listened from the car, it struck me that his accent could have charmed half the mothers present into bed with him! With the car window open, Caoimhe saw, heard and smiled.

'He's such a flirt,' she said to me. 'I saw it in the parish often enough and consider, if you will, the effect it had on me, but as a priest, it was endearing but safe. He'll need to learn a different way now.'

'And how do you think he's coping with what he's learned of his mother's other identity?'

'He's said little and I haven't pressed him. It is only a week since you first made contact and so much has happened and at such a pace that I think he's going to need a fair amount of time to process everything that's happening inside him, including me. I really hope we shall not become any kind of burden to Nicola and you, but he needs the safety and security of your nest.'

'We're hoping you will stay as you need to. Nicola's starting her new part-time work on Monday, so I will welcome your company. But hasn't it also been turmoil for you?'

'Well, yes, it has, but I'm way stronger than Michael.'

'Yes, I know.'

My sons now joined us in the car, and we returned home.

Rod Hacking

36

On Sunday, with due warning, we introduced Michael and Caoimhe to the delights of Sunday lunch in Ashburton. Sam was delighted to meet up again with Maisie, and Mark had also brought visitors: Amelia and three-year-old Danny, her son. Fiona was more than up to catering for a larger gathering than normal, and Amelia and Danny had already been on the previous Sunday when we were away, so it was only Caoimhe and Michael who were new to Nicola's mum and dad.

'Are you over here on holiday?' asked Mark innocently, and at once Michael looked at me.

'No,' I answered for him, 'and trust me, Michael can usually talk without need for help from me, but the answer to that question is slightly complicated. Caoimhe and Michael are living with us and the reason for that is that I have recently discovered that Michael is the son I didn't know I had.'

'What on earth do you mean?' Mark asked incredulously.

'What I mean is that Michael is my stepson, my former husband's son, whom I met for the first time on Tuesday, Sam's big brother and, of course, your sister's stepson-in-law. I would have thought that was not too difficult to grasp! So where does a son belong but with his mother, even when she is only three years older?'

'I'm just wondering whether I'm inhabiting a bizarre dream world.'

'Oh no,' said Michael. 'It means that you're my uncle Mark!'

We all laughed.

'I'm glad we've got that cleared up,' said Tom, 'wine for

232

everyone, provided his mummy will allow Michael to have some?'

We all laughed again as we moved to the extended dining table for roast beef and perfectly risen Yorkshire puddings.

There was no mention of Helen. Mark, Maisie and Angus were now living in Honiton with Amelia and Danny, and Mark said he had put his own house up for sale, though the children were still spending time with Helen's mother in Newton Abbot, though less than before. Amelia had already changed schools.

'Will you be having more children, Dee?' asked Mark, somewhat facetiously, 'or are you going to stick at two?'

'Well, you may laugh, Mark, but it's not impossible, and even likely. IVF for same-sex couples is now well established. We have no immediate plans given everything else in our life, but we're still young enough.'

Once we were home, Michael said, 'IVF has transformed lives and given genuine hope to so many couples, though in Ireland it's only in the past year that it's been state-funded. I'm not sure what the situation is for same-sex couples though; as a nation we're still playing catch-up with the rest of Europe.'

'And if someone had come to you as their parish priest asking your views, what would you have said?' I asked.

'From the standpoint of moral theology, I would have summoned up all my extensive knowledge and said nothing, just listened and recognised pain, before encouraging them to follow their hearts.'

'And would that be the same for a same-sex couple?' asked Nicola.

'I'm certain a gay or lesbian couple would not be seeking advice from a catholic priest! But I very much hope that had there been such a couple, I would have said to them, as I do to you: "Go for it!", and rejoice with them. If ever you decide to go forward, I would hope for another brother. Three of us could make up the front row of a scrum.'

'That reminds me,' I said, 'do you two need to do something about contraception? I'm not sure I want to be a granny just yet!'

'I'll make an appointment tomorrow. I've already found a women's clinic on Wednesday in Totnes' said Caoimhe. 'My period's just started in any case.'

'Have you some towels?'

'Yes, I bought some on Saturday in Exeter.'

'Do you know,' said Michael, 'I have never taken part in a conversation like this before?'

'Well now,' said Nicola, 'there's a surprise! A perfectly good reason for only those with sisters allowed to be catholic priests, and when I say sisters, I don't mean nuns, with whom your track record is not so hot, if I may say so.'

'I disagree,' said Caoimhe. 'His track record with one former novice is remarkably hot!'

Michael laughed.

'I am on the biggest learning curve of my life and enjoying every moment!'

'Have you spoken to your mother since leaving?'

'Not yet, but I checked online before lunch and a there's been payment into my account of €200,000 from an American Bank.'

'That's good news, Michael. It's a sort of compensation and long overdue, albeit wholly inadequate.'

'Yes, but I owe receiving it to you, Dee. You made this happen.'

'All I want for you, Michael, are the means of making choices so you and Caoimhe can make the life you wish.'

On Monday morning, Michael announced he would like to visit André's grave in the churchyard at St Mary's.

'It's unmarked as yet, other than with a small wooden cross marked AB. Go to the north side of the church and the newest graves are along on the left.'

'I'd like to do it alone.'

'Of course,' said Caoimhe. 'I'll read or do something or other on my laptop, but it's colder out there today, so wrap up warmly.'

'That's the first would-be-wifely thing you've said to me,' he replied with a smile.

'The first of many, I hope.'

'As long as "warmly" is added, that's fine,' I added to the proceedings. 'Omit it, and it changes things completely.'

Nicola had just come into the room.

'Wrap up, Dee!' she said, and we all laughed.

He was away for well over an hour.

'Did you find the grave?' I asked.

'Oh, I saw it, but truly it meant nothing to me. I never knew the man beneath the soil.'

'Nor, it seems, did I?' I said.

37

Shortly after lunch, a police car pulled up outside. It was Abi who had come to see Nicola on what was in theory at least her first day of work. She was carrying, ominously to my mind, three or four blue files.

'Abi, come and meet our new residents, Michael and Caoimhe,' said Nicola. 'Michael is Dee's other son, well stepson, to spare your brain having to work overtime to encompass apparent impossibilities.'

They shook hands.

'I work in the police family liaison and support service, so, to be honest, I have long since ceased being surprised by anything any family can throw at me in terms of how they are related.'

'I gather you are Nicola's new boss,' said Michael.

'More of a non-boss boss if that doesn't sound too complicated. We shall work closely together, but she will not be answerable to me nor to the police service, but to the courts who will be paying her. Nicola will accompany me on all my involvements with families and victims of domestics to ensure I do not cross any lines which may encroach on subsequent legal proceedings.'

'Working together and knowing each other well must make that be difficult.'

'I don't think so. Nicola's a real professional and the main idea of her work is to protect me rather than fault-finding. It's because I know her so well that I can rely on her to tell the truth without favour.'

'We must get to work then, non-boss boss,' said Nicola with a grin. 'A likely description! I'll believe that when I see it!'

With Sam resting and Nicola working with Abi, Caoimhe suggested she and I go for a walk, leaving Michael to the inevitable games with his brother when he woke up. It was a colder November day than we had been used to, so we wrapped up well and headed towards cups of tea and toasted teacakes in *The Green Table*.

'For me, one of the great attractions of life in community was order, the daily round, everything at the right time and in the right place,' said Caoimhe as we walked. 'Life as a student was the exact opposite, and then we were all having to come to terms with the new order in Irish society. The Catholic Church had been overthrown by a combination of the ballot box and moral failures on a massive scale. So, I took refuge and for a year I could live with order, and that part of me which craved it found a relief from the surrounding chaos, but I can now see that the elements of my departure were already present in my annoyance with things that were simply petty. When Michael turned up, I might almost say as an angel sent from above, I was ready and waiting, ready and wanting to read what I chose and loved.

'I certainly had not anticipated falling in love on day one of my newfound freedom, and there seemed no chance of anything coming from my visit to the Presbytery – he was a celibate catholic priest, after all. You and I laughed when we saw him flirting, but that's a wonderful way of keeping people at arm's length. He never flirted with me. As I drove him into the enemy's country, the North of Ireland, as we both thought of it, I wanted to stay with him and he wanted me to stay, albeit in a hotel until I found a tiny flat, and it was there I joyfully surrendered my virginity to a catholic priest and with a great deal of laughter. I remember as we made love, he stopped, looked at me and said we couldn't use contraception as it wasn't allowed! We laughed so much I do not know how we could go on. What has happened since simply awaited your arrival, as I had awaited Michael's in the convent.

'We loathed being up there in the North, and when Brighid came, that was strengthened by her own long-standing hatred of Protestants and the UK defending them at all costs. She's

Michael's mother, but there was something about her hate that me feel uneasy, though I said nothing to Michael, and I always felt far from at peace when I was with her, though she has never been less than kind to me.

'However, Dee, the reason I wanted to come out with you this afternoon is that whilst Michael was out this morning, using my old university library card which I discovered was still active, I rooted about and discovered that his mother had been active in the IRA very close to the top, and that her work was recruiting from convents and so-called "care homes" those girls and young women who had been outcasts in their own communities for falling pregnant, to serve as whores seeking information in enemy beds, but also for IRA men to use and dispose of as they saw fit. To my mind, that makes her complicit with the worst crimes done in the name of the civil war. We knew already knew her Bernadette Murphy, but in Republican circles she was called "Bernadeath Murphy", and that young women feared hearing it.'

'Following my long conversation with Brighid,' I said, 'I told Nicola that I thought she hadn't told me the whole truth about her activities, and you have filled in the missing parts. Have you told this to Michael?'

'No, or at least not yet.'

'I understand that, but he needs to know. The thing is, my love, he will feel even more cut off from everything: his appalling parents who have betrayed him and his God, in whom he placed so much hope, if not actual faith. All of which means, Caoimhe, that upon you lies the burden of his soul, if I might be excused my unlikely choice of language.'

'No, you're right, it's exactly that, and nothing less.' She smiled. 'Nicola and I might agree I have to be his Beatrice.'

'I know little, but my beloved has introduced me to enough Dante to know who she was, and yes, that's your task, but according to Nicola and who am I to question it, Beatrice could be there with the poet, but he had to do the work. Is that right?'

'I think Nicola would warn us against taking any analogy too far, but it will have to be something like that, though it's possible Michael may need professional assistance if he is to save his soul. He is badly damaged and needs careful healing.'

'But more than anything, and I'm not sure whether he needs counselling, he needs to be loved and held, literally by you and metaphorically by me.'

'But, Dee, for the love of everything that's good, haven't you just described your own needs? Madness, death, and betrayal more rightly belong in a play by Shakespeare, not the afflictions of such a wonderful and beautiful woman as you are enduring.'

There, in the middle of the road, we held one another and cried, and it being November we were spared being hit by a car driven by tourists.

'When I worked in *Betty's*,' I told Caoimhe as our food and drink were placed before us, 'I always believed that an afternoon cup of tea and toasted teacake could work wonders, and as we are in need of a few of those, let's test out my theory.'

'And from your observations, how do you think they do things here at the café?'

'They're pretty good. Our staff were older and mostly stayed with us, whereas here the turnover is considerable, mostly young people wanting temporary employment and there is no real training offered. They collect from the pass and deliver – politely, of course, but it's not the same. The manager, Esmé, knows where I worked and I often tease her, but she knows I approve because we come back so often.'

'You and Nicola are both amazing cooks, so do you not fancy getting back into catering? You would be snapped up at once, I'm sure.'

'Nicola's mum runs the Ashburton Catering School and has offered me work there if I want it, but I'm not sure I fancy working with students. Fiona has the infinite patience with them I don't think I could match, but Sam has to be my priority now Nicola is going to pick up some part-time work. From a financial standpoint, I wouldn't need to work again if that is what I wanted, but what I'm really looking for is something else.'

'And that is?'

'I've no idea!'

'Then you are truly in an enviable position – just like me!'

The wind had risen a little whilst we ate and drank and on our return to we enjoyed the falling leaves, almost like a heavy brown snowstorm. We avoided the intensity of our earlier conversation and as the light was falling as fast as the leaves, we increased our speed.

I'm feeling a little guilty for having left Michael with Sam for so long.'

'Well, make sure you're just a *little* guilty and no more. Michael loves Sam so much.'

'From a catholic, the idea of being a "little guilty" is highly amusing.'

'People always get confession wrong. It's actually a form of therapy in which people may own up to the darker side of their being and find acceptance – another form of the talking cure, a psychotherapist might perform and charge the earth for it. It's kept many a catholic sane.'

'But hasn't it also offered a cheap way of enabling people to go on doing the same things over and over?'

'It was never perfect,' said Caoimhe with a huge laugh in which I joined as we arrived home. 'But nothing is, and for me, that's always been a huge consolation. G K Chesterton said that original sin was the one doctrine that didn't require faith to believe. I agree and Dee, so do you.'

I laughed.

'Oh, my darling,' I said to her, 'I only hope Michael can keep pace with you,' and I kissed her on her lips.

38

By the time we had returned, Abi had gone, and I joined Nicola in the study where I could see her avoiding looking at the files Abi had brought by playing a game with Sam.

'How was Abi?'

'Ok. However, I'm uneasy about the prospect of reverting to being a police officer again.'

'I thought it was meant to be different, being there to observe to protect fair play.'

'And yes, it is, but I fear it may become a half-way house, a stepping stone, and I don't want that to be the case.'

'Is it too late to refuse?'

'No, because I am only paid for each visit and report I write, and obviously I haven't done one yet, but neither do I want to miss the chance to do something I can see as serving a purpose, nor miss the chance of working with Abi. But how was your walk with Caoimhe?'

'Intense, centred above all on her worries about Michael, a concern I share especially in the light of she has found out this morning and needs urgently to share with Michael.'

'Who's cooking, by the way?' she suddenly said.

I couldn't stop myself laughing.

'That's your response?' I asked.

'Of course not, but there is a world of difference between something important and something urgent. The important can wait, the cooking is urgent!'

'In which case, my beloved interpreter of the English language, it's you

It was never going to be possible to withhold from Michael know what Caoimhe and I now knew about his mother's involvements in the Troubles, and entirely inappropriate to do so. So once Sam was in bed, the four of us sat together and allowed Caoimhe to inform Michael what she had found out about Bernadette, his mother, often known as Bernadeath Murphy.

To his eternal credit Michael did not interrupt his fiancée once but listened intently throughout, occasionally looking to me, almost for confirmation that what he was hearing was true. Caoimhe was especially clear about the fact that she had found this out simply because it was there in the university's own domain to which she had continued to have access long after she had left.

'Are these documents and files still accessible?'

'I haven't looked again since this morning but I would imagine so, unless my stirring of the pot has been noticed and prompted a security service on this or the other side of the sea to close it down.'

'When did you find it?'

'This morning and I told Dee about it when we went out for a walk. I didn't want to talk about it in front of Sam and I wanted to find out what, if anything Dee already knew."

'I did know a little because of your mother had told me when we were in Longford,' I said, 'so it didn't come as a total shock, and if anyone held Caoimhe back from telling you immediately, it was me.'

'I suppose I'm gratified that she didn't kill anyone, at least not directly, but as I have been part of the institution that took young pregnant girls away from their families, I recognise the terrible part played by the church in this, yet again. Oh, those poor girls. However have they recovered? And in that sense, all I have experienced is to learn about something that happened even before I was born and soon after. The effect on them is far greater than on me. War is a terrible thing, and all sorts of atrocities take place other than to take life. At least my mother did not do what Nancy Carmichael did, but I guess we cannot know that. Whether there are those who might still want revenge on her I cannot say. Do you think, Dee, she felt any sort of remorse?'

'I didn't detect any, but you and I were not taking part in their war, and who knows how any of us might behave when pressed and motivated by those who fought and killed, destroying lives in one way or another. It's not my place to offer some kind of reconciliation and I think the word forgiveness would be meaningless in such a context, as I was not affected other than sharing here and now the profound pain you must feel. I have my own profound pain visited upon me not by her but by the man who betrayed us both and made far worse by the knowledge that those who have claimed friendship over the years have colluded with that, hiding behind a spurious justification.'

'Indeed, you have. I know it's hilarious in one sense, but I already think of the three years that separate us having expanded considerably to encompass my feeling that you have already been much more of a mother to me than she ever managed to be. You even manage to be more concerned for me than is warranted when what you have been enduring is so very much worse. It's a real wonder that Nicola came into your life when she did, as she did.'

'And I think it will prove to be so that Caoimhe came into yours at the right time.'

'That's odd,' said Michael. 'What do you mean by "will prove to be"? Are you implying she's not that now?'

'No. It seems to me you are made for each other, but Michael, both you and I are engaged on journeys of discovery in dark places that some claim, as your mother has, believe are over and done with, part of a past best forgotten. Mine are more obviously immediate, but your own journey encompassing the betrayal of your parents and your turn to priesthood, are no less active within you. It's why I want you to remain here for as long as you can bear us, because I would like to think that here can be the place of safety and security, and above all truth, of which you were deprived. Thanks to your almost non-existent father, my former so-called husband, who in effect was bigamous, we live in large house which can hold us all.

'I may be completely mistaken, but I am learning day by day that to enable me to face the demons that have been unleashed in my life, I need to be held by Nicola, and in a safe enough place. You are my son and I care for you so much, love you in fact, that I want you also to be safe and held.'

'To face my demons, you mean?'

'Well, I can't think you could improve on being held by that beautiful young woman you saved for literature and love.'

For the first time Nicola spoke.

'We had a thought in the night, Caoimhe. We are missing someone who should be able to come and share in your joy – your mum. Might you be able to go back and bring her for Christmas with us.'

Caoimhe burst into tears and Nicola who was sitting with her on the sofa drew her close and held her as she wept. Eventually she managed to speak haltingly through her tears.

'Why, when you're facing so much, do you seek to care for us? I don't understand it.'

'I think that you and me, Caoimhe, have something in common Michael and Dee do not, and that is that we were born and grew up in the certainty of knowing how much we were loved. I overheard you saying to Michael in the kitchen (and I genuinely overheard and wasn't listening if you take my meaning) that you were missing your mum, and so are we. We would love to have her here with us if she would come.'

'It would be splendiferous. I can't add to that!'

We laughed with her and as I looked at Nicola still holding Caoimhe close, and for a moment I wished I was as beautiful as this young woman, I smiled to myself.

As we lay in bed, I confessed my sinful thought about Caoimhe's beauty.

'I'm afraid Fr Donahue isn't allowed any longer to give you absolution, but if you would allow me to shower you everywhere with kisses and more, would that do instead?'

'More?' I said, feigning astonishment. 'I might moan but I

promise not to complain!'

39

Sam was at nursery, I had done my poetry walk and Nicola had finished writing, and and we were about to gather for coffee when we heard a car arrive. It was Chief Inspector Ro Lehmann.

'Ro,' I said, as I answered the door and let her in, 'it's good to see you, or at I hope it is.'

I introduced her to Caoimhe and Michael, who brought in coffee for us. I asked a risky question.

'You worked alongside André closely for a time in the security services. You may well answer you are bound by the Official Secrets Act, but Ro I hope you will give us an honest reply. Did you know he had a son and a partner with whom he took American holidays in Ireland? Did he confess all to your interrogations which is what you did together? Well, Michael is his elder son.'

Caoimhe realised the tone of my words suggested she take Sam out of the room, for which I was grateful.

'Yes, I know you are André's son, Michael, and the resemblance is remarkable, but I only found out this information this morning when the Chief Constable summoned me to her office.'

'Have you come to tell me I'm *persona non grata* and to be deported back to Ireland?'

'Not at all. As far as the UK government is concerned, you're more than welcome, and as the son of a British citizen you are entitles to dual citizenship. Choosing to be here with Dee and Nicola shows good taste. They are two of my favourite people, though your father was also very special to me because we worked together as we did. He was generous and kind, even to those we had to regard as the enemy brought to us for questioning. I never knew him to lose patience with anyone, however appalling nor ever heard him raise his voice or get angry.'

'Thank you for telling me that,' said Michael, 'but I can't think a senior police officer was summoned by the Chief Constable and ordered just to come and say nice things.'

'Alas, no, but I'm glad to have been able to do so. I have been sent to say things, but not to you, but to Dee and Nicola.'

'Should I leave?' asked Michael.

'No, please stay,' I said. 'I think you ought to hear what the Chief Inspector says in her role as the mouthpiece of MI5, which I assume, Ro, is why the Chief Constable has sent you, because I'm pretty sure it concerns you, Michael, indirectly. Isn't that right, Ro?'

She smiled.

'Your father, Michael, was a clever man, but he told me once that he thought he might have met his match when he married Dee.'

'I don't think you needed to tell me that, Chief Inspector,' said Michael, looking at me.

'There has been a breach of security in a section of the security service pertaining to Northern Ireland. This was made by a former member of the service who self-reported. I gather it was a minor breach passed on to a spouse, but inevitably even a minor breach can snowball, and this information was passed on to you, Dee, and led to the uncovering of protected material and persons involved in the Troubles.

'The Chief Constable acting under direct instruction requires a reminder be given that possessing that original information binds you to the Official Secrets Act which you signed when you were worked for the service, and it is the same for you, Nicola, as a former police officer. You passed it on to citizens of a foreign country, which is a serious offence against the Act, and you may be liable to prosecution.'

'I see,' I said. 'I guess saying all that will have taken a lot of effort. Would you like a piece of cake made with my fair hands to go with your coffee?'

'Oh God, yes please.'

Michael was looking utterly bewildered.

'I don't understand what's going on. You've just accused Dee and Nicola in effect of being spies facing potential arrest, and now you're having a piece of cake with them. What am I not getting?'

'Oh, come on, Michael,' said Ro. 'You have been a catholic priest and grounded in philosophy. Surely your moral theology encompassed the notion of "First Order: Principle; Second Order: Rule"? I would have thought that was essential to all your functioning as a priest.'

'Now, I'm lost,' said Nicola.

Michael laughed.

'Don't be. What the Chief Inspector has pointed out is something utterly basic to all moral philosophy and theology. First, you have a Principle, something utterly basic and unchanging, a fundamental law. Then you have Second, the Rule, whereby you function within all the chances and changes of this law. And you're quite right, all priests operate that all the time, but so I imagine must every police officer. The law is an absolute, but for sensible reasons, you do not arrest everyone for every breach.'

'Exactly. So I've done justice to the first order principle of the Official Secrets Act – now we have cake!'

'It's called casuistry,' added Michael, as I handed him a piece of chocolate cake, 'that part of Ethics which resolves cases of conscience, applying the principles of religion and morality to particular instances in which circumstances may need to amend them or if there might be a conflict of duties.'

'Which even the Chief Constable understands is almost certainly the case, allowing me to eat cake with these wicked people.'

Sam and Caoimhe had rejoined us. Sam could detect cake at a hundred paces!

'May I ask a question, Ro?' said Nicola. 'Why did the Chief

Constable send you, and I mean, send *you,* a senior to do what a junior could just as easily have done by telephone or even the great personage herself?'

'She knows how well I know you, and to keep it all unofficial and low key.'

'Except it *is* official,' said Nicola 'and if it's come from the top, what haven't you said because you assume we will understand it without being need to be told?'

'Do you mean that I'm to tell you not to do it again and not to pursue further any enquiries you might make, though of course that cannot apply to Michael and Caoimhe?'

Nicola laughed.

'Yes, that was what I had in mind.'

'Oh, what a loss you are to the Force, Nicola. I could do with you on my team.'

'But would that preclude Michael telling you what he knows about André?'

'No.'

'Are you willing to do that, Michael, to tell Ro, who worked with your father something of what has now been unearthed about her former colleague, except for those about which neither of us know – the happenings in Dundalk in the Troubles?'

To give credit to Ro, she did not interrupt Michael, though he was clarity itself as he told of André's unusual lifestyle involving two families, an enormous amount of money and a wife he made use of, omitting only material related to his mother's activities. When he had finished, she was clearly.

'When the attack was made on the Carmichael woman, the assumption was always that it was an intended attack on André,' she said.

'From what I understand, and clearly Dee cannot tell you this, my father knew he was perfectly safe, though experience was enough to cause the loss of life of my twin siblings-to-be. I gather that besides the skill of Mr O'Callaghan, Dee owes her life to you driving a Land Rover at breakneck speed into the hospital in Exeter.'

'I had help from my colleagues who blocked the traffic just

about everywhere to get us through.'

'Then thank you, Ro, for saving my stepmother's life.'

I'm completely stunned by what you have just told me, and ironically, even though a foreign national informed me, I also am now bound by the Official Secrets Act not to repeat it to anyone, including the Chief Constable.'

'"Oh what a tangled web we weave when first we practice to deceive",' said Caoimhe.

'Was that Shakespeare?' asked Ro.

'Sir Walter Scott,' she replied.

'I must do a great deal of sorting out in my mind in the light of what I've learned. Thank you all of you, and most of all, to the cake-maker. You and Michael, Dee, are the victims in all this. I have to say, though, I'm impressed that your friend Kim reported herself,' said Ro.

'Kim is a retired full army colonel and former deputy director of MI5. You don't get to be those things without a great deal of integrity, though perhaps a measure of casuistry on her part might have spared me a great deal of hurt by a full disclosure of what she knew about André a long time ago. Though, had she done so, I wouldn't now have Sam and Nicola, Michael and Caoimhe. Shakespeare it was who wrote "All's Well That Ends Well".'.

'To be perfectly honest, Chief Inspector,' added Michael, 'if Dee and I are victims, then, as she has just said, perhaps it's worth it for what we have now. The thing about today is that it is always followed by another day, and that suggests hope and possibility.'

40

Many days have now followed, and it is 1st July again, as Nicola and I have come, as we often do, to the banks of the river Dart near Dittisham, where exactly one year ago, we met, the event we recall rather than the one that brought her to me.

Mary Kelly, Caoimhe's delightful mum, came and joined us for a memorable celebration of Christmas. In the nursery tableau Sam almost got his wish, when Joseph was taken poorly and he substituted alongside Mary and the doll serving as the baby Jesus. He loved it, though leaves nursery next week and begins pre-school in September. Most of his friends will be with him. His hair is changing colour, becoming more like mine than his father's. His big brother has already taught him how to spin-pass a rugby ball!

Mary took to Michael in a big way, and he and Caoimhe invited her to come and live with them when they bought a small cottage that had become available on the Dartington Estate, into which they moved at the end of January. They were married in Dartington Hall in March and already a little Kelly is on the way, Michael having chosen, sensibly, to adopt Caoimhe's name and leave Donahue behind.

Michael speaks occasionally speaks to his mother on the telephone, and did try to access the files at Dublin University about her, but apparently, they have since been redacted. At the moment, he is an estate worker and enjoying the freedom to be himself that it brings as he drives his tractor about the place.

Caoimhe is working in Ivybridge as a locum English teacher during a maternity leave but, even more looking forward to her own maternity leave. She and Nicola are very close, and she has produced a series of poems which Nicola has shared with Viv and Emily, which they have agreed are "worryingly good"!

Mark married Amelia in April and has changed his job, now working as the manager of a hotel in Honiton. It was a lovely occasion in his new hotel, but for me tinged with a measure of sadness too. The house in Newton Abbot was sold, and the proceeds divided between him and Helen. Maisie and George spend most of their time being shuffled between Honiton and Helen's parents.

Helen is now having supervised day release and working part time in a café in Dawlish. I think of her often and wish it were possible for her and me to meet as it was when we first did so. Something went badly wrong for her, triggered by me, and a further meeting is not possible. I long for her healing and hope that one day she might use the writing talents I recognised, albeit without their content.

I have, however, become close friends with Lillian Pilling, now in happy retirement in Kenn, just outside Exeter, with her partner of many years, Floriana, who has also just retired from her work as a Consultant Paediatrician at the Royal Devon and Exeter Hospital. Lillian has become my surrogate mother, and Nicola and I call in on them and welcome them here as often as possible. Lillian is so wise, and in retrospect, relieved to have stopped work when she did. She is still registered as a psychiatrist but does not see patients, though is often consulted by those who do.

Still working at the Devon and Exeter is Brendan O'Callaghan, and Mary too is expecting a baby. I imagine most expectant mums will be overjoyed to know that their care is in the hands of Mr O'Callaghan, the same hands which knew me intimately as he saved my life. Nicola and I have not yet decided about IVF but we know who we can talk to about it should we ever do so.

There seems to have been a complete breakdown of relations between Sharon, Kim and me, which is hardly surprising, though I honestly don't think it was my fault. The last I heard from them was a change of address card for their new home in the Forest of

Dean. Although she came to speak well of Nicola's writing, I'm not sure she ever got past her initial wish to keep me to herself. However, had it not been for the feelings I once had for Sharon back in Ilkley, I might never have known that I was capable of the sort of love I have for Nicola, so I will be eternally grateful to her for that. All the same, it is sad to have lost her from my life – at least for now. I hope that one day we may love one another again as friends.

My sister, Hermione, says she goes to see my mother as rarely as possible, and apparently I am still exiled into the outer darkness of her concerns, where I can happily survive. Hermione does, however, try to get to see Peter and Colin as often as possible, and reports that Polly must have done a wonderful job with them in the time she was their mother, as they are such smashing lads. Apparently, they would love the chance to come and stay here and I am trying to persuade Hermione to bring them. Catastrophically (not too strong a word in the circumstance) they have both taken to supporting to Burnley rather than Blackburn Rovers, so if they come, I may make them sleep in the garden shed!

And most important of all is the beautiful poet sitting here with me on the bench. She has another collection with the publisher at the moment, including the poem she wrote for me and about me, almost at the beginning of our time together. Viv and Emily came to spend a few days with us in May, though Viv and Nicola speak just about every Sunday morning using Zoom – they are such great friends.

Nicola is still supporting Abi in her work though that may not last as Abi is due to be promoted in the. She does, however, have a lovely man in her life, called Carl, who plays rugby for the Cornish Pirates and she goes to watch him play in every match, and I'm not surprised, for even a lesbian like me can see how stunningly good looking he is!

I have little further to say about my beloved Nicola because increasingly as I read poetry, I have learned that less is more. She has enabled me not just to weather the storms of last year but to be more capable of loving her, and I hope others too, because of them. If that sounds less, it is very much more.

Printed in Great Britain
by Amazon

27068851R00145